My Soul to Keep
& OTHERS

The DeChance Chronicles Volume Three

By David Niall Wilson

There was a commotion in the street, and they both turned. The crowd had thinned some, and they could make out a tall, sleek stallion passing down the street at a leisurely pace. Just for a second, Donovan met the animal's gaze, and would have sworn it watched him as well—measured him. Then it passed, and a long black carriage of polished wood rolled even with the alley, and came to a halt.

"My God," Rathman said. He took a step back, and then stumbled. Donovan moved quickly and caught him, holding him upright. He felt the old man tremble, and, though he had no idea what would come next, or why it seemed important to support his own tormentor in that moment, he held on tight.

The door of the carriage opened. The crowd split, as if parted by a long, cold knife. From the shadowed interior, a lanky figure emerged. He was tall, well over six feet and thin like a cadaver. He wore a silk hat that made him seem even taller, polished boots and a long, dark suit-coat with buttons of polished brass. Donovan had never seen anything like this dark man, and he stared outright as the creature—he seemed more that than a man—unwound from the carriage and stepped into the alley.

Rathman turned then. He gripped Donovan's shirt and dragged him close. The old man's breath was fetid and foul, but his grip was like iron. He tore Donovan's attention from the apparition they faced.

"We are too late," he said. "He must not get the book. When I'm gone, the cards. Remember the cards. Reversed. Remember the cards and save them."

Copyright © 2019 by David Niall Wilson
Cover Art by Cortney Skinner
ISBN 978-1-949914-38-2
All rights reserved. No part of this book may be used or reproduced in any manner
whatsoever without written permission except in the case of
brief quotations embodied in criticalarticles and reviews
For information address Crossroad Press at 141 Brayden Dr., Hertford, NC 27944
A Mystique Press Production - Mystique Press is an imprint of Crossroad Press.
www.crossroadpress.com

First edition

Dedication

This book is dedicated to the magic of stories, and words, and the way they can take you places you never expected to be even if you are the one writing them down. This is not the first time, and will likely not be the last time, that something intended as no more than a flashback led me to something larger and grander. I also dedicate this to Crows, Ravens, the Old West, and my buddy Steven Savile, without whom there would not have been a town of Rookwood in which to set the title story.

Author's Introduction

When I set out to write the next novel in my series, The DeChance Chronicles, I started with the notion that I'd write a quick flashback where Donovan DeChance shared his origins with his lover and partner, Amethyst. I figured it would help me to define the character, and after they snapped back to the present, I'd start Kali's Tale and move on.

One day I'll learn not to plan the beginnings of novels around flashbacks. When I started writing the story of how Donovan set out on his long, strange journey, and how he met Cleo, the Egyptian Mau that is his constant companion, I got drawn in. I found myself fascinated with the story, and as it sometimes happens, the words just flowed. I was three chapters into the flashback before I admitted to myself that it was a separate story altogether from *Kali's Tale*, and that it was never going to work as a part of that other book. What I had on my hands was a new book, albeit a short one, and it was going to run its course no matter what I thought, or planned.

My Soul To Keep takes place in the fictional old west town of Rookwood, setting of the novel *Hallowed Ground* that I wrote with author Steven Savile. This story takes place many years before what Steve and I wrote, but fans will recognize some of the characters. I have very seldom been as happy with a story as I am with this one, and I'm proud that it's finding its way, at last, into print.

Another thing I've discovered as my career progresses is that all of my stories blend. I have a number of fictional settings that I make use of, Random, Illinois, San Valencez California, Friendly California, and Old Mill, North Carolina. All of these are loosely based on places I've lived, and most of my novels and stories over the years have touched on them, taken place within their borders, or connected to them in one way or another.

The novel *Kali's Tale* happened when I was finished with *My Soul to Keep*. In that novel, I take Donovan and all his team into the world of Old Mill, North Carolina, on the border of the Great Dismal Swamp. He meets one of my favorite characters there, Cletus J. Diggs, and so that people will have the whole picture before moving on to *Kali's Tale*, I have included the first Cletus J. Diggs novella here, *The Not Quite Right Reverend Cletus J. Diggs & The Currently Accepted Habits of Nature*. It's important to me that the references are clear, and I dearly love this character, and the story.

Also included in this volume is a novella titled *The Preacher's Marsh*. It's an excerpt from the novel, *Gideon's Curse*. In *Kali's Tale*, Donovan and company visit the main site of *Gideon's Curse*, the Pope Plantation outside Old Mill. *The Preacher's Marsh* is the very beginning of that novel, a tale of post-Civil War North Carolina, swamp magic, the north—the south. It's a dark, powerful story that I'm very proud to have written, and it helps build on the setting of Old Mill, North Carolina. All of it is important, and as I've discovered, all of it seems to be one big fictional world. I guess that's how it really works. All of us have a story in us... the hardest thing is finding the connections that bridge the chapters, the bindings that link the characters, and the magic that shapes the worlds.

The characters from the Cletus J. Diggs novella also appear, and have major roles, in my novel *Nevermore, A Tale of Love, Loss, and Edgar Allan Poe*. As does Donovan. I love history, and I love The Great Dismal Swamp. I hope after you've read my stories, you'll come to love them too.

David Niall Wilson
January, 2013

My Soul to Keep

The Origin of Donovan DeChance

Chapter One

The Promise

Donovan DeChance sat back in the comfort of his plush, leather desk chair and contemplated the floor-to-ceiling bookshelves across from him. Volumes of every shape, size, color and description were lined up like soldiers, some leaning at precarious angles, others jutting out from between their fellows or teetering atop piles of similarly endangered texts. The floor at the base of the shelves was piled high with boxes holding more books, manuscripts, scrolls, and notes. The library had begun to expand into a second row of boxes, creeping inexorably closer to the small living space he'd carved out for himself. He knew he'd have to take decisive action soon—possibly even bring in an apprentice to assist with storage and scanning. At that particular moment, however, the books weren't really the focus of his thoughts.

The scent of roasting meat wafted from his kitchen. He had cleared the surface of what served as his dining room table, and a silver candelabra rested on it, dead center. There were two places set, and a bottle of very old wine waited between them. Amethyst would arrive soon, and Donovan was anticipating—for once—a relaxed, uninterrupted time with the woman he loved. After a recent series of chaotic events, he felt as if they were due.

There was a growling purr at his feet and with sudden, intrusive grace, his familiar, Cleopatra, leapt to the surface of his desk and regarded him with dark, enigmatic eyes. Cleo was an Egyptian Mau, one of the only spotted cats in the world.

She should have been a small- or medium-sized animal, but Donovan was no ordinary man—and Cleo was not your average cat. She had grown over the years, in size, speed, strength and wisdom into a hybrid at least twice the normal size for her breed. Donovan reached out and scratched between her ears and Cleo head-butted his hand, purring happily.

To the right of Donovan's desk was an ornate fireplace. A fluttering sound broke the silence, and both Donovan and Cleo glanced up. From the top shelf, black, glistening eyes regarded them with what might have been affection, or jealousy, or hunger, or no emotion at all. Asmodeus was a hard read. The bird launched, floating in a slow spiral to perch on the back of the chair at Donovan's shoulder. Cleo's tail twitched. Donovan sighed.

"Not tonight, you two," he said. "You will both be on your best behavior while I have company, or I will toss you out into the alley for the night. Do we understand one another?"

Of course, they did. Donovan and Cleo had been bonded psychically for so long they often shared vision and thoughts. Asmodeus, new to their odd family unit, had linked to Donovan so fully and completely that Donovan wondered, at times, if the bird and cat could not share in the same way. The thought of a cat soaring above the city, or a crow sitting on a fence, watching to pounce on some helpless rodent, always made him laugh.

Asmodeus ruffled his wings once more, and settled. Cleo watched the bird, but made no move to pounce. There was a dubious truce between the two—their natural enmity was blunted by their bond with Donovan.

There was a knock on the door, and Donovan rose too quickly. Asmodeus screeched and launched back toward the mantle. Cleo jumped to the floor and nearly tripped Donovan as he rounded the desk. A moment later he had the door open, and Amethyst stepped inside, smiling and shaking her hair back over her shoulders. This caused a cascade of color to glimmer along the crystals she wore braided into her long, fire-red tresses.

"What were you doing, standing on the inside of the door waiting for me?" she asked.

"Something like that," Donovan said. "I've missed you."

He closed the door and watched her as she slowly circled the room. First she leaned to scoop Cleo up off the floor and drape her over one arm. As she scratched the cat's ears and up under the chin, Cleo rolled half onto her back in ecstasy and purred loudly enough to be heard on the next block. Asmodeus let out a short, mournful caw and Amethyst laughed.

"I'll get to you, featherbrain," she said. She turned and caught Donovan staring. "You too."

He laughed. "I only hope whatever comes our way next doesn't involve any more familiars. It's already beginning to seem like a zoo in here."

Amethyst had reached the table, with its place settings, candles, and wine. She put Cleo down and picked up the wine.

"Old," she said.

"Very," Donovan agreed. "I've been saving it for the right moment."

"Something smells good too," Amethyst said. "If I didn't know better, I'd think you were trying to soften me up for something."

"Lately it seems like the only time I see you is when some dark power is trying to destroy the city. I thought, since there is no pending emergency that I know of, it would be nice to show my appreciation."

"Appreciation?" she repeated. "So...you appreciate me..."

"You know what I mean." He crossed the room and wrapped her in his arms, turning her to face him. She was smiling. "I appreciate you too, though," he said. Then he leaned in and kissed her before she could reply, letting his hands slide up and into her hair and making the crystals she wore there tinkle.

"It's good to be...appreciated," she said. She pressed against him more tightly, and he matched her pressure, just for a moment, and then pulled back.

"It's time to eat," he said. "When we're done, we'll have some of the wine, and then I want to show you something—I have a new toy, and I have a promise to keep. I thought I'd see if we could kill two birds with one stone."

At this, Asmodeus squawked, and they both laughed.

"Not you," Donovan said.

He lit the candles on the table, and then pulled out one of the chairs for Amethyst to sit.

"See if you can get the wine open," he said.

As she reached for the bottle and the antique corkscrew lying beside it, Donovan turned toward the kitchen. He'd planned this for a long time. He'd taken the recipe for the roast and accompanying vegetables from a very old book, enhanced it with a couple of tricks of his own, and laid a charm around the oven to prevent burning or overcooking. As he approached the stove, he chanted softly under his breath, releasing the wards. He didn't often cook with the oven in a protective circle, but this was important and he knew his own penchant for distraction would ruin the meal if he gave it half a chance.

He slid the pan out of the oven and lifted it to the stove top quickly. The food smelled wonderful, and despite all his precautions, he breathed easier. He already had two large bowls ready. He carved the meat, ladled on some gravy and vegetables, and carried the bowls back to the other room. He placed one in front of Amethyst, who breathed in the aroma of it appreciatively, and set the other by his own seat.

"There," he said with a flourish. "Cooked to perfection, and not spilled. What more can I ask?"

Amethyst stared at him.

"What are you up to?" she asked. "You've cooked for me before, and it's never been such an elaborate display. You are nervous, and I don't know that I've ever seen you less comfortable."

Donovan smiled.

"I told you," he said. "After we eat. If I am nervous, it's just that I have been looking forward to this particular evening for a very long time. I wasn't sure, at first, that we'd come so far together, but..."

"How far *have* we come?" Amethyst cut in.

"Far enough that I trust you with my life," Donovan said evenly.

She glanced up, and he met her gaze.

"Are you going to eat?" he asked.

She smiled. She did not lower her gaze, but she did reach for her knife, and her fork. She cut a small piece of roast without once glancing down, brought it to her lips, and slid it into her mouth, teasing it with her tongue.

Donovan sighed. "Incorrigible," he said.

"Absolutely," she agreed.

He sat back, then, and poured the wine. They ate slowly. The food was every bit as good as the old book had claimed it would be, and the wine lived up to both age and reputation. It was deep red with a hint of fruit and nuts, and a spice that Donovan could not quite place. It was the perfect companion to the roast, and he finished his quickly, returning to the kitchen for seconds. Amethyst ate more slowly, but with equal enjoyment, he thought. Neither of them spoke until both bowls were empty, at last, and the final goblets of the wine had been poured.

"So," Amethyst said at last. "That was wonderful. Magic, books, and the man can cook. What more can there be?"

Donovan rose and took their dishes to the kitchen. He wiped the surface of the table carefully, and then slid the candelabra off to the side, leaving a clear space between them. There was a leather bag on his desk, and he grabbed it, carrying it back to the table. He opened the drawstrings and pulled out a wooden tripod carved from a single chunk of Dogwood. He placed it on the table and stood it up, testing to be certain it was steady.

When he was satisfied, he drew out a ball of clear crystal and placed it on the stand. The ball was perfectly round, but riddled with flaws and frosty images. Amethyst leaned in for a closer look, but he stopped her.

"Not yet," he said.

Next he took out a smaller bag. He opened this, and it was filled with bits of wood that had been burned to charcoal. He withdrew a sliver of this and began to draw a circle around the crystal. When it was finished, he drew a second around the perimeter of the first, and between the two, he etched a number of odd characters. When he was satisfied, he opened his desk drawer and brought out four small braziers. He placed them at the four compass points of his circles.

Amethyst glanced up at him. He knew that she was aware of what he was doing. It was her specialty, her gift. Crystals, stones, dirt and dust. The earth. Donovan's knowledge was broader—more all-encompassing, but there was no way he could hide his intent. Thankfully, she granted him the moment's silence to complete his preparations. He wasn't certain, if she'd distracted him or given him an option, if he'd have had the courage to continue.

He lit the braziers, different herbs in each, different words whispered to the archangels of each quadrant. The room grew very still. Energy rippled in the air. In the center of the circle, there was a flicker of light—then a soft glow—and then the crystal blazed. Donovan seated himself directly across the circle from Amethyst and spread his arms, laying them outside the twin circles, his hands palm up.

"What is this?" Amethyst whispered.

"You know what this is," Donovan said. "I found the proper enchantments in a book you left in my care. I owe you my life several times over now. You have asked me, time and again, of my past. I never answered, but I promised that, when the time was right, I would. This is that time."

She took his hands and met his gaze.

"You are certain?" she asked.

"I am," he said. Then he smiled. "This is a story I have never told. These are secrets I have never shared. When this is done, you will know me as no other man or woman in the last hundred and fifty years has known me. Do you accept?"

She nodded, and then whispered. "I do."

"Then let it begin," Donovan said.

The lights in the room dimmed. Cleo settled on top of his desk and stared intently at the circle, and the crystal. Asmodeus, perched high overhead, scanned the room. His gaze flitted from side to side, as if he watched not only the room, but places beyond. Donovan closed his eyes. Amethyst stared deep into the smoky depths of the imperfect crystal, following the faults, sliding through the mist and the crackling fractures.

"In 1842," Donovan said, "I was a sixteen year old boy, indentured to a man who called himself a doctor. That was the year that everything changed. That was the year I became a man."

The mist swallowed them both, and Donovan's story came to eerie, surreal life.

Chapter Two

Rookwood

The old wagon smelled of sweat, leather, cheap liquor, and a miasma of spices, herbs, and chemicals that would have driven a bloodhound crazy. Donovan leaned back into a pile of old rags and tried to peer out through the crack between two of the wagon's warped boards at the passing countryside. He knew they were getting close. Whenever they neared a town, or a settlement, Rathman picked up the pace. The two old ponies scented fresh apples and hay, and the old man scented whiskey and women. Donovan knew he would work long into the night, but hoped, in the end, it would mean a hot meal. Sometimes, if he could keep his distance from Rathman and find an hour's work sweeping, or scrubbing, or shoveling out a stable, he could earn a decent meal before the old man's screeching, bullying voice dragged him back to the wagon. At least it was something to hope for.

The town they expected to run up on next was called Rookwood. Donovan had never seen the place, but Rathman remembered it from many years back. Donovan hoped it was a lot of years, because the old fraud was seldom welcomed back to a place a second time if anyone remembered his previous visit, and it wasn't easy to forget. For one thing, the decrepit old wagon was painted over with brilliant, garish designs.

"Dr. Hugo Rathman, Healer, Mystic, and Clairvoyant" was painted dead center in paint so bright and so red that circling buzzards had mistaken it for blood and spiraled down to have a closer look. More than once Donovan had peered out into the driver's seat of the wagon to be certain the carrion feeders weren't after Rathman himself. The old man could drink himself into a stupor so deep that he seemed dead. Finally they passed by the first small grouping of board and tar shacks. Donovan caught sight of a thin boy with wild hair and no shirt. For just a second he'd have sworn the kid met his gaze, right through the boards. A second later, the boy was off, flying barefoot across the desert toward town. Apparently visitors weren't common in Rookwood. Donovan frowned. The rarer they were, the more likely someone would remember Rathman. It was possible that the old man hadn't cheated anyone on his last visit, but that would make this a rare visit indeed. At least three lawmen were watching out for the wagon because ill townsfolk had taken one or more of Rathman's potions and either fallen deeper into their illness, or died outright—poisoned.

Whatever the situation, Rathman didn't hesitate. He aimed the wagon dead-center down the main road of the town, bumping through potholes and jarring Donovan's teeth with each jouncing yard they progressed. The wagon creaked and moaned, but it held together. It always managed to hold together. Like Rathman, it seemed there was no force on the road or in the desert that could put the final nail in its coffin.

"You ready, boy?" Rathman grated, turning so that his unshaven face, wild dark hair and red-veined eyes glared back into the shadows. There was no way he could see into the interior, but he still managed to stare directly into the particular shadows where Donovan rested.

"Yes sir," Donovan said.

Rathman stared a moment longer, then nodded. He turned back to the reins, steered around a corner a bit too quickly, nearly tilting the wagon up on two wheels, and a moment later they came to a halt. Donovan rose, stepped up to the front of the wagon and peered out around the edge.

It was an alley between what looked to be a stable, and a taller wooden building that might have been a saloon or hotel. Rathman dropped the reins, stood, and stretched, pressing his knuckles tightly into the lower half of his back. He'd been sitting in the same position for nearly thirty miles, and Donovan knew it would take more than an hour for the stoop to leave him.

"I'm goin' to see about getting the horses taken in," he said. "You get this wagon ready—hear? We'll be settin' up in the morning, and there's no time for delays."

Rathman seemed to drop almost into a trance, as if listening to a voice Donovan couldn't hear. Then he turned back.

"Put out the books and the rheumatism tinctures. Arrange some of the other cures behind. Then get this place presentable and set up my table. I believe the spirits might just speak to me here. There's something in the air."

Donovan thought that all there was in the air was dust. He thought, very briefly, of his father, sickly and barely able to carry himself to work in a mine shaft so dark and deep it swallowed men whole. He thought of his mother, though he could barely remember her face. He thought of the tiny room that had been his, the bed that had grown too short to contain his long, lanky legs, and he sighed. At that moment, he'd have traded half his life to be back there, caring for his father—assuming the old man hadn't passed on—and getting ready to take his own turn in the mines.

"Apprentice," was the title he'd been granted so long ago. "Assistant to a man of books and medicine. A learned scholar with the ear of the spirits and the mind of a professor. What it had boiled down to was the life of an indentured manservant. He'd learned to read, but only by his own dogged effort, and stolen moments with Rathman's precious books. When he proved he could earn a dime or two by reading from the old tales to those who passed by, the good "Doctor" had taken an interest and taught what he could between drunken binges and fits of curse-spewing malevolence. He was obviously torn between the fear of teaching too much and having Donovan run off on his own, and the greedy desire for his apprentice to be able to shoulder a share of the burden of making their living. It was also true that no listener had ever asked for their money back, or threatened to run Donovan out of town on a rail, and likely Rathman held that against him too.

As the old man climbed down and disappeared in the

direction of the stables, Donovan set to work. The wagon, for all its wear, was a wonder of engineering. The sides opened out like the doors of a great house, latching to the front and back at angles. When they were in place, another panel could be lowered by ropes until it rested on its own unfolding legs and jutted from the side of the wagon like a vendor's table. Donovan set it all up in silence, working slowly and methodically and trying to ignore the scent of roasting meat that floated to him from down the street. Once the table was in place, he climbed back up into the wagon and began sorting through the boxes. He wished he could light a candle to see what he was doing, but if he wasted the candle on something like this, it would be taken out of his hide. He found the boxes of books easily, they were larger and heavier than most of their merchandise. They sold the books, but only for very high prices. They lent them for much less—and, of course, they would be on display to be read to those who had a few coins to spare. This happened more often now that they didn't have to depend solely on Rathman's raspy, whiskey-soaked vocal cords to do the recitations.

Donovan carried the crates of leather-bound tomes out into the alley and unloaded them, lining them up carefully on the shelves above the table. There were fables, books of law, stories about kings and castles, picture books depicting strange animals and legends, folklore and herbal cures. More than anything he'd encountered in his life, the books fascinated Donovan. He liked the way they felt, the way they smelled, the way the words and letters lined up with such symmetry, recording the world for anyone with the talent and ability to draw the images back from the ink.

The moonlight was bright, and he found himself lost in the mysterious titles and supple leather spines. The library was worth a small fortune, despite the wear the volumes had seen, and the rough handling. Books were rare in the west. There were few printers, and they had to be typeset, hand bound, and carried across mountains and rivers. Of all the things Hugo Rathman claimed of himself, educated was the only one that was undoubtedly true. Wherever he'd come from, he'd brought the books out with him—some remnant of a better life, or the ill-gotten gains of a long past robbery. Donovan didn't know but he thought—given the chance to record it—that the story would probably make a fine book all on its own.

There was a scuffle of sound near the entrance to the alley, and he was suddenly alert. He kept a dagger in a sheath in his boot, and there was an old club that Rathman insisted on calling "Me Shillelagh" in a ridiculous Irish brogue tucked up under the driver's seat. Donovan put the book he'd been thumbing through on the shelf and turned to scan the alley. He saw nothing, but that didn't mean anything. He felt the telltale tickle at the base of his neck. Someone was there—likely watching him—and he knew if he lost the books or any of the merchandise, to another thief he'd be beaten within an inch of his life. Good incentive to put it on the line in the wagon's defense, where he had at least a chance of protecting himself.

He was glad for the brightness of the moon. No one was likely to slip up on him. Even the shadows along the base of the buildings were too shallow for proper cover. Then he saw a flicker of shadow near the end of the alley. It wavered, long and stick-thin, before resolving itself into the figure of a young boy. He realized a moment later that it was the same shirtless boy who'd run ahead to announce their arrival.

"Hey," he called out. "What's your name? What are you doing out so late?"

The boy didn't answer. He just stood at the end of the alley and stared. Donovan thought about walking over to introduce himself, but he was afraid the boy would bolt. For some reason, the thought of that saddened him. He'd been alone in the wagon for far too long. He reached out and grabbed the first volume that popped into his hands.

He glanced down. It was a slender book of verse by George Gordon –Lord Byron. He flipped it open, turned to the boy, and without preamble or explanation, he began to read:

I stood in Venice, on the Bridge of Sighs;
A palace and a prison on each hand:
I saw from out the wave her structures rise
As from the stroke of the enchanter's wand:

A thousand years their cloudy wings expand
Around me, and a dying Glory smiles
O'er the far times, when many a subject land
Look'd to the winged Lion's marble piles,
Where Venice sate in state, thron'd on her hundred isles!

The boy hadn't moved. In fact, when Donovan looked up to check, he saw that his reluctant visitor had come a step closer. "It's from Childe Harold's Pilgrimage," he said. "Did you like it? I'll be reading more tomorrow—maybe the whole story. I've always liked it, because it's about a young man...like me. He travels to strange places, though he isn't very happy. What's your name?"

The boy continued to stare. There was a sound from the street, heavy footsteps. Donovan knew it was probably Rathman returning.

"I'm Donovan," he said.

"He's comin'," the boy said. The voice was like a whisper, but it carried. Donovan heard it clearly, as if it had been whispered in his ear, or blown to him on the wind from far away.

"It's my master," Donovan said. "Dr. Rathman, he..."

"No," the boy said. "Another. He is dark. Like the night. Watch for him."

Then, like a wraith, the boy's shape flickered out. One moment he stood in the shadows, and the next Donovan stared at nothing but brick and darkness. Rathman rounded the corner then, a bottle in one hand, his steps uneven. He staggered into the wall, clinked the bottle on the bricks, and Donovan held his breath. If the bottle broke, it would end badly. It did not.

"That you, boy?" Rathman called out. "Get them horses. Get 'em inside. Got feed an' water waitin', and they need brushed down."

Donovan scanned the shadows behind Rathman, but the boy was gone. Not a flicker of motion indicated he'd ever been there at all. He closed the book carefully, slid it back into place on the shelf, and moved toward the horses without a word. He liked the animals, and he was glad to hear they would be stabled. With luck, he'd find a softer bed in the hay nearby than he had in the back of the wagon. At the very least, Rathman would be passed out before he returned.

The old man made it to the wagon, glanced at the display, and grunted. It was the closest to satisfaction he ever showed.

"You come back and help keep an eye on this," he said, turning toward Donovan. "Too many out on the street for you to be sacking out in the stable. Understand? We start early."

Donovan controlled his breathing and nodded. He knew that anything he said would end up being twisted in some way he didn't intend it to be. He consoled himself with the knowledge that Rathman would be out cold before he returned, and would still be that way when he woke. When the old man said we, it always meant Donovan.

He unhitched the horses and led them slowly to the end of the alley, turning right toward the main doors of the stable. Out of the corner of his eye, he saw a flicker of shadow. He turned, but there was nothing, though he would have sworn he heard a voice whisper.

"He comes."

Chapter Three

He Walks in Darkness

The morning sun leaked over the eaves of the saloon that bordered the alley and highlighted the dancing dust motes around the wagon. Donovan had been up for nearly an hour, quietly setting up shop. He had brought down the round, wooden folding table that Rathman used to hold his cards, and his crystal. When he was in the right mood—when he could keep himself from drinking too early in the day and his voice from slurring—the old man read the cards. It wasn't like the other things he did. During those rare, lucid periods, the man's intelligence shone through. He spoke to Donovan, and to others, in an entirely different manner, more animated and almost human.

Donovan put the inlaid wooden box that held the cards on one side of the table. Beside it, he placed a number of crystals and geodes in a cross pattern. If Rathman read the cards, he'd use the crystal cross to divide them into quadrants, the past, the present, the future, and the things that influenced the reading. Donovan had watched, and he had listened. He'd found a book in one of the boxes that explained the cards and their meanings, the symbols and their interactions, and he knew them almost as well as the old man. He hoped this would be one of those days.

Despite the shady nature of his medicines and tinctures, Rathman's relationship with that pile of colorful images and patterns was eerie. Though his messages were not always positive, they *were* accurate. To Donovan's knowledge, Rathman had never been run out of town for a card reading, and that alone was enough to make him hopeful. If they set up the 'medical' equipment, vials, potions, and bottles, he knew he'd have to plan how they could get the horses out of the stable through the back door, bribe the owner, and get the wagon beyond the border of the town before Rathman was tarred and feathered, or shot in the back.

The mystery of the man was that he seemed capable of so much more. Donovan believed Rathman had read every book in their library, and knew most of them by heart. He was not good at creating cures, but he was knowledgeable about the diseases he claimed to be able to cure. He knew the cards, and once, before he'd grown too drunk to stare into the night sky without falling over backward, he'd pointed out a dozen constellations. He should have been studying or teaching at a university, or any of a dozen reputable professions with a future, but instead he drank, and he drove from town to town, risking his life on an almost daily basis to no more purpose than paying for the next bottle, and stealing from men and women more honest, but less intelligent, than himself.

And Donovan was chained to him for another five years. That was the price of his "apprenticeship". That was the deal his father had struck to help him escape. Ten years of service in exchange for knowledge. In exchange for teaching and care, food and a place to sleep. The deal had been for a boy's future, conceived in the mind and heart of a dying man.

He stroked the top of the box of cards. He wished he dared to open them, lay them out, and ask about his own future. He wondered if Rathman would do it for him if he asked. Somehow, he didn't think so.

"Boy?"

The old man's voice was weak, but coherent. Donovan turned to see that Rathman was watching him. The old man did not sneer, or frown...he looked very tired.

"They hold secrets, you know?" he said. "Those cards. If they could talk..."

Donovan waited, but the moment passed.

"Get me coffee," Rathman rasped, waving at the growing light of the sun as if he could brush it away. "Black and strong.

The people will be here soon, and I must be ready."

Donovan wandered out into the street. It was his first clear view of the town, and he drank it in. He spent so much time isolated that even a small settlement like Rookwood captivated his imagination. There were a few businesses gathered together along a wood-plank sidewalk. A general store was fronted by a barrel with some sort of fruit piled high on top—might have been apples, but not too fresh. There was the saloon and the stable. He'd seen both by night, lit up and tossing shadows to the street, but by day they had a different sort of feel entirely. Sunlight scrubbed away the gloss and the glitter from the saloon, leaving it grimy and stained with dust-covered windows. The stable seemed solid and clean in comparison.

The saloon also advertised rooms and food, and Donovan figured it was his best bet to either find coffee, or to find out where it could be had. He entered tentatively, glancing around the dimly lit interior at the tables with their chairs upended on top. Glasses that probably glittered by candle and lamplight sat like dusty soldiers on the shelves beside rows of bottles. He'd seen places just like it a hundred times in their travels, but there was always something about the bars that drew him.

The heartbeat of a town flowed through the same doors he'd just entered. What passed as night life, anything new or interesting, and most of the passions, dark or otherwise, would center in this room. The scent and taste of it lingered, though stale and lifeless with sunlight cutting through the windows.

"Can I help you, Son?" a man asked. He was a tall man in a striped vest and a wide-brimmed hat. He stood leaning on the bar, watching in amusement as Donovan jumped back and cracked his elbow on the door frame.

"I...I came to fetch coffee for Dr. Rathman," he said. "I thought..."

"Thought right," the man said, turning and reaching up onto one of the shelves. He brought down a chipped ceramic mug and set it on the counter. Then, giving Donovan a good once over, he reached up and grabbed a second mug. "You look like you could use a drop yourself," the man said. "My name's Boone," he added. "Cornelius Boone. This here's my place. You might see my boy Silas running about. If you do, don't you let him waste his money on that old fraud you're traveling with, you hear?"

Donovan watched as Boone passed through the doors behind the bar into what must have been the kitchen, and returned with a tin coffee pot in hand. He poured until both mugs were filled, and passed them across to Donovan.

"What...what do I owe you?" Donovan asked. He had Rathman's wallet—it was his job to carry and watch the money, though that duty would pass soon enough when the sun went down and the saloon opened for its real trade.

"These are on the house," Boone said. He winked. "You just remember what I said about my boy. Seen your 'Dr. Rathman' once before, out in the Dakotas. He was younger then. Can't say as how he left a good impression."

Donovan's heart sped. If this got around, their stay in Rookwood might be a short one indeed. Boone must have caught the fear in his expression.

"Don't worry. Havin' him out there will be good for business, while it lasts. I won't say nothin' to the sheriff, or anyone else. Just lookin' out for my own."

At that moment, the kitchen door opened again, and a thin boy with a blond thatch of hair sticking at odd angles from his head and shoulders—he looked like he might grow into in a few years—stepped into the room.

Boone turned.

"Silas? I want you to meet my new friend," he turned back and cocked an eyebrow.

"Donovan...my name is Donovan."

"Donovan," Boone finished. "You get all the stories out of him you want, but I don't want to hear about you wasting any money on that wagon out there—you hear? Donovan has promised to keep an eye on you...haven't you, Son?"

"Yes, sir," Donovan replied. He caught the boy's eye, just for a second, liked what he saw, smiled, and reached out to take the steaming mugs of coffee. "I'd better get back with this while it's hot. I'll bring the mugs back before lunch."

Boone nodded, and Donovan turned with the coffee in

hand. The boy, Silas, slipped past him and held the door as he left.

The cards were already spread on the table when Donovan returned to the alley. There were a few townsfolk hanging around out by the street, peering in curiously. An older woman stood next to the table. Rathman had the cards spread, separated into their quadrants. Donovan held back for a moment, watching.

"There's someone you're waiting for," Rathman said. He leaned in close and stared at the cards. "He's tall, bearded. He's been gone a long time."

The woman's hand actually fluttered to her breast, and Donovan grinned. He'd read the expression in old books, but had never understood it until that moment.

"Raymond," she said. "You're talking about my Raymond. He's been gone these five years—gone back East to bring supplies. How did you..."

Rathman didn't wait for her to finish her question. He pointed at a card, then tapped his finger in the center of it. "Knight of wands," he said. "Young, powerful, always moving."

"Yes," she said. "He's my son."

Rathman reached for the next card in the deck, and more of the townsfolk gathered near. He was in his element, and he didn't seem to be asking them for anything. There was a single coin on the table, but the old man hadn't even bothered to snatch it and make it disappear into his pocket.

"He's coming home," Rathman said. "Soon. By Christmas, I'd say. He's strong, and healthy, and..."

Then he stopped. The woman actually reached out and touched his arm, as if she could coax him to go on, but Rathman's eyes had gone blank. He shook his head from side to side, and reached for the cards.

"What is it?" the woman said. "Is he all right? Is he..."

"He's fine," Rathman gasped. He gathered the cards hurriedly, knocking the crystals that formed the cross askew in his haste. He was nervously shuffling the cards almost before they were all in his hand. Then, suddenly, he started slapping cards down with a quick, nervous speed that brought Donovan up short. It wasn't the old man's way to hurry it. It was all about the drama, and the reveal (Rathman's words). Donovan brushed past the onlookers, and stood beside the table with the two cups of coffee. Rathman glanced up, took a cup without a word, and drained it, despite the heat. It must have burned—Donovan was only able to sip his—but if there was pain, there was no indication of it on Rathman's face. His concentration never wavered. Donovan glanced down and started to examine the spread.

The crowd had begun to shuffle, some grumbling, others curious and trying to press forward. Before Donovan could make sense of any of it, Rathman reached out and tore the cards from the table again, rippling them up off the table in a sweeping motion, like a card shark getting ready to shuffle. Donovan saw the Magus, and The Universe. He saw Death, reversed, and the Ace of Cups. He could not see the full pattern of the reading in his mind, so he had no idea which quadrant they'd rested in, or what the surrounding cards might have been.

"What is it?" he asked. "What's wrong, sir?"

At first, Rathman didn't seem to hear him. The old man kept shuffling the cards, rippling them over the back of his hand, and then under, flipping them absently through the air. As he did this, he muttered under his breath. Then he stopped and flipped the top card into the center of the table.

It was the Magus.

Rathman gave a sharp cry and pushed back from the table. Donovan reached out instinctively. He caught the old man's empty coffee cup before it could fall to the ground and crack, clinking it together with his own and splashing hot coffee onto his leg. Then he reached out with his free hand and caught the card as it flipped up into the air and fluttered from side to side. He caught it without thought, neatly between his thumb, and his forefinger. The card was face up, and he could see it clearly.

He turned to Rathman, who looked pale.

"Boy, we have to pack," the old man said. "We have to pack, and get the horses. It's probably too late—probably been too late for a long time. I've got things to tell you, things I should have told you long ago, but..."

There was a commotion in the street, and they both turned. The crowd had thinned some, and they could make out a tall, sleek stallion passing down the street at a leisurely pace. Just for a second, Donovan met the animal's gaze, and would have sworn it watched him as well—measured him. Then it passed, and a long black carriage of polished wood rolled even with the alley, and came to a halt.

"My God," Rathman said. He took a step back, and then stumbled. Donovan moved quickly and caught him, holding him upright. He felt the old man tremble, and, though he had no idea what would come next, or why it seemed important to support his own tormentor in that moment, he held on tight.

The door of the carriage opened. The crowd split, as if parted by a long, cold knife. From the shadowed interior, a lanky figure emerged. He was tall, well over six feet and thin like a cadaver. He wore a silk hat that made him seem even taller, polished boots and a long, dark suit-coat with buttons of polished brass. Donovan had never seen anything like this dark man, and he stared outright as the creature—he seemed more that than a man—unwound from the carriage and stepped into the alley.

Rathman turned then. He gripped Donovan's shirt and dragged him close. The old man's breath was fetid and foul, but his grip was like iron. He tore Donovan's attention from the apparition they faced.

"We are too late," he said. "He must not get the book. When I'm gone, the cards. Remember the cards. Reversed. Remember the cards and save them."

Donovan started to speak. He never got the chance.

"Hugo," a voice boomed. Donovan spun back to the stranger. "Hugo Rathman. Doctor, is it now? How quaint. How perfect. It's been a long time, old man. A long time in which I've grown a bit...impatient."

"Get away," Rathman rasped. He pulled free of Donovan's grip and stood with surprising strength. "Leave this place— these people. You don't belong here."

"That may be the first thing we have ever agreed on, Hugo. I do not belong here, nor do you. Make it easy on yourself. Give me what is mine, and I'll be on my way. Otherwise, I'm afraid I'll have to take up residence for a while. I grow...hungry...over time. I will be at the hotel. If you come to me before sunrise tomorrow, and bring me what I seek, I may take pity on you—or at least," he turned to Donovan, "on the boy."

Without another word, the man—if he was a man at all—turned, and walked back to his carriage. He climbed inside, and Donovan would have sworn that the doors closed behind him without being touched. The horse started off once again, and the carriage passed from sight. There was no creak of wheels or leather. There was no sound at all. Even the people standing at the end of the alley seemed not to breathe.

Rathman stumbled forward and caught himself on the table. Donovan reached to steady him again, but the old man shook him off. He stood, and he turned.

"Pack the wagon," he said. "Pay the man in the stable, but don't get the horses yet. When night falls, slip in and get them. Be ready to move."

"That man," Donovan said. "Who is he?"

"He isn't a 'who' at all," Rathman said. "He isn't anyone you should be thinking about. You should forget that he exists, except that he may be on your trail. If you don't see me by midnight, you should forget me as well. You know the horses, you can drive the wagon, you know the books and the cards... I've seen you watching, I know you could read them. If I don't make it back, you remember what I told you, and you get out."

"But what did it mean?" Donovan asked. "What you said..."

"Was all you need," Rathman snapped. "I won't repeat it. He might hear. Someone might hear. If he..." The old man fell silent. "Just do as you're told, boy. I'm going to get a drink."

And with that, Dr. Hugo Rathman turned on his heel and walked out of the alley, leaving Donovan standing by the table, and the cards, with the wagon open and the curious crowd still gathered, watching. Donovan pulled back the chair and sat at the table. He grabbed his mug and drained what remained of his tepid coffee. He pushed it aside and slowly slid the crystals back into place. Then he started to shuffle the cards.

"Maybe you won't read them for me, old man," he said, "but

I *will* read them for you. I know you want me to run, but I've seen what that has done to you."

He stopped talking and then he stopped shuffling. He cut the cards once, and then, very slowly, he began to flip them over, three in each quadrant of the cross. He considered, just for a second, going for the book—to be sure he read them properly— but as they dropped each one, the vivid images sprang from their surface. He didn't see them as individual squares of cardboard. He saw symbols. He saw patterns blending with other patterns. He sank deeper into his mind and remembered. Four quadrants. Past, Present, Future—and influences beyond your control. The elements of truth. That was what the book called them. That was what Rathman had called them, though when he said the words his voice rolled and slipped like serpents into the ears of befuddled strangers looking for entertainment, or a thrill. It had cheapened them, tarnishing the magic so Donovan could not quite see. Now, he looked, and he saw, and he knew that, whatever happened—whatever came next—he could not run.

He gathered the cards and packed them carefully into their box. He packed the crystals, wrapped in silk, into a leather pouch. He carried them to the wagon, and then, as the dwindling crowd watched with almost hurt expressions, realizing there would be no show—no magic—no entertainment at all, he started packing. By the time Donovan had stowed the table and piled the books back into their cartons, they were all gone.

When he closed the side of the wagon, a cold wind blew down the alley. Leaves danced around his feet, and he glanced up. There was no one there, and yet, he saw a slow-moving shadow, taller than a man, slide across the mouth of the alley and into the street. Against all logic, in the hot, dry heat of Rookwood, the wind felt cold.

Chapter Four

In a Cat's Eye

Once he had climbed into the semi-seclusion of the wagon, Donovan took a few moments to think. He had no doubt that, whatever was to come; Rathman would be as good as his word on the drink. The question—as always—would be whether he could exercise enough control to make it back under his own power. This time it seemed like a good question whether he'd even have the chance.

If felt like a turning point. Just at the moment it had all gone bad, Donovan had been mired in the unending boredom of his existence, wondering if he'd live through enough towns to win back his freedom, and whether Rathman would actually grant it when the time came. Now things had shifted. For a long time he'd been handling most of the business end of things—watching the money to see that enough was set aside to feed themselves and the horses, keeping the wagon neatly packed, and the stores up to date. It had seemed natural— Rathman bellowed, and Donovan did whatever it took to stop the bellowing.

Now Rathman seemed to have extricated himself, and the weight of it all had dropped firmly on Donovan's shoulders. He ran over everything that had happened, and everything the old man had said. An old drunk he might be, but he was not stupid. If Rathman said he'd told Donovan what he needed to know, then the clues were there. He closed his eyes and sank back through his memory. He'd always been able to recall things with particular clarity when he had to, but he'd never seen a use for the ability before. Now he hoped it wouldn't fail him. *He must not get the book. When I'm gone, the cards. Remember the cards. Reversed. Remember the cards and save them.* He broke it down. The book. There were close to fifty books in the old wagon, and they ranged from old and ratty to thin and cheap. None among them had ever seemed particularly valuable, except in the rarity of their existence in such a wild, unsettled land. He ran through the inventory of all that he'd seen, and he brushed them aside. It could not be any of the books he was familiar with, so he started with that. There was a book—the man who'd come to them wanted it. He had to find it.

The next thing Rathman had said was to remember the cards. Did he mean to remember them physically—or did he mean to remember them they way they were in the reading? Donovan had only a glimpse of the spread that had been on the table to go on—four cards and no order. He had his own reading, and he suspected—no, somehow he knew—that what he'd found in the cards related directly to what had gone before. He'd always thought it was a good parlor trick, that Rathman was just a great judge of those around him and able to pick things from people's minds and eyes, tell them what they wanted to hear, and collect their money. Now, thinking back over the miles and the years, he realized there had to be more to it—and that he'd always known it. He'd just never had the opportunity, or the reason, to investigate. Certainly the book he'd read—the one that had taught him the layout and the symbols—indicated there was more.

But reversed? If he couldn't remember the spread, and Rathman must have known this, how could he possibly remember them reversed? He took the box in his hands and studied it. He turned it and studied the design. He'd never been allowed to handle the box, other than to carry it to the table, or the cards. He'd read the book, but somehow he thought Rathman had intended for him to read it. He also thought that it was possible that the book he'd read—and the cards—were not linked in any important way for the old man. Rathman never consulted the book, only the cards.

Donovan flipped the box on its edges, turned it to each

corner, and then, with a sudden inspiration, he flipped it upside down. The bottom, at first glance, was a single, solid piece of wood. There were no knots in it, no cracks or easily visible seams. He ran his thumbs over the surface, back and forth, starting in the corners, and then, halfway across the back, the wood gave, just slightly. He pressed, and there was a sudden, very solid click.

The bottom of the box opened then, a door swinging out to reveal a small cavity within. Donovan pulled it open and glanced inside. There was a silk-bound object resting in the base of the box. He lifted it free, and pulled back the silk. Something made him glance up then, but there was no one in sight. The only place anyone might have been to see into the wagon was the driver's seat, and it was empty. Still, the act of touching the silk-wrapped object seemed to enhance the solitude of the moment. He was aware of the silence, of every whisper of wind and crackle of dried leaves beyond the walls surrounding him. He sensed how far away the horses were, and how empty it all seemed without Rathman present.

He shook it off and laid the box down. Very carefully, he pulled the silk the rest of the way from the small, leather-bound book within. He'd never seen anything like it. The binding was very fine. The leather was smooth and supple, and the touch of it made his skin crawl. In fact, some instinct made him slide it quickly back onto the silk. He used this to tip the cover open.

"The Grimoire of Alexis Silkstone," was penned in elegant black strokes across the title page. It was handwritten, but the letters were so even and precise that they rivaled any printing Donovan had ever seen. He tried to remember the name, but he was certain that he'd never heard it before. The next page was only a short note..."begun this day, the seventh of July, 1733."

Donovan gasped. 1733? It certainly didn't belong to Rathman, then, or to the strange, elongated stranger. Still. Something about the inscription itched at his mind, and something in the script seemed oddly compelling, and familiar.

There was a sudden scraping sound, and he spun, nearly toppling the box of cards and dropping the box in his clumsy, far-too-slow attempt to conceal it. Framed in the opening at the front of the wagon, he saw the boy's face. The boy who'd preceded them into town. The boy who'd warned him.

"You think too loud," the boy said.

Donovan stared at him dumbly.

"The old man, he is in danger," the boy said. "If you want to help him, bring the book."

"Who are you?" Donovan asked.

"They call me Bones," the boy said. "There is no time."

Images flashed through Donovan's mind then...the cards... the black carriage...the horse that had looked at him with such intelligence. Other images intruded. Insects, thousands of them. A cemetery. A cat. The cards, as he'd read them, unrolled before him, not in a cross, but in a string, tied to one another by tendrils of silken energy.

"Silkstone," he said.

The boy nodded. "That is what they call him now. He is like your Doctor. Not what he seems. So few of us ever are."

Then Bones disappeared from the doorway, and tucking the silken bundle into his pocket, Donovan climbed through after him.

He'd been inside longer than he thought. The sun was dipping behind the stable, and he knew that it would be less than an hour before it disappeared entirely. In the desert, when the sun began its descent, it sped as it neared the horizon. The last few seconds could pass without notice unless you concentrated and managed not to blink.

"Dr. Rathman is in the saloon," Bones said. "I sense he is readying himself for a confrontation."

"He's drunk," Donovan said flatly. "If he confronts anyone in that state, he'll have no chance."

"Without the book he has no chance," Bones said. "The liquor gives him courage. We cannot help him. The other comes. Silkstone comes. If you want to help, we must find his wagon—and his things. We must find his power, and take it before he uses it to consume the Doctor, and the town. If we wait, he will feed. I have followed him for a long time—I don't want any more to die."

"Who *are* you?" Donovan breathed.

"A very old boy," Bones replied. "Very old and very tired. I have followed him a long time."

"Why?" Donovan asked.

"He ate my parents," Bones replied. "He took their power. I cannot rest until I take them home."

Before Donovan could say another word, Bones turned and disappeared down the alley. He moved so quickly, so close to the wall and deep in shadows that it was difficult to follow. Donovan almost had to run. When he hit the street, he did his best to emulate the boy's movements. He pressed close to the walls. He willed the light to ignore him. He averted his gaze from those who passed and thought of an empty street. He had no idea why he did these things. They came to him, and he acted without question. The time for questions was clearly in the past, and the decision whether to follow Rathman's orders and go for the horses, or try to help, had been made for him.

They circled the end of the boardwalk and came up to a narrow, rutted road that ran behind the businesses. Donovan saw that, near the far end, just past the Saloon and at the base of a wooden stair that led down the back wall of the building, the dark carriage had been parked.

Bones stopped just inside the alley and pulled Donovan to the side.

"The horse will be there," he said. "I have no time to explain. If it senses us—if it knows what we are doing—it will try to stop us, and it will call to him. Once that happens, our time will be very, very short. Silkstone keeps the things that hold his power in that carriage. Like the book, they will be hidden. If we do not find them before he returns, we will not survive. He will consume us."

Donovan stared down the alley. He saw that the boy was right about the horse. Despite the fact that it made no sense, the animal was still harnessed to the carriage. It should have been stabled, fed and watered, brushed down and cared for. It was a magnificent animal, and that made the poor care seem even more illogical.

"It is not just a horse," Bones whispered. "You have got to

let go of everything you believe. Nothing here is what it seems. Do you believe Silkstone is a man?"

Donovan shook his head.

"Then why would you believe that that," Bones nodded toward the carriage, "is a horse?"

They moved silently down the alley. Each time they passed a gap between buildings, Bones sped up, flashing like a thin sliver of darkness across the gap, and Donovan did his best to follow. By the time they reached the rear of the saloon, they were moving so slowly Donovan felt his footsteps synchronized with the thudding of his heart, and he was certain that the creature they approached could hear it.

Then the silence of the night was broken. There was a harsh cry, and the crash of breaking glass from the saloon. Donovan turned, startled, but Bones grabbed his arm.

"I'll go," he said. "Get into that carriage. Find his power. If you don't, this is our last night on earth."

Then the boy was gone, slipping into the back door of the saloon with no more sound than a passing breeze. Donovan turned toward the carriage. He heard the horse blow, and then stamp, but then it settled. Fighting the urge to hold a breath he knew he'd expel too loudly, he started down the alley, willing himself part of the shadows.

Chapter Five

Silkstone

Rathman was seated at the bar with a mug of beer, and a shot of whiskey—his third—when the rear doors opened. There was a small crowd. They had a boy, probably not more than eight or nine, named McGraw. He wore a striped shirt and a straw hat he tilted at a cocky angle, and he could bang out quite a tune on the piano. He'd been playing since late afternoon, and beneath and behind his music, the hum of conversation, slap of cards on the poker table, and clatter of glassware had remained steady. When the doors opened, and the stranger walked in, all of it stopped. The music continued, just for a moment. Then, one by one, the notes trailed off. Everyone in the room, except Rathman, turned and stared.

The stranger unfolded through the doorway. That was the only way to describe it. He stood a foot taller than the doorframe. His suit, so finely tailored it seemed almost a second skin, was as dark as night, and his hat, tilted just slightly and rising another foot above his head, was of the finest silk. His boots were black and polished to a mirror sheen, and he carried a walking stick in one hand with a crystal top. It was very long, and very slender, and when he stopped and leaned on it, scanning the room with a laconic grin, it gave him the aspect of a giant, articulated insect leaning on an impossibly tall splinter.

The silence held for several heartbeats, and then Cornelius Boone, trying to appear nonchalant, turned to face the slender giant. He forgot the glass he'd been polishing, and it slipped from his hand, dropping to the floor and shattering. The sound was impossibly loud, and it snapped the stranger's spell.

"Dr. Rathman," the man said, "I have been waiting. I asked you to bring me something that is mine, but instead, it seems, you have chosen to spend time with your old friends, whiskey and beer. Such a shame."

Rathman turned then. He reached out, grabbed the shot glass, and downed its contents with a quick twist of his wrist.

"I have nothing of yours," he said, standing to face the newcomer. "I have nothing, to speak of, in fact. I have a wagon, some books, a pair of horses who have seen better days, and a boy barely able to fetch coffee and stack bottles."

"We both know that's not true," the man said. "I've followed you a long time, *Doctor*. I've followed your footsteps when they were gummed up with tar and feathers. I've got a collection of wanted posters rolled in a tube in my carriage. I've got requests from lawmen in three different states of the union to bring you to justice. None of that matters, of course."

Rathman actually laughed. He turned and stared at each of the others in the room, one at a time. Then he turned back.

"And you," he said. "Since we're making introductions... Alexis Silkstone. How many bodies have you left along the trail, I wonder? How many broken towns? How many souls did you steal, before you slithered in here?"

He turned back to the rest of the bar and continued.

"Our friend here, he's not really a man. Not like you, or me. He's quite a bit more—and less—I'm afraid. He isn't a very nice person, as I'm sure you're all about to find out, and he has the mistaken impression that I have something that belongs to him. It's been a long time since I last stepped foot in Rookwood," he said. "But one thing I remember from my previous visit. I remember that there is law in Rookwood. I remember that an honest man could find protection here."

"Oh, my my," Silkstone purred. "You can't be serious. You know me, and you would still use these innocent, honest folk as your shield. A weak, shallow move from a tired old man. I should have expected no less."

"You should have expected me," a voice spoke up from behind him.

Several things happened in that moment. Silkstone whirled, searching the shadows for the source of the voice. Rathman, seeing his chance, reached down and pulled a gun from his coat pocket. He aimed and fired without thought. The bullet slapped into Silkstone breast high and spun him around. The tall man swatted at the air and growled.

The shot barely slowed Silkstone, who ignored Rathman, and dove toward the shadows. He came up a second later and staggered back into the bar. He held the boy, Bones, by the throat, dangling him off the floor with no effort at all.

The momentary distraction was all it took for Cornelius Boone to get into the act. He ducked behind the bar and came up with a long-barreled shotgun, and he leveled it at Silkstone, though his hand trembled.

"You want to drop that boy, mister," he said. "You want to drop him and hightail it on out of here before I see if two rounds of shot can do what Doctor Rathman's pistol couldn't. You seem pretty tough—I wonder if you're ready for a wager?"

Rathman didn't wait. He fired again. This time the bullet passed through where Silkstone's stomach should have been. The tall man paused, and just for a second his grip loosened. In that instant, Bones appeared to melt, just for a second. His body went limp and then liquid, like a splash of shadow, and he was free. By the time he dropped to the floor, he was a boy again, and it all happened so quickly that none who witnessed it could later swear to what they'd seen. To most, it seemed Silkstone had simply released his grip.

Now there were men moving all over the bar. Guns were drawn, and those with no weapons dove for cover behind tables and around the far corner of the bar. Someone slipped out the front door, and Boone called after them, "Get the Sheriff! Get Sheriff Crawford."

Silkstone drew in on himself, and then, with a flash of darkness and shimmering silver light, he expanded. There was no longer a pretense of being a man. The thing's arms and legs stretched, and the top of the silk hat brushed the beams of the ceiling. The crystal tip of the cane flashed and a bolt of light shot across the room, knocking the gun from Rathman's hand.

Rathman screamed in pain. The impact spun him around, and though he managed to keep his feet, he clutched his hand to his chest as if it has been burned to a stump. Silkstone drew back the staff again, but before he could unleash its power, Bones launched himself from the floor. As he did, he spread out, as Silkstone had done, but in a black sheet of shadow. One second he was a young, very thin boy, clutching the tall, gaunt creature's wrist, and the next he flowed around the staff, and the arm, coating them in a black sheet of darkness. Silkstone cried out in surprise and rage. Boone let loose both barrels of the shotgun, and the tall creature staggered backward, shaking his arm as if to release it from something sticky.

Rathman, seeing his chance, pulled something from his pocket with his good hand. It was a bit of stone, no larger than a coin. Its surface shone like polished metal. He gripped it tightly and held his hand high, then he began to chant in a loud voice. He spoke in Latin, and though none present knew what he said—with the probably exception of Silkstone himself—the words rang bright and pure. Their meaning—while not clear—was implied by the quality of the sound. He spoke of light. He spoke of banishing the darkness. He cried out a warning and a shield, and for just a moment, Silkstone wavered. He staggered back a step, and then another. Bones clung to his arm and his staff tenaciously, and the driving power of Rathman's words pressed him back. Boone reloaded the shotgun and steadied it, waiting for another good shot.

Chapter Six

Cleo & the Night Mare

The carriage shuddered as the door closed behind Donovan. He gripped the doorframe from the inside and rode it out. He knew the creature harnessed to the front was aware of him. He didn't think it could release itself from the harness, and he didn't think it could get to him as long as he was inside the carriage. What he was afraid of was that it would raise enough of a fuss to alert its master. Whatever was going on inside the saloon had everyone busy for the moment, but how long could it last?

He glanced around him and got the lay of the strange vehicle. There were no windows, for one thing. He'd never seen a carriage with no windows for the passenger to peer out through. There was a single seat, dead center, and it was oddly placed and sized. It didn't seem as though a man could sit in that seat comfortably. His feet would dangle off the floor, and the angle of the back was very rigid. There was no upholstery. The seat was the same hard, black polished wood as the carriage exterior. He studied it for only a moment, and then began scanning the rest of the vehicle's interior.

The light was dim, but he found that his eyes had adjusted well enough. He saw there were several doors in the back wall of the chamber, and he went to them quickly. He opened the first. He saw a row of books and small cases, an array of pouches, cups, and braziers, and a dagger in a long, slender leather sheath. He had no idea what he was looking for, but nothing in this cabinet called out to him, and he felt that whatever held Silkstone's "power" would leap out at him—that he would know it.

He opened the right-hand cabinet that stood farthest from the wall. He thought, maybe, that what he sought would be there, because it *was* the farthest, and so the most protected. This door hid blankets, clothing, candles, and a variety of odd grooming implements that Donovan neither recognized, nor understood. None of it seemed important. Not in the way that the boy, Bones, had intimated.

He stood before the center door for a moment. There was a bumping sound, and his heart nearly stopped. He stumbled to his feet, and could not, in that second, tell whether the sound came from before him, behind him, inside or outside the carriage. He cried out then, abandoning caution, and flung the center door open wide. There was a low growl, something warm, soft, and heavy launched from the cabinet's interior and struck him dead in the center of his chest. He gasped and closed his eyes, certain he'd breathed his last, but when nothing further happened, he opened his eyes and stared.

On his legs, staring at him intently, was a cat. It made no move to escape, nor did it attack. It was almost as if it were waiting for him to speak, or to make the first move. He sat up slowly. The cat didn't budge, and a moment later, they were face to face, the cat on his lap as he sat, facing the open cabinet behind it.

"Move on now," he said softly. "I have to find something, and there's not much time."

He picked the animal up gently and placed it on the floor beside him. Then he dropped forward to his knees and peered into the interior of the cabinet. There were three jars inside that were filled with something dark and grainy, like dirt—or sand. Behind them, there was another row of similar jars stretching so far to either side that they disappeared into the shadowy compartment's interior. In front of all of it sat what appeared to be a brass clock. It had a glass dome covering its works, and inside were four heavy brass balls that spun back and forth slowly, beating like a heart.

He glanced at the jars, but his gaze was drawn back, again

and again, to the ticking, mesmerizing motion of the clock. Could that be it? Could it be that simple? Was it—in fact— simple, if time itself was involved?

Donovan leaned forward and reached for the clock. The cat, watching intently from where he'd placed it at his side, leaped. It crashed into his hand, and instead of touching the clock, he struck the one of the front three jars. It tilted, wavered for a moment, and then spun out of the cabinet. Donovan tried to catch it, but he was too slow. It crashed to the floor and shattered. He cursed, started to turn to the cat, and then cried out as something spewed from the broken jar, whirling and filling the air with a dark miasma of grit, sand, dust, and something more. There was sound, like a long, agonized scream. Donovan fell back, and the force, ignoring him, whirled in the air and battered at the carriage door. It struck once, recoiled, and then with an incredible burst of power, shot straight through the wood. The door exploded outward in a wash of splinters and shards. The horse reared and the carriage tilted up on two wheels.

Donovan tried to stand, but the jerk of the carriage swept him off his feet again and he tumbled back. The cat, caught off guard, also tumbled. Without thinking, Donovan reached out, caught it, and tucked it against his chest as jars tumbled from the cabinet, crashing against one another, into the floor and against the walls, and jostling the clock. Each time one of the jars was broken, the screaming, whirling grit filling the carriage increased in volume and power, driving Donovan against the back of the strangely designed seat.

The cat dug its claws into his shirt, but not his skin. It clung tightly, and Donovan curled around it protectively. As he did, he felt an odd sensation creep over him. His own screams quieted, and his mind, which had threatened to spiral out of control into darkness, or madness, calmed. He glanced up carefully and took in the small space with new clarity. He saw the clock. It teetered, and somehow, just in time, he realized that he could not allow it to fall, or to break. He didn't know why, but he knew he had to protect it, as he protected the cat, and that he had to get it out of that carriage. Without any further thought, he acted.

It wasn't easy. Whatever was breaking free of the jars was powerful. It was also angry, and he was the only thing in range. He sensed he was not a target, but that this did not mean there was no danger. He plastered himself to the far edge of the carriage from the door and began, very slowly, to work his way around to the cabinet once more. Not all of the jars had broken open, and though the carriage still shivered and shook now and then, the horse seemed to have realized its mistake and quieted. Something in Donovan's mind made him bypass the clock once more. He ripped at the jars. He drew them forth and flung them out the door of the carriage, hearing them explode and scream and feeling the buffeting power of whatever—whoever, he thought—was escaping.

He didn't stop until the cabinet was free of everything but the clock. Then he reached for it again, but the cat—once again— knocked his hand aside. He turned toward it and glared.

"I have to get it out of here," he said. "I..."

The animal leaped past him to the first cabinet he'd opened. It scrabbled inside, dragging things free with its paws in a mad scramble, until a dark, folded sheet of silk spilled free. It spun, claws piercing the material, and leaped back to Donovan, though the silk was nearly torn free by the escaping energy. It was lessening. With the final jars tossed free of the carriage, and the dust whirling up and out and away, the sound, and the power that had blasted Donovan's senses was dying toward silence. He wanted the clock in his hand and his feet on solid ground before that silence was complete, though again, he had no idea *why* he wanted it.

He took the silk as the cat backed away, watching him again with bright, glittering eyes. This was another thing he was going to have to look into shortly. In his limited experience of cats—they did not communicate on a human level. They did not save people from killing themselves over magical clocks. They did not dig around in cabinets. He didn't allow himself to question it, or even think about it. He knew he had only moments, and he acted.

He slipped the silk over the clock, wrapped it tightly, and lifted. It was heavy, and he nearly lost his grip as it slid off the shelf, but he grunted, dug in his nails, and managed to lower it to the floor. He quickly knotted the silk about it, being careful to cover every inch of the brass and glass. Then, thinking it might be important to have his hands free, he knotted the loose ends of the silk tightly to his belt. It banged against his hip as he moved. There was a walking stick by the door. It was topped by a black stone. He grabbed it and clutched it tightly, thinking it would make a decent club, and he had no other weapon.

He jumped down from the carriage to the ground, and he turned toward the saloon. In that moment, the horse struck. It spun, tilting the carriage and ignoring the weight pulling on it. Its eyes flamed and its jaws were open wide. With a screech of rage it lunged. Before it could strike, a blur of spotted fury launched from the interior of the carriage. It struck the horse on the side the head, clung, and its claws dug into the soft skin of the snout, and the nearest eye. Donovan cried out and fell back. The carriage tilted, teetered, and then toppled over, dragging the horse back with it. The cat leaped free, landing at Donovan's feet.

Before either of them could move—the back door of the saloon blew outward and darkness poured out after it. Through the sound, somehow, Donovan heard Rathman's voice. Or maybe, he thought, he heard the words in his mind.

"Run, boy! For God's sake run."

He scrambled to his feet, gathered up the cat in his arms, and did as he was told.

Chapter Seven

In the Hands of Time

Inside the bar, there was silence. Rathman lay very still in the center of the floor. He breathed, but barely, and he would not be rising again that night. Where the boy, Bones, had been flung aside, a ragged, half-wraith, half-corporeal form leaned against the wall. It shimmered, and slowly, as if thousands of spiders wove patterns across the rends and tears of its fabric, the boy's body repaired itself.

Cornelius Boone lay where he'd dropped behind his bar. He was fine, and he intended to stay that way. When things had gone from bad to insane, he'd dropped, curled up against the backside of the bar, and waited for something to give. He held the shotgun cradled and loaded. If anything, or anyone, had rounded the bar at that moment—even his son—he probably would have shot them dead without a thought.

The customers who'd fallen into the periphery of the conflict either sat still as stone, shocked into immobility by the events they'd just witnessed, or limped and crawled and scrambled for the door. They did not look back. They did not try to help one another, or call out for Cornelius where he'd fallen. They did nothing that might attract attention. There were too many hours until the sun would rise, and they would never be the same after this night. Nothing would be the same.

The boy, McGraw, sat at the piano. His hands were very still, hovering just above the keys. He didn't play, but his lips moved. Anyone close enough would likely have heard him whispering the familiar words to some bawdy drinking song —or maybe a hymn.

Later, no one would be able to say exactly what had ended the confrontation. One moment Silkstone was there, looming over them like a giant walking stick, or a Praying Mantis, dark flashes of power streaming from the cane in his hand, and the corners of his mouth pulled back in a grimacing rictus-mask that might have been his version of a smile.

Then another sound had arisen. It seemed in that moment that a swarm of tiny, whirling black insects burst in through the back of the bar. As they came, they screamed, and insect or not—those screams had been human. Pain, and anger, terror and rage—the spectrum of human violence and hatred was embodied in that wail. As it grew, more voices joined in, some high and screeching and others low and menacing. Silkstone had batted at them with his cane. He cried out in rage of his own and tried to turn and flee. His way was barred. As he spun toward the door, the black mass caught him up and spun him faster. He reached up with his long arms toward the beams of the ceiling and planted his strange, elongated feet on the floor, but it was no use. He held, and the very frame of the building strained, but as more and more of the black flecks invaded and circled, he was slowly erased from sight in a black vortex that dragged him around, and again, and then whirled him out of control as he scrabbled and tore at anything within reach, fighting to free himself, and failing.

Whatever it was that had invaded the saloon had no interest in any other, except the boy, Bones, and the old man, Rathman. Bits of the cloud spiraled out and engulfed them, just for a moment. Remnants of this otherworldly touch began to sew Bones back together. Nothing could be done for Rathman, but he lived. Despite all that he had experience, he lived. It was unlikely to be a long respite, but the man breathed, and Silkstone, in an explosion of sound, power, and a great sucking pop of air, was gone.

That was inside…

At the end of the back alley, Donovan paused and turned. He

had very little experience with strange voices in his head, but he knew on some deep level it would be wisest to listen to them. Still, he hesitated. Rathman was still inside, and Bones, and as much as he wanted to be away, and safe, he knew he couldn't leave them. He also knew he couldn't live the life he'd watched the old man lead, running from city to city; drowning his fears in whatever was handy. A lot had become clear in a very short time, and there were far too many questions he was going to need someone alive to answer.

Whatever had burst through into the street was gone. The carriage was down on its side in the street. The horse that had drawn that carriage and tried to kill him was gone. Somehow none of this helped still the hammering of his heart.

"I have to get in there," he said. He didn't know if he was talking to himself, or to the cat, or which would be crazier.

As he spun, the clock thumped into his thigh. His thoughts focused again. He had to hide it. Before he could go back, before he could help, he had to get it away from Silkstone, and make sure the creature never found it again. He had nowhere else to go, so he spun and ran for the alley. He passed the mouth, glanced at the wagon, and then kept going. It was too obvious. He couldn't risk going there.

The next door he passed was the front of the stable. There was no attendant—everyone in the town was either running to or away from the saloon. Donovan used that as a screen and ran through to where the horses were tucked away in warm stalls. They were nervous, shuffling about and rolling their eyes. Donovan slipped into the stall with the first of them and grabbed its halter.

"Shhh," he said. "It's okay."

He glanced around the stall. The horse had been fed and watered, and it looked as if the groomsman had even given him a quick brushing. There wasn't much in the stall, and Donovan had to think quickly.

A bale of hay had been tossed in the corner. He crossed to it, rolled it up on its side, and began digging frantically at the bottom. It was harder than he'd thought it would be—the hay was bound tightly—but after a moment he'd cleared a hole a little larger than the clock. He untied the package from his belt, checked to be certain that it was still wrapped tightly, then knelt and tucked it up inside the bale of hay. Next he took clumps from the floor and pressed them in tightly beneath it, sealing it as fully as possible. He turned to the cat and waited. He felt ridiculous, but the animal had steered him right so far, and if what he was doing was a mistake, he was certain it would let him know. It made no move to stop him, so he rolled the bale back over and tossed more straw around the base, scuffing it with his feet.

He picked up the cat and tucked her under his arm, then stepped over to the horse again. His presence had calmed the animal, and now that the horrendous sounds and screaming had died away, it only shivered lightly. The other horse was in the next stall, and Donovan took a moment to reach over and stroke its nose.

Then, without looking back, he stepped out of the stall and closed it behind him. He knew he needed to get out of the stable without being seen. He needed to divert whatever might be waiting for him out there from the stable at all cost. He started for the front of the building, but the cat squirmed free then and bolted back into the depths of the building.

"Where are you going?" he called out. He turned and followed. He passed several stalls and a ladder leading up into a hayloft, then turned a corner to his right, and he saw the cat. It stood by what appeared to be a rear utility door. It was probably where the hay was brought in, and it led into the back end of the alley where Rathman's wagon was parked. Donovan pressed it open and glanced outside.

A few moments before the silence had calmed him, but now it felt ominous. Whoever, or whatever Silkstone was, he was still out there. He might be hurt, and he might even be dying, but he was dangerous, and if things were quiet, it might mean the tall man was hunting. If so, Donovan didn't want to make it easy. He had nothing to do battle with such a creature, and from the sounds of things, neither Rathman nor Bones had had much luck at that either, though whatever had been trapped in the now broken jars had been a different story.

He glanced at the back road, where the dark carriage had been parked, then turned toward the street. He slowed as he neared the wagon. It shook slightly, and Donovan froze. Could Rathman have made it out of the bar after all, or the boy? Did they need his help?

Something grabbed at his leg and he glanced down. The cat had hooked the claws of one paw into his pants leg. It tugged him back, and away from the wagon. Donovan stared. Then he turned back to the wagon, and started walking parallel. The street was only a few yards away, and once he reached it, he could duck into the saloon and try to find Rathman. He needed to find out what he was up against.

The wagon shook again, more violently, and Donovan broke into a run. The cat dodged around the corner at his feet, keeping pace with him. They found the front door of the saloon open wide. When they entered, they were greeted by the sound of a shotgun action, and for the second time in only a few moments, Donovan froze.

Cornelius Boone stood behind the bar. His hair was wild, and his eyes were wide and staring. He aimed the gun straight at Donovan's chest, and the boy raised his hands.

"Don't shoot, Mr. Boone," he said. "I'm not here to hurt anyone."

He saw Rathman then, and ignoring the shotgun, he cried out softly and ran to kneel at the old man's side. He lifted Rathman's head and held it in one arm. His old master's breathing was shallow, and it wavered like wind whistling through dry reeds. When Donovan touched him, his eyes opened. He gazed up and almost managed a smile. It faded quickly to a grimace of pain.

"The book?" he croaked.

Donovan stared for a moment, and then he remembered.

"I have it," he said. "It's with me."

"You have to run," Rathman said. He broke into a fit of coughing, and then got it under control. "He has the clock...he can't get the book."

"He doesn't have the clock," Donovan said. "I hid it. And I'm not going anywhere. You ran—and now..."

"Now I'm dead," Rathman said. "I know. I only have a few

moments. You have to destroy him. If you have the book, and the clock, you can do it. But the souls...the jars..."

"Free," Donovan said. "The jars are broken. Whatever was in them came for him. The carriage tipped and that horse..."

"Not a horse," Rathman coughed. "Familiar."

Donovan frowned. Suddenly the cat stepped forward. It leaned down, ducked its head, and rubbed against Rathman's cheek. The old man's eyes flew open wider. He almost sat up.

"Cleo?" he said.

"What?" Donovan asked. "You aren't making sense."

"Cleopatra—the cat—thought she was dead. Cleo is here?"

"She saved me," Donovan said simply. It was crazy, but it was also the truth. "At least three times."

Footsteps sounded, and Donovan glanced up. The boy, Bones, was crawling across the floor toward him. He looked even thinner and more emaciated than before, and his eyes were dull, but he was better off than Rathman.

"Fire," Bones said. "It must be fire. It is the only way."

Rathman nodded weakly.

"Fire," he agreed.

"He is in the wagon," Donovan said.

Rathman reached up and gripped him by his shirt. The old man pulled, and lifted slightly off the ground, dragging Donovan down.

"Burn it!" he said. "Now, before it's too late.

"But...the books. The cards."

"Damn you," Rathman choked, "*Burn it!*"

The old man grew stiff, his eyes bulged, and his back arched. Donovan shook him gently.

"Rathman. Rathman!"

It was no good. The old man was gone, and Donovan laid him gently on the floor. He turned to find Cornelius Boone leaning down, holding out a wooden box.

"What is it?" Donovan asked. He was fighting a rush of tears he did not have time to shed and trying to struggle to his feet.

"I heard," Boone said. "You'll need this."

Donovan glanced down and took what was offered.

It was a tinderbox.

Chapter Eight

The Burning

Donovan took the tinderbox and turned. The street was empty. He felt the pressure of many eyes, but none of those behind them had the courage to join him as he walked out onto the boardwalk and turned toward the alley. The cat, who he now knew was Cleo, though the knowledge left him with more questions than answers, trotted at his heel. The boy, Bones, had started after him, but it was a slow, laborious effort that would take more time than Donovan was willing to grant it, so he was on his own.

He turned at the mouth of the alley, and saw the wagon, parked as he'd left it. It still shook, though with less violence. He heard the crash and tinkle of breaking glass. He stood and stared for a moment, and then started forward. It was crazy. Everything he had ever known—everything that he owned and hoped to inherit—was packed away inside that wagon. The horses that should pull it were safely tucked away next door, and here he was, ready to—what?—stand at the tail end of it and toss sparks until it caught.

"Donovan."

He turned. Cornelius Boone's boy, Silas, stood a few steps behind him. He held out a torch almost sheepishly, though he shook with terror.

"Saw you leave," the boy said. "Saw my pa give you the tinderbox, and I thought maybe you could use this."

Donovan took the torch and almost smiled. The expression died short of his lips, but it must have reached his eyes, because the boy relaxed.

"I'm still trying to figure out what to do," Donovan said. "That thing, whoever, or whatever, is in the wagon. If I just light the wagon, I'm afraid it'll catch your saloon on fire. If I try to get the horses, well, whatever that is isn't going to stay in there while I haul it out into the desert to light it."

"Your Pa said to burn it," Silas said.

"He wasn't my Pa. I worked for him. It was his wagon—guess it's mine now. Another reason I don't want to just burn it. But there's more."

"What?" Silas asked. He didn't really sound curious, but the question was dutiful—Donovan's comment almost demanded it.

"Whatever is in there is alive," Donovan said. "Evil, good, light or dark, it's got two arms and two legs and it talks, and I'm not sure when it comes down to it I can just light it up and watch it burn like cordwood. Not sure at all."

The wagon gave a mighty shake then, and the point became moot. Silkstone, or what was left of him, stood up at the front of the wagon. He turned awkwardly in the driver's seat, found Donovan, and locked gazes with him.

"Boy," Silkstone hissed, "give it to me."

Donovan stood his ground. He made no move toward the wagon, nor did he back away. He returned Silkstone's gaze, and he waited.

The thing on the wagon tried to climb over the side and clamber down. Halfway through the motion, it tumbled, and it fell. The heap of rags and bones that rose from the dust was only a thin, wavering wraith of what had been. It was still too tall, but now, instead of giving it a menacing aspect, its emaciated height made it fragile. Every motion seemed destined to snap a brittle limb, or send it tumbling again. A stiff breeze would have dropped it to the ground again, or spun it into a wall.

Still, it came. One pained step after another, it made its way down the alley toward Donovan, who held the torch, and the tinder box, as though they were a shield.

"Light it," Silas said. "Light it, mister, before it's too late."

Donovan glanced down at the torch. He handed the tinder box to the boy, and he held out the torch. "I can't hold it and light it. If I try, he'll be here before I'm finished."

Silas Boone was scared. He was way out of his element. For all of that, the boy held it together like a battle-scarred veteran. He took the tinder box, fished out the flint, and struck. Sparks flew, just missing the end of the torch. Then again, and again. On the third strike, tendrils of smoke rose from the torch, and on the fourth, it burst into flickering life. Donovan pulled it up and away from Silas, and the tinderbox. When he turned, Silkstone stopped. Only about five yards separated them.

"You have something that is...mine," it hissed. "You will give it back, or I will drag your soul through hot coals."

Even as it spoke, it wobbled, barely able to remain upright.

"What I have belonged to Hugo Rathman," Donovan replied. He was surprised how steady his voice sounded. His heart was hammering.

The thing laughed. The effort nearly tore it apart, but still, it laughed, a dry, wind-through-reeds sound.

"There is no Hugo Rathman," it said. "There is only Silkstone. He created me. He dragged me from the pits and gave me form. He bound me."

"What are you?" Donovan asked.

"You would not understand the answer. Trapped. I am trapped, and I am wearing thin. The book, and the clock...I must have them. I can give you power. I can show you secrets. You must...give them to me. I must...feed."

"The clock is long gone," Donovan said. "If Rathman's name was Silkstone, then the book was his as well. You will never see either again. If you do not turn, and depart, I will destroy you."

Again, the thing that had called itself Silkstone laughed. It shivered and made strange, hiccoughing noises in its throat. It stumbled another step forward, and another.

"Burn it!" Silas cried out suddenly. "Burn the damned thing! Can't you see it's comin' for you?"

Donovan shook his head. He held the torch before him steadily, but made no move to use it.

"There is nothing for you here," he said.

The thing tottered forward again. This time, instead of stuttering steps, it lurched at him. Whatever was holding it together had begun to give way. It was a last ditch effort, a primal rush. Donovan didn't move. He held out the torch, and he waited. From behind him, another cry rose, but he ignored it. If he turned, he knew it would be bad. What approached him was hurt badly—weakened, possibly beyond recovery—but that didn't mean it wasn't dangerous.

The sound of rushing feet approaching from behind echoed through the alley. The boy, Bones, looking only slightly better than the creature advancing on Donovan, rushed past. He threw something—a small jar—and it shattered at the creature's feet. Liquid splashed from the shattered glass, and Bones, crashing into Donovan from behind, knocked him out of the way, and grabbed the torch.

Even as he fell, the scent of kerosene rose and Donovan knew.

"No!" He cried out. "It's dying..."

He hit hard, and rolled. The kerosene caught in a sudden blaze, and the boy tumbled into it headlong. He gripped what remained of the creature near where its throat had been and shook. The fire raged. The kerosene had ignited it, but there had not been enough in the jar to explain the sudden heat, or the raging flames. Donovan rolled, over and over, until he came up against the side of the stable. Silas Boone had backed into the street. In the center of the alley, engulfed in red flame and dancing smoke, Bones choked the essence from the skeletal cadaverous demon he had hunted.

Donovan rolled to his feet. He tried to rush back to where the blaze roared in the center of the alley, but it was too hot. He fell back, watching in stunned silence, as the fire engulfed the boy, and the creature, feeding on some energy he could neither see nor sense. The flames burned so loudly that he saw the cloud billowing from the street behind the saloon before he heard it. Dark, seething, like a huge swarm of locusts, or bees, the power he'd released from the jars in the carriage poured into the alley.

Silas turned tail then and ran. Donovan stood his ground. The cat, Cleo, brushed up against his leg. They watched, captivated, as the swarm whirled up to and around the flames.

In seconds, the blaze was obscured by a spinning vortex of darkness that screamed and wailed and pounded in on itself in relentless waves. Donovan had seen tornadoes in the desert. This was like that, only more focused, and more violent. He could make out individual voices, saw faces swirling past in the grit and the shadow, and now and then highlighted by bursts of flame. The air spun fast and faster, and he realized with a start that it was sucking him—and everything around it—inward. With an effort, he leaned and snatched the cat off the ground. Without a glance back, he turned and ran. He dove around the corner in front of the stable, rolled to the wall, protecting the cat with his body, closed his eyes and pressed back into the wood.

It seemed to last forever, beating the walls and the ground and the street with waves of slashing wind, and then dragging things back into itself, as if the flames sought sustenance, anything to keep them burning. When it ended, it was so sudden that Donovan sat in shock for a full minute afterward before he realized it was done. There was no sound. There were no flames. The wind was simply—gone. He sat the cat on the boardwalk and rolled to hands and knees. He crawled to the edge of the stable and peered around into the alley.

Inside the stable, he heard the animals screaming in terror, and he knew he—or someone—would have to get to them before they hurt themselves. There were suddenly a thousand things calling for his attention, concerns he'd not even dreamed of the day before, but for that moment he pushed them aside.

The alley was empty, except for the wagon, which, while canted over a bit toward the saloon, seemed intact. Where the thing he'd known as Silkstone had stood, there wasn't even a scorch mark. The glass from the kerosene bottle was gone. The flames and the grit and voices and souls—Bones—they might as well have never existed. It was so quiet that he feared, just for a moment, that he, the cat, and the horses were the only things left alive.

Then, starting slowly, but growing in volume and power, he heard something new. From the saloon, the strains of an old hymn broke free of the old piano. The boy, McGraw, had found his courage, and begun to play. The notes of the song wound out through the town, and all around him, Donovan heard voices and saw people stepping into the street. He rose, shook off the dust, and turned toward the stable and the panicked animals. There was a lot to do and even more to think about... but for the moment he went where the need was strongest, and most imminent.

The cat, Cleo, trotted at his heels. Neither looked back.

Chapter Nine

Promises to Keep

Rookwood came back to life very slowly. The saloon had sustained the most damage. The backdoor frame and part of the wall were gone. The edges of that hole were scorched, as if they'd been burned in some sort of fire. There was no scent of burning wood, however, and after a half day of steady hauling, sawing, and pounding, Cornelius, Silas, and Donovan managed to repair the damage. The wood was discolored in places, but the wall itself was sound.

The interior had taken only minor damage. The finish on the bar and the piano had been scuffed by whatever had whirled out of the broken jars out back. There was a faint bloodstain where Rathman had fallen for the last time that had proven particularly stubborn. It wasn't long before the magic of entropy settled in, and people's stories started to twist away from what Donovan remembered to more mundane, though creative, explanations of the past few day's events.

Some said a twister had touched down out back of Boone's Saloon and actually wound its way in the door, killing Rathman and causing all kinds of frightened misconceptions among the patrons. Silkstone shrank back to the size of a man, and folks said it was a shame that his magnificent horse had broken free of the carriage as it had, disappearing in the confusion of the storm.

There was no mention of the boy, Bones, at all. When Donovan asked, only Silas Boone had a vague recollection that something had come in the back door of the saloon and attacked the stranger. They all believed that, when Silkstone burned, Donovan held the torch. They also believed that Silkstone must have somehow spilled the kerosene on himself. None of them offered an explanation for why there'd been nothing left of the body. None of them seemed to *want* to know. It was better if it all faded to pale. Things should have rational explanations, they said. Things should be "normal".

Donovan wished them all luck with that. For him, everything had shifted so far to the left of normal that he suspected the effect was irreversible. Cornelius Boone had suggested that Donovan go through the dark carriage out back and see what he could find. No one in the town wanted anything to do with what might be in there, but they were clear on one thing. The trouble had followed Rathman, and thus Donovan, into Rookwood. Whatever was in that dark wreck was his to carry away. They needed it gone, so they could forget.

He'd cleared out everything he could find. There were jars and vials, some articles of clothing, a silk hat much like the one Silkstone had worn, several very old and very strange books, along with a rolled parchment, and a journal. There were more of the jars that had held the black dust, but they were all empty. All of this Donovan dug free, packed carefully, and tucked away in his wagon. Everyone agreed on that point too...he'd come in with the old man, and since Rathman was dead, what he'd owned would go with Donovan. He was nearly seventeen, and old enough to care for himself. He had a little money, and he had some skills, dubious as they might be. He could get along, and as far as most of the town was concerned, it wouldn't be too soon.

Still, he set up the table outside the wagon, and he read from the old story books. His audiences were small, at first. Mostly children showed up, and for them he read from a tattered copy of *Aesop's Fables*, and from an illustrated book of fairy tales he'd found in the back of one of Rathman's trunks. When the adults came around, he pulled out Shakespeare, and Herodotus. He often read passages directly from The Bible, and these drew the biggest crowd. The town was currently without a minister, and they were starved for the Good Word.

He spent his early mornings and late evenings clearing out the damage from Silkstone's fruitless search, repacking what seemed useful and discarding things he didn't want. There was one comfortable bed in the wagon. He carefully laundered the bedclothes, cleaned the interior of the wagon until it was spotless, and turned it into—if not luxurious accommodations—at least the most comfortable he'd ever known. Rathman had been carrying a watch and a pouch with nearly a hundred dollars in gold. That, plus the change he earned telling stories, and helping Boone rebuild his tavern, gave him enough for a good start. He also made ten dollars for the wood from Silkstone's carriage, which he sold to the local undertaker to use in making coffins.

The most important things he did, however, he did at night, with only Cleo for company, and a lantern burning at his side. He had the book that had been hidden beneath the Tarot cards. He had the book about the cards that he'd read once before. He had the clock, and he had Silkstone's journals. What these all opened up to him was beyond anything he could have imagined, or comprehended, without experiencing all that he had. The books spoke of portals, and visions. They explained incantations and spells. They also, in the end, gave him purpose.

The clock and the book that had so enraptured the stranger were a pair. The book explained how the clock, which had begun its existence as a very mundane, if expensive, timepiece, had come to be enchanted. There was a spell of binding in the book that tied one to the clock, which existed, as the book put it, in more than one dimension. In its other existence, it rested on a forgotten shelf. Time in that place moved at only the tiniest fraction of the speed that it does on Earth. When the spell of binding was performed, the holder of the book, and the clock, would live a lifespan determined by another version of time.

The cards were the biggest revelation. As he'd suspected, after seeing the visions in Rathman's reading, they were not really cards at all. They were symbolic keys, and with them he was able to unlock still more secrets. And then there was Silkstone's journal.

The book was scribed in thin, spidery letters of incredible

precision and elegance. The story it told was of one of the longest and most bizarre hunts in the history of the world. Rathman, then still simply Herbert Bloom, had happened upon a book of spells. The book had contained one particularly effective summoning ritual, and, arrogant and foolish, the young Rathman had performed it. At that point he was already in possession of the clock, and had bound himself to it. He had renamed himself Silkstone the great, and he believed himself nearly immortal. The summoning of a demon did not hold the terror for him that it should have.

There were, of course, consequences. Everything has rules, magic most of all. Rathman, or Bloom, or Silkstone—whatever you called him—did not provide the necessary sacrifice, and when the demon arrived, it needed the blood of that sacrifice to seal it to its new realm. When Rathman withheld it, albeit because he didn't *have* it, the demon lost control and attacked. For all his foolishness, Rathman *was* a reasonably powerful mage. He escaped the circle and left the demon partially trapped inside. He failed, however, to seal the rift once he'd stepped through, and over time, the prison had failed, and the thing that crawled out stole his name, calling itself Silkstone.

Bloom, changing his name to Hugo Rathman, had fled, taking his book and what he could get away with. What he was not able to take was the clock and Cleo. The clock he would have lived without, though not nearly as long. Cleo was another story. The clock had been within the protective circle, and when he trapped the demon, it had remained inside. He knew that the demon would not destroy it, because—since there had been no sacrifice present in the circle at the time of summoning, Rathman himself had assumed that role. The demon could not allow anything to happen to the clock, because if Rathman died, it would be destroyed as well. All it could do was feed on the souls of those it encountered—sealing their essence into the jars it had carried in the dark carriage to sustain it on its long hunt.

The chase had continued for many years. As Rathman traveled the west, criss-crossing from town to town, doling out the remnant of his power and drinking himself into oblivion, the creature tracked him. Every stop along the way was recorded meticulously in the journal. Every life that was taken, every soul that was stolen.

As Hugo Rathman grew older, and weaker, the creature known only as Silkstone drew nearer. It knew that, should it ever gain custody of the book, it could rebind the clock, stealing the days and years remaining to its summoner. There was no plan beyond this. The thing was intelligent, and focused, but it was not human. It could never have been human. Its wit and black humor were remnants of Rathman's personality, stolen through Cleo, who it held prisoner in the carriage.

Cleo had guarded the clock. She had watched over it, waiting for Rathman to return, waiting for him to figure it out and regain the upper hand. There was a link between the two—a strong link—and Silkstone used it to his advantage. He stole bits and pieces of Rathman's mind when the link was strong, and he used the link for tracking.

Eventually, other books and other rituals came to the demon. It summoned its own familiar—the horse that had never really been a horse. Theirs was not a bond of love. Silkstone summoned it in the same manner he himself had been summoned. In the horse form, it relied on him for sustenance—for souls. Given half a chance, it would have consumed Silkstone himself and retreated to whence he'd summoned it. Silkstone treated it as if it were truly his familiar. He created the bonds through incantations and enchantments, mimicking the life Rathman had led and trying to build a shell he could inhabit once both book and clock were his.

There was a lot of other information in the book. There were spells discovered along the way, powers the demon already possessed that, for whatever reason, it had recorded. The journal felt almost like a forced confession, or a record. Donovan did not know who the thing had recorded it for—and he was certain he never wanted to know.

The day after he finished reading the journal, he packed it, along with Rathman's book, back into the bottom of the box that held the Tarot cards. He packed the wagon carefully, and then he walked around to the saloon to say his goodbyes. He knew he couldn't stay. Somehow he sensed that sitting in one place for too long might never feel comfortable again. At least, not for a long, long time.

And there was another thing. He'd read most of what Rathman had to offer. There were some new books collected by Silkstone, but they were thin, obscure, and dangerous. There had to be more. He had a sudden thirst for knowledge. He felt a great balance all around him—a balance that the events of the past weeks had challenged severely.

He'd read enough to know that what Rathman had done, while well within the realm of possibility, had come with certain risks. The old man had not been careful. He'd allowed his concentration to slip, and he'd used the power for his own gain. Most of the great magical stories of the world showed the lives of those who misused power going astray in bad ways and dragging the world along for the ride. How much greater must the risk be in magical things? How many Rathmans were out there? How many creatures like Silkstone were loose in the world? Who was there to figure it out and to make sure things didn't fly out of control?

Cleo paced him as he entered the saloon, and he stooped to scoop her up and carry her inside. He'd experienced some strange sensations around the animal. His senses were keener. More than once, he'd felt a nauseating slip in his mind, and seen things from an entirely different perspective, low to the ground, moving too quickly, and then back to his own thoughts. He thought it would grow stronger as time passed. If he'd judged the days and years of Silkstone's journal rightly, the cat was at least eighty years old, and thus, not a cat at all. There was so much to learn—having her as his companion made that task seem less imposing, and a lot less lonely.

"You're in early," Cornelius Boone said as Donovan entered.

"I'll be heading out today," Donovan said. He tried to keep his voice nonchalant, but despite all that he'd seen and experienced, he was only a boy on the brink of his seventeenth birthday. He wasn't yet used to speaking with grown men on a familiar basis.

"Thought you might," Boone said. "Seen it coming for a while. Know where you're headed?"

Donovan shook his head. "I need to find places where there are more books," he said, working to try and get the thoughts out of his mouth the way they formed in his head. "I think there's a lot I need to learn. I don't want the life that Mr. Rathman had, but I don't think I'm going to settle anytime soon."

"Well, Silas is gonna miss you," Boone said. "That boy actually started working on his reading. You know he reads verses to me from The Bible every night now? Got you to thank."

Donovan smiled. "He's a smart boy. He'll pick it up just fine, now that he's started. I'll leave him a couple of books—books with stories in them, and not just verses. Just in case he's interested."

Boone nodded. "Got a preacher coming to town in a couple of weeks. New fella from back east. Don't reckon I'm going to ever be able to tell him what happened."

"It makes a better story for a late night and a beer," Donovan agreed. "You're more likely to find believers. The folks out in town, they've already put it behind them. They're convinced you were struck by a freak storm, and Hugo Rathman died of a heart attack. It's the story they'll tell."

"Reckon you're right," Boone said. "It will sound better at the other end of a whiskey bottle. You headed west?"

Donovan nodded. "For now. I want to hit some of the bigger cities, and then I'll probably turn back east. The universities and libraries on that coast are the greatest in America. Then there's Europe. I have the feeling I'll be collecting words for a long time."

Boone sat a plate of eggs, bacon and fresh bread in front of him, along with a mug of coffee.

"Better eat up then," he said. "That sounds like a lot of miles, and a lot of words. You're not gonna make it on an empty stomach. I'll have Silas pack you some supplies. I figure that'll just about leave us even."

"Thanks, Mr. Boone," Donovan said. "I appreciate it."

"Cornelius," Boone said. "Call me Cornelius. I'm happy to call you friend."

Donovan smiled, and nodded, and then he ate slowly. He knew it would be harder to find a meal like this once he got back on the road, and wanted to savor it. He picked off a bit of bacon and held it out to Cleo, who ate it gently from the tip of his finger.

"What do you say, Cleo," he said. "Shall we do some traveling?"

The cat held its silence, but as he gazed deep into her eyes, he thought, just for a second, he was gazing out into his own. He shivered and stroked her gently.

"This," he whispered, "is going to get interesting..."

Chapter Ten

The Man Behind the Mask

Donovan slowly opened his eyes. He gazed across the circle at Amethyst, who, still entranced, had an expression of deep concentration etched across her lovely features. At some point during the sharing, Cleo had jumped up onto the table, and sat watching quietly. The four braziers had burned low, and the crystal, which had swirled with light and shadows, had faded to its normal, opaque stillness. Donovan squeezed Amethyst's fingers, and she raised her head slowly. She turned her head from side to side, glanced down to where Donovan still held her hands, and then up to meet his gaze. She returned the pressure of his touch, and then carefully extricated her fingers and sat back.

Donovan watched as she stretched, looking like a fire-maned cousin to a lioness. Then he rose and began clearing away his paraphernalia from the circle. The crystal went back into its bag. The braziers he tested with his fingertips, found cool enough to touch, and carried to dump the charcoal in the waste basket before wiping each carefully clean and returning them to their place in his desk drawer. He cleared the table meticulously, wiping away the marks that remained of the protective circle. All the while, so softly it would have taken a very sharp ear to hear him, he chanted, releasing the wards on the cardinal points of the circle, banishing the images of the past, and clearing the air.

When all of this was done, he brought out another bottle of wine, uncorked it, and poured some into their glasses. Then he returned to his seat.

Amethyst watched all of this in silence, but it was a

comfortable silence. She took a grateful sip of the wine, whirled her goblet distractedly, and at last, she spoke.

"1842, huh?" she said softly. "You were sixteen, and Cleo was?"

"Cleo was, Cleo," Donovan said with a smile. "It's not polite to ask a lady her age, you know."

At that moment, the cat leaped down from the table top and landed in Amethyst's lap with a soft thunk. She stood on her hind legs, pressed her front paws into Amethyst's shoulders, and met her gaze. Then, with a soft thump Cleo head-butted her in the chin and began to purr. Amethyst burst into laughter and hugged the cat.

"I always knew I had a thing for older men," she said at last. "I guess I knew you'd been around a long time, as well. I just didn't know how long. You still have the clock, then?"

Donovan nodded.

"I didn't perform the binding until many years later. I realized over time that a single lifetime was not going to allow me to complete the work that I'd started—that, in fact, the work might never be finished. There are a lot of dangerous books out there. Scraps of paper that hold the keys to souls and other universes. Scrolls and etchings and even paintings that should not fall into the wrong hands. The balance is very intricate, and I'm afraid most of those with the ability to manipulate it don't have the proper respect for what can happen if it's broken."

"So you watch over us all," Amethyst murmured.

"Let's just say, I try," Donovan said. "You know me. I'm as big a bumbler as the next. I have studied and learned and practiced and still I only have a tiny shred of the knowledge that exists. There are others older and more powerful. There are certainly plenty of others that are dangerous in one way or another, both to themselves and to the universe. Tracking them down keeps me busy."

"So I've seen. But what about the settling down? Your younger self seemed pretty certain on that point. That you never would. What happened to the horse and wagon, and the traveling?"

"I still get around," Donovan said softly. "You've seen the

portals. I've explored a great number of them, with more to wander down when the mood hits. There are focal points in the universe, places where the great lines of power meet. San Valencez rests atop one of the greatest junctions. It's what drew me here, and likely what drew you as well, even before you were aware of it. Rookwood, as it turns out, was another such place. Mine was not the last strange happening in that remote town, or even the most powerful. I'll tell you that story one day. It involves gunslingers and an angel. It's a good story. I have a lot of stories. Remind me, for instance, to tell you what really happened in the events that became 'The Scarlet Letter.'

"As for me, I traveled for many years. At one point I even took the name of Silkstone, as Hugo Rathman had done, and lived the life of a traveling illusionist. I was well-known in those days, and in the end, that was why I had to give it up. If those who you entertain can find you—so can those who would like to see you destroyed. I came to San Valencez when it was nothing but a gold town. There was Lavender, with its hidden mines, and there was San Valencez. In the end, it was San Valencez that boomed and grew. The money was here, and the power. The lines of force that bisect beneath this place affect more than our kind. The crossing is a catalyst.

"So I took the fortune I'd built and invested it, and I built myself a home. This building is the second to rest on the same foundation. I own it, and most of the next couple of blocks. The library I had collected during my travels was growing rather large for a wagon, or even a train—I spent a few years living on one of those, as well as a long summer on my own riverboat. When I first built this building it housed my library. As technology has improved, computers allowed me to digitize much of it, and to move the truly dangerous items out of reach. My need for space shrank, and so, to cover my own tracks, I began renting out rooms, and floors. Now I live on this single floor that most of my tenants don't even know is here. I come and go as I wish. I have Cleo, and you, and there is very little missing in my life."

There was a loud squawk, and Asmodeus, who'd been quiet through the entire process of the sharing, and the aftermath, launched from his perch far atop the fireplace and did a lazy circle of the room. He circled again, and then, like a feathered stone, dropped to land on Donovan's shoulder with a plop. Donovan and Amethyst both laughed, and Cleo, still seated in Amethyst's lap, glared up at the bird haughtily. She did not, however, launch at him, or chase him away.

"Okay," Donovan said, scratching the old bird under its chin, "maybe I don't have everything just yet, and maybe there *are* plenty of surprises still waiting for me out there.

"What about you?" he asked, turning to Amethyst. "I have only known you for a few short years. You didn't come to your own power, or collection, or knowledge, by attending San Valencez University and cheering for the dragons."

Amethyst smiled up at him almost coyly.

"You wouldn't want all our secrets to be revealed in a single day," she said. "Surely not. I will make you the promise that you made to me. When the time is right, I'll tell you everything there is to know. For now, we have wine, and I have a lot to think about..."

She ran her gaze up and down his form slowly.

"And I have some things I want to...explore."

She placed Cleo gently on the ground at her feet, rose, and wrapped Donovan in a tight embrace. He met her gaze, and then leaned in close to kiss her. Then, in a single, swooping motion, he slid his hand down her back, turned her, and lifted her into his arms. As Cleo hopped back up onto the table to walk, Asmodeus standing nonchalantly at her side, Donovan carried Amethyst out of the room and down the hall toward his bedroom. The lights, as if of their own accord, dimmed.

Somewhere in the darkness, very quietly, a clock ticked.

The Preacher's Marsh

An Old Mill, North Carolina Tale

ONE

In 1868, Old Mill, North Carolina was no more than a smudge on the map. There were roads leading north and south, maintained for the most part to transport cotton. There was a cotton gin, a general store, a scattered spread of housing for those who worked in town.

Near the edge of town on the way up from the south road the Baptist church gleamed and glittered. Its walls were brilliant white wood, and the steeple held a shiny metal bell that was polished and cared for as if it might have been cast from the Holy Grail itself. On the north road, a smaller Methodist church sat back a ways from the road. It wasn't as brightly painted as the Baptist building, but it had colorful stained glass windows and wood trim.

The fields surrounding the town stretched out along bumpy dirt roads toward the Great Dismal Swamp on the Virginia side and the Perquimans River on the southern boundary. Owned by a very few families, this land was planted almost exclusively with cotton. Some of it was farmed by sharecroppers, a few acres by squatters, but the majority of it was worked in much the same way it had been for the past hundred years. The local gentry had been forced to release their slaves from bondage, but other than the formal release, little had changed. The cotton still had to be picked, and the slaves who had worked the fields for so many generations had nowhere else to go. In most cases they'd stayed on, either remaining with the families who'd owned them, or putting up shacks and hovels nearby and working as freedmen for little or no wages. The south did not leap into the new America. President Lincoln's war brought change, but it was slow, seeping change.

When Reverend Gideon Swayne walked into town in late August, the sun was just setting over the cotton fields. The streets were all but bare, only a couple of barefoot, grimy kids pushing wagons of produce and other goods back to wagons for their parents. Most shopping in town took place on Saturdays. Reverend Swayne arrived in Old Mill on a Tuesday, and any man, woman or child with two good legs and the use of their hands was picking cotton, sunup to sundown.

He was a tall man with coal black hair that was a little long for the time, swept back over his ears and his collar. He had several days' growth of beard, but it was difficult to tell if this was by choice, or just from the lack of a place to shave. The dust of the road was heavy on his pants legs; his face was drawn and thin. He couldn't have looked less like he belonged if he'd flown in on a broom, and gossip had flown about from mouth to mouth and house to house since he first appeared on the road outside town and was spotted by a group of field hands picking cotton.

He stopped in the road in front of the Baptist church and stared up at the steeple. He put his hand over his eyes to shade them from the bright sunlight and took in the gleaming paint and the polished metal bell. He glanced in through the windows and caught sight of wood paneled walls and flashes of color behind the pulpit.

Brother Dan Cumby was pastor of the church, and he lived in a neat, well-kept bungalow situated on the lot next door. His grass was cut close to the ground. The bushes that lined his porch were trimmed to geometric perfection. Not a speck of dirt besmirched the purity of his paint, nor a smudge the clarity of his glass windows. It was a comfortable home by the standards of the day. Reverend Swayne had seen dozens of homes on his way into town, and none of them approached this one for comfort.

Inside the house, someone pulled the drapes aside, just a fraction of an inch. Reverend Swayne felt the weight of eyes staring, but he did not return the gaze. He continued to study the church, as if he were considering walking up and knocking on the door, or stopping by to visit. Then, with a quick shake of his head, he leaned down, grabbed his bags, and turned back to the road, continuing into town.

When he was out of sight, the drapes fell back into place over Pastor Cumby's window. No one came to the door, or watched Reverend Swayne's progress. He rounded a corner and stepped up onto a boardwalk that lined the front of the town's few offices and stores. There was an awning, and he stood for a while, relieved to be out of the sun.

As he stood, he scanned the storefronts. There was no one in sight, but he didn't seem upset, or even particularly surprised. He spotted the Walz's General Store, and shouldered his bag again. A few moments later he pushed the door opened gently and stepped inside.

Devon Walz glanced up from where he was arranging cans on a shelf. He hadn't expected business—during the workday in the middle of the week he might as well have closed the doors and gone home. When the door opened and a tall stranger stepped through, it caught him off guard.

Gideon Swayne stood in the doorway, hands clasped before him and his bags on the floor at his feet. He was a big man, but he was quiet and made no untoward moves. Devon put the can he was holding down on the shelf, wiped his palms on his pants legs, and stepped into the main aisle of his store.

"Howdy," he said, keeping some distance from the stranger. "Can I help you?"

"I hope so," Reverend Swayne said. He smiled, and the smile was contagious. His eyes were a deep, chocolate brown. His clothing was clean, but not too expensive. The coat was cut in a style Devon didn't recognize, and there was a twang in the voice that screamed "Yankee."

"I've come a long way," he continued. "My name is Reverend Gideon Swayne. No reason you'd know it, or that it would matter, but it's what my mother gave me, and it has served me well."

"Pleased to meet you, Reverend," Devon said. He wasn't sure what to make of the strange greeting. A man's name wasn't something he'd be inclined to question, and no one in Old Mill was going to need to be told that this man had come a long way. Everyone within forty miles of town knew everyone else, and very few outsiders stayed more than a day or two. Family came in to visit, at times, but for the most part Old Mill was a world unto itself.

"We got two churches here already, Reverend," Devon said. "Pastor Cumby preaches at the Baptist church to the south, and Reverend Winslow leads the Methodist worship to the North. Most folks here go to one, or the other. No disrespect, but if you've come looking for work, you hit the wrong town."

Reverend Swayne's smile never wavered. He stepped forward and offered Devon his hand, which the grocer shook.

"There is always work for a man of God," Swayne said. "Times are changing. The country is changing. I have heard a particular call, and I've come in answer."

"I don't think I get your meaning, Reverend," Walz replied, frowning.

"There are many rooms in my Father's house," Reverend Swayne said. "I've come to check on the souls of the newly free. I've come to make sure God is part of their lives, as He is so obviously part of the lives of those who worship here in town. Tell me, sir," he turned to Devon and there was a light in his eyes that had been missing only moments before, "who preaches to the freedmen? Where do they worship? Do they have a church, or do they meet in their homes."

Devon stared. Color rose to his cheeks, and his pulse slowly rose to his throat and pounded.

"I take it," Reverend Swayne said, studying the grocer's face, "that they do not worship here in town."

"They do not," Walz growled. "Mr., you've come to the wrong place to be spouting that Yankee crap. You want to make nice with the niggers, you go do it, but you won't find them here in town. Not if they know what's good for them. They get fed, and they work, just like they always have."

"There's no call to get angry," Reverend Swayne said calmly. "I don't intend to herd them into your store like a cattleman, or to drag them into your churches. I've only come to do the Lord's work in best way I know to do it. Our Lord did the same. His apostles were stoned and beaten for teaching in the streets and spreading the message of his love to the low, the criminal—the poor. How can I do less?"

Footsteps sounded outside, and both men fell silent for a moment. The door opened, and another man stepped through. Reverend Swayne stepped aside to make room.

"Howdy, Devon," the newcomer said in a booming, forceful voice.

"Howdy sheriff," Devon said, nodding.

Sheriff Hawkins was a tall man with broad shoulders and a belly just beginning to protrude over his wide, leather gun belt. He glanced around the store and made a half-hearted effort to pretend he was there to shop, then turned to Reverend Swayne. He swept his gaze up and down the stranger's tall frame, and then he smiled. He held out one big, meaty paw to shake, and he met Gideon Swayne's eyes. There was no humor behind the smile, and there was just the hint of controlled violence in the man's grip.

"I don't believe we've met," he said. His voice had the timbre and inherent threat of a growling bear.

Reverend Swayne took the offered hand and shook it firmly. He met the sheriff's gaze easily, and his smile was genuine.

"Reverend Gideon Swayne," he said. "I've come a long way, sheriff, all the way from the great state of Illinois."

"That is a long way," Hawkins replied. "If you don't mind my asking, Reverend, why? Don't you have a church back there waiting for you to lead them to the Promised Land? You wouldn't be running from someone, would you? Pardon my asking, and I mean no offense, but we're a pretty tight-knit little town. It's my business who comes, and who goes—how long the stay—you know?"

"No offense taken, sheriff," Gideon said. "I was just telling Mr. Walz here that I've come on a mission. I did have a flock in Illinois, a little town called Random. We've done a lot of praying these past few years, a lot of soul searching. The war hasn't been easy on anyone. I can only imagine how much worse it must have been here.

"A lot of men and women who looked to me for guidance

had family who died here, or near here."

"We all lost kin," Walz cut in.

Reverend Swayne nodded, but went on without pausing.

"A part of what we prayed for," he said, "involved the reasons behind the war—the people we were fighting for. A lot of our prayers involved freedom, and the release from suffering. Men died—young men, old men, fathers and brothers, and it seems to me, gentlemen, that it's important we be certain they didn't die in vain. Wouldn't you agree?"

Neither the sheriff, nor the grocer trusted himself to answer. The words sounded reasonable, and the man delivering them had a wide, friendly smile, but there was something lurking behind the words that they didn't trust.

"Thought you said you came here to preach to the niggers," Walz said at last. The words came out too quickly, as if he wasn't sure whether to speak or spit. Sheriff Hawkins turned to the grocer, studied his expression, and then turned back to Gideon.

"That true, Reverend? You come to make sure the darkies find their way to glory?"

Gideon refused to be riled so easily. He'd been traveling for a long time, making his way across country, mostly on foot, and as he traveled he told his story. Despite having fought a war that nearly tore the country in two, setting family against family and town against town, he'd found very few sympathetic audiences. He'd expected a less-than-friendly welcome to the south, and he was prepared for it as well as a man can prepare for such a thing.

"I understand how you might disagree with my message," he said at last. "I didn't come to start trouble. A lot of hours of prayer are behind me. The money, love, and spirit of a small church brought me here, and my intention is to make them proud of me."

"You got any niggers in your congregation back home, Reverend?" Walz asked. All hesitation had evaporated as his anger heated. "You even got fields to be worked back there? Crops? You ever see a field of cotton go bad because no one was there to pick it, and the weather hit?"

Gideon remained silent.

"I think maybe you'd better carry your message a little further, Reverend," Sheriff Hawkins said slowly. "Around here, we've got two churches, and they're about all I can handle. I keep the peace; we get along, white and colored, just fine."

"Just like you have for the last hundred years, I suspect," Gideon cut in. The words were sharper than he'd intended, and he gave himself an inward kick in the seat of his trousers for letting them get to him so quickly. He'd been on the road too long. He was far enough south, and if any place he'd come across in his travels needed his work, this appeared to be it.

"I apologize, gentlemen," he said quickly. "I have been on the road a long time, and I'm very tired. If you'd be kind enough to point me toward a place I might spend the night—a barn, or a room I might rent, and a place where I can find a meal, I'd be much obliged to you."

At first it appeared as if he would receive no answer at all. He stood his ground, but sweat dripped down the back of his neck and under his collar. His hand trembled, just a little. He hoped they didn't notice, but there was nothing he could do.

"You want to keep that attitude under lock and key," Sheriff Hawkins said at last. "We don't take to strangers easily, and you don't know a thing about that war. You sat back in your quiet little town, prayed on Sunday and sent your boys off to fight. We lived in the middle of it.

"This street you see outside? Every building on the other side of it burned four years ago. It's all new, and we built it together, every man, woman, boy and girl within forty miles was here. Those who had money donated it, those who didn't worked. They didn't have the time to spare—the cotton needed picking. They didn't have as many workers to do the picking because their fathers and brothers and sons were dead, or in prison, and the slaves were set free, asking for money, or running north.

"People starved here, Reverend. Good people. People died here as well, and since then we've been rebuilding our town, and our lives. We've gotten the workers back into the fields, and we've gotten them back under control. You aren't waltzing in here in your funny suit with your holier-than-thou ideas and tearing it back down. Understand that I'm telling you, not asking you.

"You can stay in my barn tonight. There's hay in there, it's warm enough, and it's soft. Watch out for snakes. I'll see to it that someone brings around some food, and some water. I'll even bring enough to get you to the next town if it will get you there quicker, but don't you think for a minute you're staying around here."

"I appreciate the offer of shelter," Gideon replied, "and you are right, I don't understand. There are a lot of people, towns, even states that don't understand. Not the way you do. Not the way we should. I do know one thing, sheriff. If we don't find some common ground in the middle where we can learn that truth in peace, this nation will crumble around us."

"This ain't your common ground, preacher," Walz growled.

Gideon fell silent and nodded slowly. There was nothing to be gained by arguing with them, and quite a lot of potential for loss. He wasn't going to find the people he'd come in search of in Old Mill, though they undoubtedly lived on the outskirts. He didn't need the sheriff's permission to spread the Lord's word, but if he angered the man now, he'd end up arrested and escorted out of town—or worse.

"If you don't mind," he said, "I'm very tired. If you could show me that barn, I'll settle down and get some rest."

Sheriff Hawkins stood very still for a few moments. Gideon wished he could hear the man's thoughts, because the hard, lined face gave nothing away.

"Follow me," he said. He turned and headed for the door. Gideon picked up his bags and followed.

At the door, Hawkins stopped, glanced over his shoulder, and caught Walz's gaze.

"Tell the boys I'll be around tonight," he said. "Make sure they all come."

Without waiting for a response, Sheriff Hawkins pushed out the door and into the street with Gideon at his heels. The door closed behind them, but a moment later, Devon Walz pushed it open again. He stood with the door open just a crack and watched until the other two men rounded the corner and were out of sight. A moment later, he stepped out onto the street, locked the door carefully behind him, and hurried off in the opposite direction. There weren't many men in town, but those that were, he would find. The others he would reach by sending messages with the workers who drove in the trailers of cotton to the gin.

Word spread fast in and around Old Mill. When the cotton was in season, there wasn't much else to talk about. When someone acted out, or some young buck was caught with another man's daughter, it was news. This put it all to shame. The sheriff almost never called a meeting, and when he did, it meant trouble for someone. Devon thought he knew what was coming, and as he walked and spread the word, he grinned.

The barn was clean and dry, and that was better accommodations than Reverend Swayne had seen in days. He dropped his bags near a tall mound of hay and turned to the sheriff gratefully.

"I truly appreciate this," he said.

"Just don't get too comfortable," Hawkins said. He didn't smile, and he didn't offer his hand a second time. "I'll send a girl around later with some food—I don't want it said Old Mill turned a man of God away hungry. Don't mind if they say we turned you away, though. When the sun's up in the morning, I'll expect to see you on the road."

"I understand," Gideon answered noncommittally. "Both you and Mr. Walz made your opinions crystal clear. I may be getting on in years, and I may be a Yankee at heart, but I'm not a stupid man. If you don't mind, I'm going to settle in and try to get some sleep. It's been a long day."

"It has at that, Reverend," Hawkins said. "It has at that."

When he was alone, Gideon settled his belongings and drew forth a worn Bible. There was enough light from the door to see by, and he sat for a long time, reading and thinking, then reading a bit more. The words were familiar and comfortable, and they helped him to relax, and to order his thoughts. He had no intention of moving on in the morning, but he did intend to get out of Old Mill. Those he sought would be in the fields, or living on the fringes of the town, and he wouldn't reach them by sleeping in the sheriff's barn, or rotting in his jail—assuming the town even had one.

Just before sunset, a young girl brought him a plate of biscuits drowned in thick white gravy and a small jug of water. He thanked her, but she scurried back into the growing shadows without a word. Gideon settled back into the straw, ate the biscuits slowly, enjoying their savor. He washed it down with water from the jug, set the dishes aside, and settled back to sleep.

When the footsteps and hushed voices surrounded the doorway to the barn just before midnight, he was sound asleep.

Gideon woke groggy and disoriented in the darkness. A sound had snatched him from sleep, but it hadn't repeated itself, and he was caught halfway between wakefulness and dreams. Then someone whispered and he stiffened. He didn't rise, and he didn't speak. He listened, wishing he hadn't left his bags even a few feet away.

"It don't seem right, him bein' a preacher and all. Can't we just wait for tomorrow?" The voice was high pitched and whiny, and it echoed in the stuffy silence. Gideon slowly rolled to his back, hoping whoever it was couldn't see any better than he could. He thought he saw a flicker of shadow across the barn door, but nothing else moved.

"Shut up, Sam," Sheriff Hawkins growled. "Keep quiet and do as I say."

No one else spoke. Gideon watched as they entered. Their shadows followed Hawkins through the shadowed doorway and into the barn, making as little sound as possible. Gideon counted five in all. Five grown men—to do what?

Gideon drew his knees up to his chest, rolled over so he could reach the strap on his bag, and lurched to his feet. He knew he had no chance to escape so many, but he thought that there was just a chance that if he made it to the door and hit the road running, they wouldn't follow. It was one thing to beat a man in the privacy of a barn, and quite another to do it in the open street for all to see. There had been hesitation in the one man's voice, maybe it would be enough to see him through.

"He's moving!" one of the men yelled.

Suddenly all of them were moving at once. Two leaped to block the door and something slid in front of Gideon's ankle. He tried to leap over it, but was too late and seconds later he was falling. It was dark and so, he didn't see the floor in time to break the momentum with his hands, or the bag. He hit hard, and the impact sent sparks of pain flashing through his mind.

By the time he shook off the cobwebs, and the real pain hit, his arms and legs had been grabbed and held tightly. A flame flashed off to one side, flared, and the light bobbed nearer. Gideon moaned, and a man he'd never seen held a lantern high. Five faces melted from the shadows. None were smiling, and the man in the center, just to the right of the lantern bearer, was Sheriff Hawkins.

"Sleep well, Reverend?" he asked.

Gideon struggled, but he couldn't free himself from their grip. Someone leaned down and swung a punch, landing on Gideon's ribs and driving the breath from him in an instant. He tried to double up, couldn't manage it, and fought for the breath to scream.

"You want to bite that tongue if it helps you stay quiet," Hawkins said matter-of-factly. We got business, but it doesn't concern the rest of the town. You understand me, preacher?"

Gideon nodded. His face throbbed, and his muscles screamed from the tension of being held prone and spread-eagled on the floor of the barn.

Hawkins spat, and it landed with as sickening splash in the dirt beside Gideon's face.

"You come down here," Hawkins said, "mouthing off about prayer groups and your church folks back home. You tell us how the country has to heal, and how you've just come down to ease that suffering. You just wandered on down a few hundred miles of green countryside to walk through the rows of cotton and tell the niggers how Jesus is their savior, and everyone is equal in the eyes of the Lord. That about right, preacher?"

Gideon could only stare, wide-eyed. His throat was too dry for speech, and someone had gripped him tightly by the hair, preventing him from nodding.

"We didn't just lose boys and fathers and brothers, preacher. We lost our lives. We lost our pride. We lost a way of doing things our grandparents learned from their grandparents. We crawled back down here to be kicked like dogs by blue-coated jackasses just looking for excuses to shoot us as war criminals, and we set the niggers free.

"You ever catch a fish, Reverend? You ever see a fish where the hook was set, and the mouth was ripped—maybe the prong popped through an eye, or sliced a gill, but you didn't really want the fish? You toss it back in the water, and it flops over on its side, or its back. It swims in circles. It gets the water all bloody and attracts predators.

"I've got news for you, preacher, that's what happened when we set those darkies free. They looked at us like we were stupid. They wandered in circles, trying to figure out what to do. A few of them got excited, like kids, and tried to take off. Some of them probably made it. The rest, though? You know what they did? They said "Yassuh Boss," instead of "Yassuh Massah" and they went back to work.

"It's their way of life too, preacher. It's what their parents taught them. It's what they know. You come in here and start preaching to them about freedom, and standing up for their rights, and being equal? What do you think's going to happen? There's going to be trouble. Folks will be hurt. Folks will hurt them. The cotton won't get picked, people won't get fed, and it will be your fault."

The sheriff hesitated for a moment, and then said.

"I can't let that happen. I told you earlier, and you should have listened. It's my job to keep things under control here. It's my job to see people aren't hurt, and that things run smoothly. I take my work seriously, reverend, as I guess you take yours. I've known your type, and when I sent you out here to rest, I knew you wouldn't just leave."

Gideon tried to struggle again, and Hawkins struck like a snake. He lashed out with one boot and sent it crashing into Gideon's ribs. There was a sickening smack, and Gideon groaned.

"We've got all the Christianity we can handle in these parts, preacher," Hawkins said, his breath heavy and his voice gone hoarse. "You aren't welcome."

They fell on him then. His arms and legs were released, and he tried to roll into a ball. Boots and fists struck from all directions. It seemed the more they hit him and the more he tried to crawl away or protect himself, the more frenzied they became. He was reaching for the straw, hoping to dig a hole beneath it and pull himself inside, when something crashed into the side of his head. He saw a brilliant flash of light, and darkness crashed around him, walling him in and the others out.

TWO

The sun rose over the cotton slowly, baking away the morning dew. The plants were nearly four feet tall, bolls thick and white and stalks rough and jagged. Sun filtered down through the leaves to draw what little moisture the soil held out and leave a cracking crust over the ground.

Workers had been in the fields for hours. The first hint of dawn brought them forth, trying to take advantage of the few hours where the dew softened the plants slightly, and it was possible to pick without butchering your hands or baking your back. That would come later in the day, but the morning, when the cotton sacks weren't yet heavy and clothing had yet to plaster itself to everybody, soaked in sweat and caked with dust and dirt, was the best time. There were few good times in the fields during picking season, so they were savored when they arrived.

Gideon woke to the sound of voices singing. He didn't hear footsteps, and he couldn't see clearly, but he heard the voices. They were low and powerful, raised in rhythmic celebration. For a moment, before the throbbing, screaming pain in his bones and muscles hit full force, and before he realized that he couldn't see, Gideon thought he might have finally taken the last walk into Glory. Their singing was beautiful.

He cried out from the pain, or tried to, but the sound that came forth was a pitiful, spitting mewl. His throat was dry and ached from multiple bruises. He clenched his eyes tightly, and then tried to open them again. All he could manage was thin slits. The sunlight was too bright, and it stabbed into his brain with slivers of light that exploded on contact with his thoughts. His cheek lay on the cool earth, still shaded—for the moment—from the pounding heat of the sun. He pressed his palms into that soil, and tried to lift himself. His shoulders trembled with the effort, and his head pounded. He managed to lift himself only a couple of inches before his arms gave out and he dropped back to the earth. This time his cry was slightly louder, though it burned in his throat.

He rolled to his back, and tried feebly to sit up.

Nearby he heard a rustle, and immediately thought of animals, or snakes. He flailed his arms and tried again to sit. This time he got his elbows beneath him. His eyes were sticky, and at first the thought they were just dry. Then he managed to get a hand up to brush across the lids. His face was matted with half-dried blood. His leg felt broken, and when he sat up and put pressure on it he nearly blacked out again. He gritted his teeth and used his sleeve to clear his eyes. They were still swollen, but he was able to make out a little of his surroundings.

The rustling sound repeated, to his left. He tried to peer over the tops of the cotton plants, but he couldn't sit up fully. The pain in his leg prevented him from doing more than pushing up off the ground. The sounds drew nearer, and he coughed to clear his throat. The sound stopped.

"Help me," he said, the words so soft they were barely audible.

The rustling began again. Something was moving toward him slowly. His heart pounded. His mind conjured dogs, snakes, gators—all the stories he'd heard and read about swamps over the years returned to him, magnified by the pain and warped by the too-bright sunlight.

"Who is it?" he called out. "Who..."

The leaves over him parted, and he saw the face of a young boy staring down at him. The child couldn't have been more than seven. He was dark as molasses with bright, inquisitive eyes. When he caught sight of Gideon he pulled back sharply. There was no sound for a moment, and Gideon called out again.

"Help me."

The next thing he heard was the pounding of feet and the whipping of cotton plants as the boy crashed through them, running away.

"No," he croaked. "Come back."

It was only a moment before silence engulfed him again. He gritted his teeth and pushed harder, trying to raise himself to a sitting position. White hot pain flashed from his leg straight to his brain. His back arched his head hit the ground hard. The darkness rose, and he fought it. The green leaves and white cotton bolls wavered and shimmered. He reached up, tried to grab the leaves, and failed. Deep, black nothingness washed over him and flies landed, crawling unnoticed through the drying blood on his face.

When he opened his eyes again, he no longer lay in the cotton field. It was dark, and the flames of a fire danced nearby. His head was pillowed on his bags, and his leg was very stiff. He realized after only a moment that it was bound in a splint. He heard someone humming under their breath, but he couldn't focus on the tune, or place the voice. It was unfamiliar, but comforting, rhythmic and smooth.

He tried to raise his head, and the sound of the motion alerted whoever it was nearby. The humming stopped, and before he managed to balance himself on his elbows, a cool, damp rag was pressed to his forehead, and a soothing voice whispered near his ear.

"Lay down. You aren't ready. Just lie down and be still."

She leaned over him, and he saw her face. She was beautiful. Her eyes were a deep chocolate brown. Her hair fell in waves over her shoulders, and her eyes were deep, wide pools.

Gideon did as he was told. He settled back onto his bags and tried to make out his surroundings. The fire, he saw, lay just outside a doorway of canvas, or burlap flaps that had been tied back to the side. There was a pot suspended over the flames, and all around him he saw indistinct mounds of cloth and board, bottles and jugs and odd shapes that might have been tools.

Every inch of his body ached. His head pounded, and if he looked too long at the fire his eyesight faltered, the world shifted, and his stomach lurched. He kept his gaze on the shadows, and on the figure of the woman, moving about with comfortable confidence.

She returned to his side with a cup in her hands.

"Drink this," she said. "It's tea—and herbs. It will help the pain in your head."

Gideon started to nod, thought better of it at the first stab of pain, and let her bring the cup to his lips. She turned it up and poured just a small amount of the warm liquid into his mouth. He felt it trickle down his throat, but he was too numb to taste it. Whatever was in the concoction, it warmed his mouth, and then his throat, and within moments, he felt a tingle of sensation in his chest. He took several more sips, and was surprised to find that, with some effort, he could speak.

"Where am I?" he asked.

"Well, that depends," she answered with an enigmatic smile. "If you was to walk straight out the tent here and keep going, you'd be as close to nowhere as this ol' Earth has to offer. That's what they call 'The Great Dismal Swamp,' and most folks who wander in there too deep don't come back. If you walked around back, you'd see a bunch of trees, and if you kept going straight, you'd hit cotton. From there, that's about all you can see."

"The sheriff..." Gideon said. His mind was clearing, and as memory flooded in, shadows forms, lantern-lit faces, and swinging boots filled his thoughts. He closed his eyes and winced, and she raised the cup to his lips again.

"He don't come here," she said soothingly. "He don't come into the woods, and he don't come any nearer to the swamp than he has to. Probably thinks you're dead. You was close, layin' out in the cotton. If Elijah hadn't found you, you'd be there still, likely snake bit and feedin' the buzzards."

"Elijah?" he said. "Elijah came to me in the cotton?"

She laughed loudly and stood.

"No prophet came for you, preacher man. Elijah is Sarah's son. He was pickin' cotton and found you sprawled halfway across his row. He ran to his momma, Jesamina, and she came and fetched me. We hid you in the shade and moved you here as soon as we was sure no one was looking."

"Thank you," he said. "But why? Why would you help me?"

"You needed helpin'," she answered. "That's all there was to it, start to finish. We couldn't leave you out there in the cotton attracting coyotes and buzzards—we have work to do. That cotton ain't goin' to pick itself."

"Thank you," he repeated.

He reached out weakly, and she placed the cup in his hands. He sipped slowly, letting the warm tea roll down his throat. The aches in his body throbbed, but it was a throb of life. Where he'd been numb before, the warmth seeped in and brought his flesh back to life.

"Your leg's cracked," she told him. "We put a splint on it, and tied it up, but it's not going to hold your weight for a while."

She turned, grabbed a stick that leaned against the tent near the door, and dropped it beside him. It had a crook in the top and about a foot down from this the stub of a branch protruded.

"You can use this for a crutch," she said. "Elijah found the wood, and I cut it to fit."

"I owe you my life," he said softly. "Would you tell me your name?"

She smiled at him and tossed her hair in a very girlish manner. He smiled back, though it was difficult to find humor through the pain.

"Desdemona," she said. "Desdemona Eyre. I've lived near her all my life. I was born to parents owned by the Pope family. It's Pope cotton we found you in—we work their fields."

"But," Gideon tried to focus his thoughts, "you don't have to work for them now."

"We have to eat," she said. Her eyes flashed. "We don't live on their property, and we don't call them 'Massa', but we've got to work. There are children to feed. Mr. Walz up at the General Store sends a wagon out and we buy what we can from him, but without the grain and vegetables Mr. Pope gives us, we'd starve."

The name Walz caught in Gideon's mind.

"I met Mr. Walz," he said, grimacing in pain. "He and I don't see eye to eye, it seems. The sheriff isn't fond of me either. I'm certain I was meant to die, or to crawl out to the road and find my way back to Illinois."

"You must have done something to rile them," Desdemona said. "Mr. Walz, he don't let colored folk near his store, and he don't talk about how he sends supplies our way, but he's never hurt anyone. At least not here. Sheriff Hawkins is different—that one has a pocket full of mean and he's looking for someone to spend it on."

"The sheriff told me there's no room for another man of God here," he replied, uncertain what reaction to expect.

"The swamp has its own Gods," she replied cryptically. "Word travels fast here, preacher man. I know why you came. You should let that leg heal, and then let us walk you out to that road when none of the folks in town is looking. You met the friendly ones, for the most part. If Reverend Cumby gets an eyeful of you, he'll be raining fire and brimstone on your head, along with another beatin', or worse. He's protective of his 'flock,' and because he comes out and stands at the end of a cotton row once a month to bring us 'the word,' he figures we belong to him—spiritually speaking."

Gideon was surprised to hear this.

"The impression I got was that none of them was much interested in your spiritual growth," he said. He picked his way through the conversation carefully. He'd already made wrong assumptions once in this place, and it had nearly cost him his life.

"Oh, Reverend Cumby only wants to pretend like he's preaching to us," she said. "I don't think he believes we'll make it to Heaven, or, if we do, it will be some lower area, or working the Holy cotton fields. That man talks a lot about sin, and about salvation, but he never comes any closer than it takes him to send a boy out with a collection plate. If the Methodists could work their way in they'd do it, but there's more Baptists, and one of them is Sheriff Hawkins, so they keep their distance."

"He comes out here to ask for money?" Gideon asked.

"He would go on down to hell and pass the plate with oven mitts to protect his hands if he thought he'd get a good take," she said. There was a note of bitterness in her voice that she couldn't quite hide.

"And now there's you, preacher," she said. "What did you come for? We don't have much out here, as you can see. Why did you walk all that way from your home up North? What do you want? Her eyes narrowed, and she cocked her head to one side in a way that made Gideon smile, despite his pain. She managed to seem rustic and elegant all at once, and with her hand on her hip and her eyes pinning him to the ground, there was something regal in her manner as well. Clearly, however many others lived out among the trees, she was one of their leaders.

"I didn't come here because I wanted something," he said, searching carefully for his words. "I came here because I was called to it. I saw the war form a different place than you did—different from those men in town as well, I guess. I saw men and boys dying, women left behind to struggle and worry and raise children who never met their fathers or brothers. I saw a whole lot of evil washing over the land and not much being done about it.

"We fought that war for a lot of reasons. Sometimes I wonder if any two men understood it quite the same way. One of the reasons, though, was that it was time for men and women in this country to stand as equals. The days of owning another human being have passed, and though those ways haven't been banished from the minds, or the hearts of the men who stood to gain most from them, laws have been passed to bring them to an end.

"Laws are just words, though. You can pass a law that says the sun won't set in the evening, and good luck with it. You can tell men who have worked their land with the muscle and hearts of men they claim to own that they no longer own those men, and that they have to be fair and pay for a day's wages, but it doesn't mean a thing if it isn't enforced."

"You think you can make Boss Pope pay us?" she laughed and slapped her knee. "That is something I want to see, preacher. I surely do."

Gideon smiled wanly. "I know I can't make a change like that on my own." He said. "I don't even know if it can be fully made in my lifetime. I only know that it's my place as an American citizen, and as a man of God, to do what I can do. We fought and killed and died in this country, so freedom could be shared by all the men and women of our country, and I came to see what I could do about sowing the seeds of that work. I came to try and make a difference, if that makes any sense."

"It don't," she said, turning away. "You'll get yourself killed, and everything will be the same as it was, except God will have one less preacher down here, and one more up there to bother him."

"We'll see," he said.

She snorted, but she didn't disagree with him again.

"Come morning, you're going to have to lie quiet," she said "They find out we took you in, and they'll kill you. Probably kill me too."

"I can't ask you to take that kind of risk," he said. He placed his palms on the ground and tried to press himself up, but the flash of pain in his leg cleared that thought from his mind quickly. "I don't want anyone to be hurt for my sake."

"You just do what you're told," she said. "You stay here, keep the flaps closed, and don't say a word. I'll leave some food, some water. No one much comes here. I keep myself further into the woods than the rest of them. Don't like late-night visitors. Don't have much use for people, truth be told. The swamp, she talks to me. The bones of the animals have their own language, and the plants give me their strength for medicine."

"You're a healer?" Gideon asked. His eyes lit with interest. "Are you trained?"

She laughed. The sound was fresh, like the breeze that leaked in through the tent-flap door. She turned to him and looked him up and down to see if he might be teasing her. When she saw that he was not only serious, but that now he was confused by her laughter, she came and sat beside him on the floor. Her eyes danced with amusement.

"You been up north too long, preacher," she said. "Where you think I been, finishing school? There's no one to teach medicine in the swamp. I learned from my mother, she learned from hers. Some of it I learned from the swamp. Sometimes you just know. You break a leaf, or make tea from something you've never tried before, and you taste it, or smell it. You rub it between your fingers and you feel something tingle on your skin. The world is full of healing; you just got to know where to look."

"God has a way of giving us what we need," Gideon said softly. "He provides when life feels hopeless. If he has given you the ability to understand plants, and to relieve suffering, you have been gifted with something special."

"My gifts come from my mother," she said. "God didn't have anything to do with it. If God put my grandfather on that slave ship and stole him away across the sea; if he left me and mine to work until we drop so some fat white man can beat us and tell us to go work some more? I don't want anything to do with that God. I'll trust the swamp, and the spirits."

"God is with you in the swamp, and in the fields," Gideon said.

"You need your rest," she said. She pushed him back, not too gently, and he fell against his pack. He tried not to smile, but failed.

"You've heard all of this before," he guessed.

"I've heard a lot of things," she replied. "Seen things too. What I've seen, I believe—what I hear is usually just someone making noise to listen to their own voice. Reverend Cumby told us how God was in the cotton. He preached to us about how children and young ladies would wear the clothing made from that cotton, how it would keep people warm and make things beautiful. He told us that from the back of a hay wagon surrounded by children, and young ladies, not a one of them wearing a new, warm, or clean bit of clothing. He stood there in his polished boots and not a child among us with more than a shredded bit of leather to tie to his feet. He talked like he didn't see us at all, smiled that devil's smile and held out his hand like we owed him something."

"I'm not Reverend Cumby," Gideon said.

She turned and studied his face.

"No, I reckon not," she said. "Still, your God left you half dead in a cotton field, and Cumby is sleeping on goose down."

"My God brought me to you," he said... "Or you to me. Either way, I'm where I was intended to be. He will guide me."

She shook her head and rose.

"Sleep, preacher man. When we're done in the fields tomorrow, I'll see about moving you closer to the swamp—farther from the Popes. They don't come here often, but when they do, there's no telling what they might tear into. I'll get you out of sight, and out of mind, and help you heal that leg."

"I'll earn my keep," he said. "I can't pick in the fields, but there are other things that need to be done."

"Oh, I'll keep you busy, preacher man. Don't you worry yourself over that. No one here eats for free."

"If I spoke on Sundays, would your people listen?" he asked.

"You'll have to ask them," she said. "There's a few who pray to your God, a few others who might if someone other than Reverend Cumby was behind the words."

"It's not the man behind the words that's important," Gideon said.

"Your Jesus was a man," she said, surprising him. "There's a difference, though, preacher. He walked into the desert for forty days and learned to heal. I walked into the swamp. We'll see who teaches who before all is said and done."

"Gideon," he said.

She stared at him, a question in her eyes, and he smiled.

"My name is Gideon—Gideon Swayne."

"Good name for a preacher," she said.

Desdemona slipped out through the canvas flaps and into the night. Gideon watched her go, then laid back and closed his eyes. He drifted into sleep to the sound of insects singing, and the low moan of the wind through the trees.

THREE

It was a week before Gideon could stay on his feet for any length of time, even with crutches. He spent his days preparing food, gathering herbs and supplies that Desdemona needed, and clearing a small patch of ground. The freedmen had come together to bring him scraps of canvas, a few boards, things they could ill afford to give up, but that they presented to him with all the gravity of the wise men carrying gifts to Jerusalem. He wasn't used to the work—he'd lived his life in relative peace. The church had called him at a very young age, and though he'd done as he was told, and studied hard, he had never faced physical challenges of the magnitude he now experienced daily.

One of the old men, an elder with very dark, leathery skin and hair the same color and consistency as the cotton, stayed behind with him most days. Ben, probably not his given name, but the only one the man knew, could no longer put in a full day in the fields. The heat of the noon sun was too much for him, but his spirits were high. He was up with the dawn, and he worked constantly. There were things to be mended. Some of the shelters needed repair, clothing was torn, and it was a constant struggle to trap, hunt and gather enough food. Gideon followed Ben on long rambles through the woods, most of which would have been shorter rambles without the crutches and the pain.

He learned to fish, set snares for rabbits and other small animals, how to avoid snakes and which were the most dangerous. He learned which plants should be gathered any time they were spotted, and which ones not to touch if you didn't want to develop a nasty rash. He learned how to start a fire, how to keep it from smoking, how to burn it low so that the coals were good for cooking.

He worked with Ben until the workers returned from the fields. Sometimes he helped serve the food, though it was difficult for him to get around on the makeshift crutches, and by the time the day had passed, he was sore, exhausted, and his leg throbbed. It was then that he started his real work.

At first he was able to spend only a few moments a day clearing weeds, dragging branches and limbs, and prying stones loose from the moist earth. He'd chosen his spot carefully-- a small clearing surrounded on all sides by tall, slender trees growing too close together to support a lot of foliage. He'd never built anything in his life. Not really. As a boy he'd helped mend fences, and had been present at a few barn raisings, but a lot of years had passed, and even in those early days he'd been more of an observer, not really involved in the construction.

Even if he'd paid close attention in those days, it wouldn't have had much bearing on the work at hand. There were no piles of lumber lying about, or well-oiled tools to work with. There were castoffs, broken axes and hand-crafted wooden mallets, and many of these were in use, or guarded carefully by suspicious workers.

On the fourth day of his labor, Gideon lay on the ground in the corner of his clearing. He had a makeshift hoe made from a broken bit of iron that had once been used to bind the slats of a barrel. He'd tied it to a stick with a strip of cloth. His back ached from hobbling about during the day. Sweat dripped into his eyes, but he ignored it. The first few times the sweat had poured down into his eyes, he'd brushed at it with the back of his hand. The dirt stung, and his clothing, already matted and filthy, was no good for cleaning it out.

He worked slowly and carefully, clearing a foot at a time. It was about ten minutes into the day's work when he felt the weight of watching eyes. He had no idea who it would be, and he didn't want to scare them off, so he didn't look up. He dragged the flat edge of his piece of iron over the ground, working out a stone here, or chopping deeper to find the base of the root of some odd shrub or weed. He'd cleared a space about a yard square, and was oddly pleased at the result.

He gathered what he cleared into a small pile. After fifteen minutes more, he was exhausted. He swung his tool out and started to drag it back across the uneven ground, but he couldn't do it. He leaned forward and laid his head on his upper arm. Sweat and dirt mingled and he thought if he rested that way for too long, his cheek would be stuck in place, and they'd find him there passed out, when the morning came.

Except they were already watching.

The first to slip out of the shadows surrounding the clearing was the boy, Elijah, who had first stumbled across Gideon in the cotton field. Elijah walked slowly and tentatively into the clearing. He came very close to where Gideon lay sprawled on the ground, and squatted, his head cocked curiously to the side.

"What you doin'?" he asked.

Gideon licked his lips, trying to replace lost fluids. With a great effort, he sat up. He let go of the hoe, not wanting to embarrass himself if he turned out not to have the strength to draw it back to himself.

"I'm building a church," he said.

The boy glanced around the clearing. He looked down at the mound of dirt Gideon had cleared, and at the odd, bent bit of metal he was using to clear the land. Without a word, Elijah stood, leaned in close, and picked up the pile of rubble. He carried two handfuls of the branches and dirt and stepped into the trees. In a moment, Gideon saw him return. Behind him, another short figure hovered at the edge of the clearing. It was a girl—Gideon didn't know her name, but he'd seen her around the camp.

"It's okay," he said softly.

He'd managed to sit fully erect, and was starting to get his strength back, slowly. In a moment he'd be able to lever himself to his feet, using the crutch, and hobble over to where he'd left a small jug of water. He needed the drink badly, but he didn't want to ask Elijah for it. He didn't want to show a sign of weakness, or ask for help he'd done nothing to deserve. He already owed the boy his life.

The girl, a year or two older than Elijah, maybe ten, sidled into the clearing. Elijah had stepped into the trees again with the last of the meager pile of stones and branches Gideon had gathered. The girl studied the cleared corner, and then she disappeared into the trees. A few minutes later, she and Elijah reappeared. Both had tools of their own with longer handles. One was flattened on the end, like the blunt end of a pickaxe; the other was a more efficient version of Gideon's hoe.

They walked to the corner opposite where Gideon had begun his work without a word, and started clearing. They worked quickly, their speed and discipline born of long hours in the cotton fields under a burning sun. There was no laziness in them, no dishonesty to their work. They saw a job that needed to be done, and they set to it. The only thing that remained was for Gideon to find out why.

He gripped the crutch, placed the tip in the soil and lifted. At first he thought he was going to fall back and re-injure his leg, but somehow he managed to gain his balance and stand upright. He hobbled over to his belongings and leaned down, using the crutch for balance, until he had the water jug in hand. He took a long drink, closed his eyes, and let the cool liquid run down his throat. After a moment, he drank again, careful not to take it all too quickly, then corked the jug and lowered it back to the ground.

When he turned back, he saw that the two children had already cleared an area twice the size of the one he'd begun. They worked quickly, shoulder to shoulder, and the pile of rubble they'd gathered was nearly two feet tall and as big around as a wheelbarrow. Gideon watched for a few minutes, and then he stepped forward.

"Wait," he said.

The girl whirled on him, jumpy—ready to flee at the first sign of betrayal. Gideon's heart went out to her. He wondered what sort of life had brought her to such a state. He stood very still, leaning on his crutch.

"You have done enough for today," he said. "You worked hard in the fields, and I don't want to be the cause of you being too tired to work tomorrow. Help me get this moved," he gestured at the mound of cleared branches and stones and soil.

"If you'll help me, after, I'll see about making a shelter in the corner you cleared."

Elijah nodded, though he still didn't' speak. He leaned his pick carefully against a tree in plain sight. The girl did the same with her hoe.

"What's your name, child?"

The girl looked up at him, shook her head with a jerk, and bent to the pile at her feet. Elijah watched her for a moment, and then glanced up at Gideon.

"Her name is Sarah," he said. "She can't talk."

Gideon frowned. He started to ask more, but Elijah didn't wait. He was already leaning down to help the girl. The two disappeared from the clearing, laden with handfuls of debris.

The mound was large. Even after such a short time, the superior tools and the hard work of his two new helpers had paid off handsomely. Gideon studied the pile, and then moved back to his belongings. He dropped to the ground and dug through his pack, searching until he found what he was after. One of the ladies of his church had given him a leather poncho. It was to have been for cold weather, or to keep the weather off of his head and back, but now he had a new use for it.

He gripped the cloak tightly and levered himself back to his feet, just as Elijah and Sarah stepped back into the clearing. The girl stared at him disapprovingly. It was obvious she thought he'd been resting while they continued to work. Gideon started to explain himself, and then thought better of it. His actions would do more than any speech might, so he swayed across to the mound and dropped the poncho onto the ground.

Working slowly so he wouldn't fall, he hand-walked down the crutch until he was seated beside both the poncho and the mound of debris. He quickly began taking handfuls of it onto the leather. Elijah caught on almost at once, and knelt on the far side of the poncho.

Within just a few moments time, they had nearly half the pile bunched near the center of the strip of leather. Gideon lifted one of the corners and folded it in toward the middle. Elijah did the same on his side. Sarah stepped to the far corner, at an angle from Gideon, and lifted another corner. She handed it to Elijah, who now held two. She let go and moved to the final corner, and moments later Elijah was dragging the bundle toward the edge of the clearing. She followed him, as if she feared to stay alone in the clearing with the large, white stranger. Gideon smiled.

He stared at the corner they'd cleared, and then he closed his eyes. He imagined the church back in Random, Illinois. He thought of how the women brought in baskets of food every Sunday, the scents of fresh bread and roasted corn mingling with spices and hot tea. He tried to imagine a steepled roof rising through the clearing and into the trees, and he could almost see it. It was bent, canted to one side and ragged, but just for a moment he could see it, and he smiled.

He was still smiling when Elijah and Sarah returned for the second and final load. It was a good day's work—the best since he'd started, and for whatever it meant, he had allies. When the last of the pile had been cleared, Sarah turned to him. She smiled, and when she did so, her face lit up like a small sun. He smiled in return, and she turned and fled through the trees, leaving Gideon and Elijah staring after her.

"I need to make a tent," Gideon said at last. "Will you help me?"

Elijah nodded. Gideon rose, and they went to the pile of materials that had been slowly growing since Gideon's arrival. There were two fairly large bits of canvas. He stared at them, and at the strips of rope, leather, and cloth piled beside them. It had seemed a simple thing a few moments before, but now it occurred to him that, once again, he had no idea what to do next.

Elijah must have picked up on his dismay, because the boy leaned in, grabbed one of the pieces of canvas and a strip of leather, and headed back to the cleared corner confidently. Gideon followed as quickly as he could. The boy surveyed the surrounding trees. He chose a tall oak with a branch broken off about the height of a grown man's chest. He took the leather, looped it around the branch, and attached it deftly to one corner of the canvas.

"What can I do?" Gideon asked, feeling silly asking

such a question of such a young boy, but at the same time overwhelmingly grateful for the help.

"Hold this," Elijah replied. He placed one of the corners of the canvas sheet in Gideon's hand and raced back into the trees. He returned a few minutes later with a tall, straight branch that was notched at the top. He grabbed the tool he'd used for clearing the ground and dug a hole, then placed the thicker end of the branch in and patted the soil tightly around it. This held it in place until he was able to get a second bit of leather and attach the front of the canvas to it.

After he'd repeated this with the second sheet, overlapping the two at the top to form a seam, he brought stakes of cut wood and pounded them into the ground, tying off the sides and corners of the canvas to drawn them outward. Gideon had seen such tents used by the army many times, but had had no idea how to make such a thing. Before he knew it, Elijah was taking the last flap of material available and fixing it so that it could be tied in place across the front of the makeshift shelter.

The boy stood back, pleased with his own effort, and stood.

"Thank you," Gideon said.

Elijah nodded. Then he turned and met Gideon's gaze fiercely. "When you build the church," he said, choosing his words carefully, obviously afraid to say the wrong thing, "my momma can come here and talk to God?"

It was a question, and at the same time, it was a statement. Gideon was touched.

"Of course," he said. "You don't need a church to talk to God, Elijah, and you don't need my permission. Your mother is welcome to come here at any time. I talk to God every day."

Elijah watched him carefully. "You do?"

"Of course," Gideon said. "He's always with me."

"In that field out there," Elijah pointed off through the trees. Gideon assumed he pointed toward the Pope cotton fields, "he was there?"

"He was," Gideon nodded.

Elijah glanced down at Gideon's leg dubiously.

"It wasn't God that broke my leg, Elijah," Gideon said, leaning down to ruffle the boy's hair. "It was men. God sent me you. Do you know where the name Elijah came from?"

The boy nodded. "My momma told me...but I don't know if she got it right. She don't read. We got a Bible, but she just remembers what Reverend Cumby says, and what the other women say."

"When Jesus was tired," Gideon said softly, staring off into the swamp, "he took some of his followers and he went up onto a mountain to be alone in a place where it was quiet. He needed something to help him go on—a sign from above. Do you know who came to him?"

Elijah shook his head, but Gideon saw in the boy's expression that he suspected what came next.

"It was Elijah, and others," Gideon said solemnly. "Just like you came to me in the cotton. I'll never forget that, son. You tell your mother, when the church is built, she's welcome here. I'll read to you all from The Bible, and if she wants, I'll teach her to read it for herself. It's why I came here. I thought I knew that before I started, but now..."

His words trailed off, and he stared at the tent, the clearing, and the trees surrounding them. The light was fading, and he knew he should start a small fire.

"Go and get some rest," he said. "I'll see you soon. You've been more help than you know."

Elijah smiled up at him, waved, and ran off through the trees, leaving Gideon standing alone in the twilight. In that moment, he felt very close to God.

The church didn't go up quickly, but as the days passed, more and more assistance arrived. Some brought materials, and others offered their time and labor. Through it all Elijah was there, never far from Gideon's side. Sarah was there most evenings, as well, and though she never said a word, despite Gideon's efforts at drawing her out, she worked steadily and smiled more often.

"You sure don't learn fast," Desdemona told him one evening, staring at the framework of the church building that had risen in the clearing. "Boss Pope is gonna find out about this sooner or later, and there's going to be hell to pay, no matter what God has to say."

Gideon smiled at the joke. He liked listening to Desdemona's voice. When he got her started on the swamp, or the cotton fields, or the families that worked at her side, she could go on for hours in her rich, drawling tones. Sometimes Gideon leaned back against a tree and found, much later, that he'd drifted off to sleep while she talked, and she'd covered him against the chill. His quarters were now a mirror of hers. He'd erected walls on three sides using trees he'd felled, or found already fallen, and shaped for the purpose. The walls stood to the height of his shoulders, and he'd made a peak of the roof using branches, moss, and some of the original canvas walls to block most of the weather.

"I have no quarrel with the Popes, other than the way they treat their workers," Gideon said. "I expect you're right—he isn't going to be happy about the church, and the sheriff isn't going to be pleased to see me still alive and close by."

"Reverend Cumby will set them on you, you wait. If none of the others get riled, he'll preach hell and damnation at them until they run out here and do something about it. You're stealing souls from him—he'll say that makes you a demon."

"What do you think?" Gideon asked softly.

She eyed him carefully and shook her head.

"Don't get no ideas, preacher man. I don't believe in your church, or your God. You have these folks working together and happy, and that's a good thing, but when the swamp is ready to swallow you, or call to them, you best get out of their way—and mine."

He studied her in return, but his smile didn't falter. Her threat lacked conviction, and he'd caught her, more than once, standing in the shadows and watching him. He thought that, maybe, she would have joined the others and helped him with the church, if she just let loose of her inner control for a moment. Despite her rough life, and the too-often frowning lines on her face, she was a startlingly attractive woman.

Gideon had never married. He'd had plenty of interested ladies back in Random, but for one reason, or another, nothing had come of any of them. His work had always come first, and though they were sweet ladies, the women of Random, Illinois, had not lit a fire in him hot enough to compete with his life's work for his time, or his heart.

Now, he wondered. He'd caught himself more than once drifting form his evening prayers into thoughts of Desdemona, wondering if she would stop by his clearing, or if he'd see her the next morning before she left for the fields. Soon he'd be strong enough to accompany the others, and he expected to spend his fair share of time working. He wouldn't take pay for the work—not that he expected the Pope family would offer it, but he didn't want to stand idly by while those around him worked. His leg was healing nicely, and he felt stronger than he'd ever felt. The work and the fresh air had done him a world of good.

"I'll start teaching soon," he said. "Will you come?"

She laughed and flashed one of her all-too-rare smiles at him. "I'll come and listen to you, preacher, if you'll come with me to the swamp the next full moon. I need to cast the bones for Laticia, Sarah's mother. She's asked me to read for her, and to see what can be done. You know the girl hasn't spoken?"

"I knew she hadn't spoken around here," he nodded, "but I assumed she was either shy, or had been hurt in some way. I didn't want to embarrass her, so I've never asked."

"Her father left after the war," Desdemona said. Her smile vanished at the memory. "He took off up north. Said he was going to send back money, then come for them and take them to a better life, but we've never heard a word. Don't expect we ever will. Either he took off on his own, or they killed him."

Gideon didn't have to ask her who "they" were. He'd a pretty good idea that Sheriff Hawkins and Reverend Cumby weren't the only men between Old Mill and freedom that weren't happy with the war's outcome. He suspected that even if the man had gotten free of the south, there would be little he could do to get back in and get his family out.

"Sarah?" he asked softly.

"She hasn't said a word since he left. First week, all she did was cry. Then one morning she got up, went to the fields, and started picking. Elijah has been watching out for her—his momma told him to, at first, and now I think he likes doing it. He talks for her sometimes, but she's been silent for over a year."

"And you think you can help?" he asked. He tried very hard to keep the skepticism from his voice, but he saw in her eyes that he'd failed.

"You come with me, and see for yourself, preacher," she said. There was a hard edge in her voice at that moment that he regretted being the cause of.

"I'm sorry," he said. "I meant no disrespect. I don't even know what you mean when you say "cast the bones," but I should know better than to laugh at something before I've seen it. I was raised to believe in certain things. The rules in my home, Random, Illinois, are very rigid. The things my parents believed and taught me were identical to the things their parents taught them. Anything new or that they didn't understand, was sinful. I've dedicated my life to their God, and his church."

"And my life was given to the swamp," she said. "I never got asked if I wanted the sight, or if I'd like to have spirits invade my dreams. When it happened, folks stayed away from me. I grew up with only mother to teach me, and talk to me, and her ways were the old ways. They didn't come from this swamp, but there are things here she recognized, and what wasn't the same, she learned. What she learned, she passed on to me. Then she died."

"I'm sorry," Gideon said. He saw pain wash over her features. It looked like regret, or loneliness, only bitterer.

"It was a long time ago," she said. "Cyrus Pope's older brother killed her. She wouldn't do what he wanted. He tried to make her, and he lost an eye for his trouble, but before it was over he'd beaten her to death. I saw the whole thing—I was too scared to help her."

"My God," Gideon said.

"Nothing to do with your God, or any other," she said. "Men. It's always men and women who bring the evil, preacher. You can pray all you want, and you might find something good in the words, or the spirit behind them—but don't take your eyes off the men. They're the demons in your woodpile. That's something my momma told me—when she was teaching me about fire."

"You miss her." Gideon said.

"I miss a lot of things," she said, turning to face him. "I miss the peace and quiet I had here before you showed up. Now we have this church here," she nodded at the building and shook her head again. "The trouble that's coming, it isn't coming from God, or from demons. It's coming from men, and it's going to be bad. When I cast the bones, I'll ask about that too."

"I'll come with you," he said.

"I know," she answered, and her smile returned. "Even if you thought I was leading you into a hell hole, you'd follow, wouldn't you preacher?"

"Why do you say that?" he asked. He couldn't help grinning in return.

"You owe me, Gideon Swayne. I healed you, and I gave you something to stare at out of the corner of your eye. You won't say it, and you might even deny it now, with me staring you straight in the eye, and calling you out, but I see what I see. You came here in search of something, and you think that thing is a church—a place to teach people about your God, and do some work you only sorta understand. That's just part of it.

"You came here because something was missing in your life that you weren't going to find back in that mud-splat town in Illinois, wherever that is. You came south, knowing what you might face, and even when they knocked you halfway to Hell, you stuck it out.

"You didn't do that because of this," she smacked her hand on the side of the church building. "Not just for that, anyway."

"Why, then?" he asked her, stepping closer.

She backed away with a chuckle. "Oh no, preacher man. You come by my place tomorrow, and come with me to the swamp. When we get back, we'll talk some more."

She turned and started out of the clearing, but Gideon stepped after her and grabbed her arm.

"Wait," he said. "You said I didn't stay just for the church." He patted the wall as she'd done. "What else? What was I missing?"

Laughing, she patted herself on her behind and danced away into the shadows, leaving him to stare after her, mouth agape and other parts of his anatomy swelling in agreement. He watched until she was completely out of sight, and then turned to his shelter with a sigh. It was going to be a long night of prayer, and he wasn't sure even that would lift his burden.

FOUR

She came for him just after sunset two days later. Gideon hadn't seen Desdemona since she'd shimmied off into the night, but he'd thought about her constantly. His work had suffered; those who helped him in the evenings had noticed, though none had spoken to him about it. They watched him out of the corners of their eyes, and grinned at him as if everyone shared a secret the preacher wasn't in on. He would have worried over it, except that he couldn't keep his thoughts focused on anything but Desdemona.

Just before she came, he was standing alone in the clearing and staring at the church. As always, Elijah was there. Sarah had gone home to her mother, but the boy had begun hanging around later and asking endless questions, some about Illinois, some about the road between Illinois and Old Mill, and some about God, and the church. Gideon did his best to answer them all, but this night he was too distracted to be coherent.

"What you thinking about?" Elijah asked.

Gideon, startled from thoughts of Desdemona, groped for an answer that wouldn't be a lie, but would certainly not give away truths he wasn't ready to part with. He answered with a question.

"What does it mean to 'cast the bones,' Elijah? Do you know?"

The boy gazed up at him with an expression that was difficult to read. It was halfway between incredulity at the fact Gideon didn't know the answer to the question he'd asked, and suspicion that he was being sidetracked from his own question.

"Just what it sounds like," Elijah said at last. "Someone has the sight, like Desdemona, they take a handful of bones. I don't know where they come from—don't want to know. Just old bones. They go and they..."

Elijah hesitated, as if searching for the right word.

"They pray, I guess," he said at last. "I don't know what else you'd call it. They go quiet for a long time. I saw my grandma do it once. She was there, kneeling in the dirt, and everyone stayed away. She had a fire, and she was too close to it—seemed to me she was too close—and it was like she wasn't even there. I saw her, and I saw those bones, but I don't know what she saw."

"Did she tell you?" Gideon asked.

"Not me," Elijah said, shaking his head. "She told my ma, and the others. I was too young."

Gideon turned back to the trees. Elijah watched him for a minute, and then tugged on his arm.

"Why you want to know 'bout that?" the boy asked. "Did they cast bones in The Bible?"

"No," Gideon replied. "I don't think they did. That was a long time ago, though, Elijah. It was a different world. Who's to say what they did, and didn't do? They had oracles, and they had prophets. They sacrificed animals—even in the Old Testament God called for sacrifices."

"Like Abraham and Isaac?" Elijah asked.

Gideon looked down at the boy proudly. "Exactly like that," he said. "Sometimes it's the things that mean the most to you that you have to be willing to let go of."

"Is that why you left your church—the one in Illinois?" Elijah asked.

"Maybe," Gideon said softly. He turned to stare at the uneven walls of the church in the clearing and smiled. "I think, though, that I gave up that church, which was never really mine at all, so that I could find this one. What do you think?"

Elijah's eyes twinkled.

"I think Miss Desdemona is coming. I'll see you tomorrow, Mr. Gideon."

He turned, and he was gone, and suddenly Desdemona was there, sliding between the trees like a shadow. She had a bag in one hand, and a pack in the other. She tossed him the pack as she cleared the trees, and he caught it easily.

"You ready, preacher man?" she asked. Her expression was lost somewhere between a smile and a mystery, and he smiled in return.

"What's in the bag?" he asked, shaking it at her.

"First rule," she said, turning her back on him and heading off through the trees toward the swamp. "When I listen to you preach I won't interrupt you. When you come with me to the swamp, you don't ask questions."

He stood still and watched her for a long moment, hefting the bag. He was tempted to peek inside and answer his own question, but the swaying of her hips and his own curiosity held him in check. He shouldered the back and set off on Desdemona's heels. He felt a small, nagging guilt at the idea of following a swamp witch out to watch her perform her "magic," but it wasn't as strong as it seemed like it ought to be.

Gideon's world was expanding, and not slowly. He'd stepped right out of one reality and entered another that was denser, richer, and felt closer to the spirit inside him than any Sunday service in Random Illinois could have aspired to. There was no doubt in his mind that he had received a calling. He had known from a young age that he was different from the boys that he played with, and that—though he was interested—the girls he knew that planned to grow up, marry, and raise housefuls of children were not the draw for him that they could have been, if he'd allowed it ... if the voice in his heart that spoke to him more often than any other had allowed it.

That voice was silent now, but he didn't feel a sense of disapproval. It was a sense of wonder that drew him into the forest -- a connection with the land, and another being, that transcended anything in his experience.

Desdemona didn't talk as they walked. At first he thought she might be drunk, or drugged, because she swayed from side to side, dodging trees at what seemed the last possible second and sliding over fallen trees sinuously. Then he realized that there was a rhythm to her motion. She danced down the trail, swaying and rocking, and as he followed, trying not to get too close, or to interfere in any way, he began to believe he could hear the rhythm that she moved to. Shadows shifted to the right, and to the left, but he ignored them. He had no idea why, but he trusted this strange, beautiful woman, and if she saw anything out of the ordinary, she paid no attention to it. Gideon followed her lead.

They eventually came out in a clearing that bordered on the swamp. The water was fetid and green. The scent was pungent, loamy, and mixed the taste of decay and fresh and deep roots. Desdemona stopped in the center of the clearing, and Gideon saw that she—or someone—had been there before. A circle of smooth stones had been placed in a wide circle, concentric with the outer ring of the clearing. Desdemona stepped into the circle, and turned.

"You better come in here, preacher man," she said softly. "What I'm going to do, the things we're going to see, they don't like the insides of things. They won't cross my circle, but if you stay out there, I can't make any promises."

Gideon crossed the circle and stood at her side. He stared out into the trees to one side, and over the brackish water of the swamp in the other. The sunlight was long gone from the horizon, and the moon hadn't quite reached the center of the sky. The shadows were long, stretching from the trees surrounding the clearing toward the circle, but somehow falling just short.

Desdemona gestured to the ground at her side, and Gideon sank down, dropped the bag beside him and gazed about the clearing nervously. He wasn't really worried about what might come—he trusted his faith, and he trusted Desdemona. Still, something kept him on edge, and he made no move to come closer to the ring of stones.

Desdemona circled him slowly. From the bag he'd carried with them, she took candles. She placed them on each of the stones. When they were in place, she took out three bags of powder. The first she sprinkled around the outer rim of the circle.

"What is it?" Gideon asked.

She glanced at him, and then turned back to her work. "Remember the rules preacher man, no questions."

He started to protest, then thought better of it and sat back.

As she finished her circuit of the stones, she dropped the pouch beside him.

"Salt," she said softly.

She grabbed a second pouch and three small bowls. These she placed at points around the circle so that if lines had been drawn through one to intersect the others, a triangle would be formed. This time, Gideon held his silence and watched as she poured the powder into the three bowls. A moment later she pulled a small tinderbox free from the bag and lit each of the bowls. Pungent smoke rose and misted around them. Combined with the shadows it made it difficult, if not impossible to see the trees or the swamp and after a moment or two an odd vertigo washed over him. He wasn't certain which direction he'd entered from, and he thought if he jumped to his feet and ran, he'd be as likely to splash into the swamp as to find his way through the trees.

He remained seated. Desdemona returned and placed her tinderbox carefully back in the bag. She took a small branch soaked in some kind of oil and lit it by placing the tip into one of the braziers and flowing on it to feed the heat. With this small torch she lit each of the candles in turn. Gideon couldn't be sure at this point if she'd lit the candle in the north first, or that in the south, but she circled in a counter-clockwise direction until they were all lit, then snuffed her torn in the soil at her feet.

There was one pouch left, and Gideon eyed it suspiciously. It was smaller than the first two, and from its shape he didn't believe it to be filled with powder. The scent of whatever burned in the bowls permeated the air near them, and seeped languidly through his senses. The glowing light from the three bowls lit the smoke and he thought he saw shapes flying, or swimming through the smoke. He ignored them. It was a trick, and illusion, and he'd learn nothing if he hooked his mind on the first thing she tossed his way.

Desdemona sat across from him. They were dead center in the circle, only a small patch of ground between them. Desdemona pulled out a carved wooden box and set it on the ground beside her thigh. Gideon watched her carefully. She grabbed the last of the pouches and opened the drawstrings that bound it. She pulled it open and dipped her fingers in. What she pulled out was two small strips of something. It was brown, and at first Gideon mistook it for jerky. She pulled the strings tight, and the pouch disappeared, though he didn't see where she'd put it. His gaze was locked on her eyes now.

"You gotta trust me, if you want to see," she said.

The words were as soft as her breath, but he heard them clearly. He nodded, and did not drop his gaze. She leaned in across toward him and held out one of the two brown strips between thumb and forefinger. With her other hand, she brought the second to her lips and slid it in. Taking a deep breath, Gideon parted his lips and accepted what she offered. He thought, just for a moment, that he saw a dark sparkle in her eye.

"Don't chew," she warned. "Let it sit on your tongue, or tucked behind your lips. You might feel a little numb. You might hate the taste. Don't' spit it out, don't swallow the strip. Let it melt as it will. Don't think about it."

Gideon thought about saying that now that she'd told him not to think about it, it was unlikely that he could think about anything but the odd-tasting, bitter thing on his tongue, but even as the words formed, she dropped her gaze and drew the wooden box around in front of her. He forgot about the odd, sticky substance almost immediately.

Desdemona didn't open the box immediately. She watched it and ran her long, slender fingers over the wooden lid. Gideon was curious, and he nearly spoke. He wanted to tell her to open it, to get it over with and show him what she'd brought him to the clearing to see, but his lips were thick and tacky and it was too much trouble to part them. Besides, he noticed something else then.

She was singing very softly. He would have almost called it a chant, but it had a melody, rising and falling in a rhythm that caught his senses and trapped them. He tried to look away, but only managed to shift his eyes, staring at things on the periphery of his sight. The mist circled them and formed a wall of mist against the outside world. Things moved in those depths, he was sure of it, but he couldn't bring himself to look directly, and a tiny voice in the back of his head suggested that if he did, he wouldn't see them at all.

Or was it Desdemona who said it? Sang it? He was disoriented, and his head was thick with—what? He vaguely remembered that she'd placed something in his mouth. Had he been drugged? Was she drugged?

There was a sharp sound to his left, and he started. He wanted to look—needed to see what had made the sound, but he couldn't do it. The sound repeated, behind Desdemona, but again he couldn't lift his gaze. This would have been an even easier motion than turning to the side, but there was no chance he'd pull it off. He watched her face; he knew she was lifting the lid of that box.

He could see it in his mind. It was small, only a few inches across and maybe six inches long. It was maybe three inches deep though, so it would hold—what?

Desdemona dropped her gaze slowly, and as she did so, he was drawn along in her wake. When she broke eye contact completely and gazed into the box, he was able to move again— and to think, a little. He didn't move. He watched her reach into the box, and one by one she plucked them free.

Bones. What she drew from the box was a small collection of white, sun worn, bones. Some were smooth, as if they'd been in running water for a very long time. Others were jagged and broken. There were teeth, tiny ribs, and one was, Gideon believed, a human knuckle. He stared in fascination as she lined them up carefully in some pattern he couldn't name.

From somewhere, she had produced a sharp stick. She jabbed the point of it into the dirt between them and drew it back toward her crossed legs. She worked quickly, and Gideon saw that she was writing something, or tracing a pattern. The stick twitched and shot from side to side so violently it nearly flew from her hands. He couldn't tell if she was moving it, or hanging on for dear life as it moved her. Her song grew louder. He knew none of the words, but the rhythm drew the pulse of his heart into syncopation and bound him to her. He didn't know how, or why, but he knew that it had happened.

As suddenly as the motion of the stick through the earth

had begun, it stopped. She tossed the stylus aside impatiently and leaned in close. Her hair fell forward, and hung over the smaller circle within a circle within a circle where she'd drawn the symbols. Her hand shot out and circled the pile of bones, scooping them from the earth in a swift, graceful motion.

"Close your eyes."

He heard the words, but he couldn't focus on a source. She might have insinuated them into the rhythm of her chant, or her song, or whatever it was. It might have come from somewhere in the mist, from one of the floating, swimming, swirling shapes. His eyes grew so suddenly heavy that nothing he might have done could have kept them open. He fought it, and they fluttered, and then closed. The world spun, and then righted itself.

He stared into the eyes of a wolf.

He tried to scream, but the sound was so distant, so quiet that it whispered through his mind and he couldn't catch it. The wolf's skin dried and cracked. Fissures ran through it, starting at the nose, and below the bottom lip. Its teeth were bared, but the skin fractured and peeled away to bone. The jaws snapped so suddenly and loudly that the air moved and washed around him and he heard a soft click in the void of silence. It was a tooth, bouncing off the ground, though he saw no dust or dirt or grass, only the bone.

Then a sequence of forms grew from the dark surface where the ground should be. There were birds, and rats, a raccoon and some sort of lizard. He saw deep brown eyes and hard scales, limbs contorting and wrapping around one another, serpents and eagles and then, very suddenly, her eyes.

Desdemona's eyes were wide and wild. They were deep and glowed with a greenish yellow light that was no reflection of the fire, or trick of the mist. He leaned closer. Her hair rose and danced, as if caught in some mystic, invisible whirlwind. He felt it, and he didn't.

She raised her hand between them, knuckles aimed at his face, fingers curled back like talons. He saw her eyes over the top, and now the flames danced across them, reflected and intensified. She stared at him with such intensity he was afraid the vision of the wolf was himself, and his skin was melting and cracking away—but he held that gaze, and after a moment, she smiled.

With a flick of her wrist she sent the handful of bones whirling into the air. They danced before his eyes, and he tried to pick them out in flight. The wolf's tooth. The beaver's rib. The lizard's spine—the knuckle. His hand ached and he fought the urge to look down. The bones dropped, but he did not follow their flight. He watched her eyes.

The fire roared and popped. Desdemona arched her back as if she'd been shot. She clasped her hands violently to the sides of her head and screamed. He could only watch. As she arched, the fabric of her dress pressed tightly to her body. Her thighs were muscled and straining, and he feared she would break in half, bowed and overwhelmed by—what? There was a rush of energy—not wind, exactly, though it fanned the flames—but something that washed over him and heated his skin. He felt as if the flames ate at his skin from within, but it wasn't pain, it was sensation. It wasn't death, it was a birth, a new life, a thing he'd never imagined, and dreamed of every night of his life in some dark moment between lucidity and prayer.

And then it was silent.

The world stilled. The mist hung like a shroud around their circle, and even the fire seemed brittle and solid. Something passed between them, linked their eyes, and then tucked itself away. She dropped her gaze, and his followed. The symbols she'd drawn in the dirt stood out dark and liquid. Their color would not remain stable, and he couldn't stop tracing their patterns, following the motions of the stick she no longer held as the earth offered the motion back to his senses.

The bones lay across the top, jumbled, warped, and scattered. He stared, and at first they broke the patterns of the symbols and interfered with the symmetry of the vision. He frowned, and if he could have moved his arms he would have reached out to brush them away. He wanted to make sense of the letters, or pictures, or patterns, but then he saw it.

The bones had fallen in a pattern of their own. They shimmered, and he stared, trying to make sense of it. It was there, just beyond his grasp. And then it was gone. He stared, but the image receded. The bones were just bones. The dirt was just dirt. He felt the cool, clammy sensation of mist on his cheeks. He smelled the suddenly cloying reek of the incense. He glanced up, and the breath caught in his throat.

Desdemona unwound slowly from her arch. She shook her head, and her hair fell in wild disarray over her shoulders. Her skin was moist—maybe from sweat, maybe from the same mist that dampened his clothes and his face and his hair. She was absolutely beautiful in that moment and he found that, though he could move again, he could not speak.

Desdemona closed her eyes for a long, endless moment, and he stared at her, unable to look away. Then she returned her attention to the bones and studied them closely. She traced each one with the tip of one long finger, trailing off at times along the symbols she'd drawn beneath. Her lips moved silently, but he didn't think she was singing, or chanting. She was thinking out loud, sorting something he couldn't fathom, or conceive, and all he could do was stare at her in fascination, wondering how he had missed that unbelievable heat, that overwhelming primal sensation, for so many years and called himself a man of God.

Could there be a sensation so intense without divine presence? His tongue felt thick and dry, and he thought about asking her for a drink, but held himself in check. He had made a promise, and that was the one rational thought remaining to him from an evening that faded more and more quickly as he tried to force it back from his memory. She looked at him and this time her smile was pretty, but just that. She seemed timid, just for a second, as if waiting to see what he'd do, or say—as if waiting for acceptance.

Gideon licked his lips and she leaned back, grabbed a small jug, and handed it to him. He took it, sniffed it, and she laughed softly.

"Water, preacher man," she said softly. "It is only water. Drink."

He did, and then it was his turn to smile, as he handed it back to her. He wanted to speak. He wanted to tell her so many things, and to ask her even more, but she held up a finger and silenced him.

"Not now. Not yet. You think about it, preacher man. I got people to talk to. My night is just starting, but you need to get back to your church, and your God. You got some praying to do, maybe, and some thinking. I got people waiting for me, counting on me. Tomorrow, maybe the next day, we'll have us a talk."

He nodded, but she was already moving. She gathered the bones, dropped them back into the small box, and packed the pouches and tinderbox carefully. She lifted each of the bowls and tossed the ashes out into the night. He was afraid they'd burn her hands, but they'd cooled long before, and he suddenly wondered how long they had been in the swamp. Clouds obscured all but a fine mist of light that came from everywhere and nowhere at once.

When everything was packed away as it had been when they arrived, she handed him the bag again, and he took it slowly, holding the fingers of her hand in his as she tried to release it. He held her like that, fingertips pressed together tightly, and then she slid away. He caught a smile on her lips as she turned, but she was gone in a quick flash of shadow, and he stumbled after, trying to keep up without running into a tree, or tripping over a root, or sliding into a puddle. He felt like he'd just awakened from a week long sleep, and his limbs were clumsy. She moved with the grace of a doe, and he felt her impatience as she stopped several times to wait for him to catch up.

As his mind cleared, he tried to run back through everything that had happened, but it faded in and out. Every time he thought he remembered something specific, it shifted and he became equally certain it had been something else. All the while, her eyes haunted him, and he followed her flashing legs and wild hair through the swamp, wondering how he'd come so far from Random Illinois, and why it had taken him so long to leave.

At the edge of his clearing, she stopped. He hadn't even known they were close, but there was the church. The shadows were lightened slightly in the clearing, and he knew that it was not as late as he'd feared. The moon was in the sky, shining in on the thatch and bark roof of God's house. It was beautiful in that light, and when he turned and handed her the bag, she was bathed in that same light. Her eyes shone, and she smiled at him.

"Pray, preacher man," she whispered. "Pray for me, and for the vision."

He put a hand on her shoulder, and thrilled at the touch, but held himself back from any other show of emotion. There would be time.

"Gideon," he said softly.

She tilted her head quizzically to one side, studied his face, and he spoke again.

"Call me Gideon. Please?"

Her smile lit the clearing and she reached up to touch his cheek with the tips of her fingers.

"Pray for me, Gideon," she said.

And she was gone.

FIVE

Gideon didn't see Desdemona the following day, or the next, and each hour that passed distracted him further from his work. He tried to concentrate on helping to prepare the food, but he was nearly fully recovered, and the menial tasks that had kept him alive and alert on so many previous days seemed pointless and too simple. The old and the very young did not really need his assistance; they had tolerated him during his infirmity. Now he was a tall, healthy man, and all of his peers were in the fields. During picking months, there was no rest. The cotton had to be picked, then it had to be picked again and if there was time before frost or bad weather destroyed what was left, there might be a third picking. They called that a Christmas picking, though it fell nearer to Thanksgiving.

The church building was complete. He worked on it every night, patching holes and filling in holes that didn't really matter. He, Elijah, and Sarah had combed the woods for appropriate logs and stumps to create rough benches, and one morning, without any warning at all, he'd entered to find that an altar had been created from stacked crates. Wood was precious in the camps, and the straight, planed wood of crates was worth its weight in gold. Still, someone had found this use appropriate, and though it gave him a chill and made him feel guilty on some levels, it brought tears to his eyes.

It wasn't enough to keep his mind occupied. He needed to see Desdemona, though he didn't like admitting this to himself. He needed to talk to her about what he'd seen in the clearing by the swamp, though he wasn't sure that the answers would ease the nightmares that haunted him. As a man of God, he was concerned for her soul, but as a man he was concerned for his own, because he knew that whether or not she was willing to embrace his faith, the burning sensation that rose inside him at the thought of her would not waver or die. If she sprouted horns and claimed his soul, he might not be able to deny her.

When the waiting grew too much, he acted. It was a morning like any other morning—a Friday. He rose earlier than usual, but he did not make his way to the fires or the gathering of food. He strapped on his boots, and dressed himself to work. His hair was growing long, dangling in his eyes and waving behind him like that of some crazed prophet. He tied it back with a colorful cloth bandana. Even at six AM it was warm, but he knew from questions he'd asked and stories others had told that it would get much worse before it got better.

Without a backward glance at his church, he strode through the woods toward the fields. A few moments later he fell in behind the line of pickers trudging toward the fields. They weren't talkative, but they smiled when they saw him. One of the children turned and ran back to the camp. He returned with a heavy canvas bag and tossed it to Gideon before running ahead to rejoin the line beside his parents.

There was a murmur of discussion, but they kept it low, and fell silent if he drew too near. There was no sign of Desdemona, but he saw Elijah in the crowd, and Sarah. They reached the fields and spread out, one to a row. Even the quiet rumble of conversation died away as they disappeared into the shoulder-high plants. It was still early, and dew coated the leaves and stalks. Gideon stepped into a row beside an older man, maybe forty, maybe sixty—Gideon was unable to tell for certain. The work, the sun, and the rough life had worn the man's features like water over stones in a river. On the other side a girl of fifteen or so started down her row, nimbly plucking the soft white bolls from the harsh, scraping, cutting pods.

Gideon had no idea how to pick cotton. He watched for a few moments, and then set to work. His hands were raw after the first hour, but he gritted his teeth and continued. His leg ached, but he wasn't moving that quickly, and the pain in his hands helped him ignore the leg.

The sun rose high and hot and drained the moisture from the cotton and Gideon's body. His throat was parched, but he'd left without water, assuming it would be provided. After three hours, his sight blurred, his skin was scorched, and he could only hobble down the row. His sack was heavy, half full of cotton, and dragged like an anchor behind him. The others had left him behind, and he moved on in a daze. As he walked and picked, bled and ached, he prayed. He started by reciting every verse he could recall from the book of Job.

When Desdemona found him, he was mumbling snatches of the Song of Solomon and crawling down the row. He was still picking, but so slowly he hadn't moved two yards in half an hour, and it was hard to tell if he was aware of the work, or the passage of time.

"Hey, Preacher man," she called out. "You better take a break and get a drink."

He didn't rise, and she stepped closer, putting a hand on his shoulder.

"Hey, she said. You gotta crawl before you can walk."

She held out a jug of water. Gideon dropped his bag, nearly fell forward into the dust, caught his balance, and gripped the jug so tightly his hands trembled. He drank greedily, and she had to snatch the jug back before he drained it.

"You can't drink like that in the heat," she said. "You got to pace yourself. Pick slower, pick better, and get you some water. You want to come out here like a fool, that's your business, but if you're gonna do the work, you gotta do it right. It won't be you they come after with their whips and their cursing. It will be all of us."

He nodded.

"Sorry," he said.

"You're tryin' Preacher man, we all know that. Just don't try so hard."

He glanced up again, and some of the light had returned to his eyes. He saw her standing, the sunlight glittering in a rainbow-hued aura around her face as he tried to force his vision to focus through a sheen of burning sweat. She might have been an angel.

*

"Gideon," he said softly.

She stared at him as if the sun had stolen his senses, and he actually found the energy and spirit to smile.

"Call me Gideon," he said. Then, without another word, he stumbled to his feet and picked up his bag. He stood for a minute, getting his bearings. He blocked the glare of the sun with one hand and gazed up and down the rows. Every now and then he caught sight of one of the other pickers. They moved with a rhythm he couldn't feel. They worked in tandem, not all progressing at the same speed, but part of the same force. He wasn't part of that. Not yet. Maybe he never would be completely, but he was aware of it, and it amazed him.

He thought of the years and years and decades of others who'd gone before. The rhythm he sensed came from the earth beneath their feet and the blood and sweat that enriched the soil. It came from the bones and endless, plodding footsteps, running up and down the rows and the stalks, plowed under with the scraggly, frizzy remnant of the cotton that sapped their souls and drained the ground of its nutrients. He's passed fields on his way south that had been seeded with cotton so many years straight that all they produced was pathetic, bent stalks that barely supported the small and often worthless cotton bolls they grew.

He'd also passed through fields burned to the ground. He'd seen homes desecrated and families begging beside the roads. He'd seen men steal for their families and others fight for their pride, but he'd seen it from a distance. He'd remained detached, stayed in the shadows, offered grace at a few meals and avoided confrontation. That was then.

Here, he yearned to be a part of what was happening around him. He'd believed that in Random he felt the Lord in the church. He thought he'd felt the light and love of his God on Sundays when the tables were heavy with food, or at services where tearful women in expensive hats and dresses awash in lace had answered the call, week after week, dedicating and rededicating themselves to their faith. To his faith.

Except it hadn't been real. He knew that now as certainly as he knew the pain in his torn, shredded palms and the deep ache in his leg. He knew it because what he felt now, the depth of emotion these people shared, was light and day to the ladies of Random, Illinois. He thought, scandalously, that they needed to be taken out into the woods by Desdemona, or someone like her, and shown how green the grass could be, how tall and powerful the trees were and how that strength had grown from years of stretching toward the light. Centuries. Life not measured in days, but in decades.

He turned and saw that Desdemona had disappeared back into the cotton rows. He was alone, and he turned back to the cotton. He worked steadily, and he picked up his prayers where he'd left off, or tried to. It was hard to tell what he'd been thinking, or doing, before the water. He was already thirsty again, but he saw that Desdemona had left the jug. He tucked it into the shade behind a couple of the taller plants and remembered where he'd left it. He'd move it a little at a time, use those movements to mark his progress.

The sun had begun its long trek back down from the center of the sky, and the promise of evening, and food, surfaced like a dangling carrot before a recalcitrant mule. He smiled at that thought, as well, and left the verses of the Old Testament behind. His favorite Gospel was that of Luke, and he began reciting it to himself, trying to match the rhythm of the words to the motion of his hands, and his feet.

He didn't see the young man riding up behind him. He heard the hoof beats, too late to react. There was nowhere for him to go, and nothing to do but to wait, and to see what would come next. He straightened slowly, and turned. He heard the horse snort, but did not allow himself to react. When he'd spun to face the row he'd been picking for what seemed years, he faced two of the coldest eyes he'd ever encountered.

The young man sat his mount arrogantly The horse was a powerful animal, dark brown and brutish with close set eyes and sharp, white teeth. It was the sort of animal you'd never turn your back on. So was the boy.

"Well, what we got here," the rider said, turning to the side and spitting a stream of tobacco juice that splattered over the mud in a vile, brown flood.

Gideon stood and watched him, saying nothing. There was a wicked looking lash mounted on the side of the saddle, and a military issue saber hung from the boy's hip. He'd have seen action in the war. He was too young, but Gideon knew as well as any that a great number of young men, and women, had left their homes behind to fight in the war. The gray slacks and tattered gray hat left no doubt which side of the war he'd fought on, and little doubt what his attitude toward the workers would be, for that matter.

"I heard there was a white man back in there with the niggers," the young man said. His face was a practiced sneer with sharp edges, and there was a twitch at the edge of his mouth that Gideon didn't trust.

"I heard you was buildin' them a church—preacher from up north. Sheriff thought you was dead 'till the rumors come through."

"I'm truly sorry to disappoint him," Gideon said. He tried to keep his voice steady and his emotions even, but it was hard. He remembered Sheriff Hawkins' cold voice, the flashing eyes and crashing boots of the others. He remembered the shadows and the pain, and his leg throbbed. His heart sped up slightly, and his already parched mouth went dry. He held his ground.

The boy studied him the way you'd watch a lion in a circus cage, or the body of a man shot in the street. The interest was cold, distant, and deadly.

"You don't belong here, preacher," the boy said at last. "Best for you if you move on."

"Seems to me," Gideon said reasonably, "that this cotton needs to be picked. Can't see a reason you should complain if one more set of shoulders bends to it."

The young man laughed. "You ain't picked as much as an eight-year-old nigger, preacher. Not much loss if you was gone, I'd say." After a hesitation, the boy sat up straighter and continued.

"I'm Isaiah Pope, and this is my land. Mine and my fathers, and my brothers. These are our niggers, and I don't care what a man in a fancy office five hundred miles away has to say about it. They been pickin' our cotton all their lives, and they'll still be pickin' it when these are gone and the little pick-a-ninnies grow up to take their mommy and daddy's places. Nothing you can do to change it."

"I'm just here picking cotton," Gideon said. "I teach the word of our Lord and Savior on Sunday, but the rest of the days, I intend to earn my keep. I hope you can respect that."

The boy spurred his horse forward, and he had the whip in his hand in a flash. Gideon cried out and wheeled, tripping backward. The leather strap cracked, and a lance of pain sliced down Gideon's side. He gripped the wound with both hands, and the lash bit again, creasing his ribs on the opposite side where he'd left an opening. He tried to lunge at the horse, but Pope laughed and cracked the whip a third time. This cut Gideon's cheek and he staggered, nearly dropping to his knees. The leather had come so close to his eye that he panicked.

As he backed into the cotton, he rolled once, twice, then found his footing and took off down the cotton row at a run.

"You better run, preacher," Pope called after him. "You better run, and keep on running. You pick cotton in our fields, you're not a white man, and you ain't no preacher. You're just another thick-headed nigger."

The words faded as Gideon crashed through row after row, afraid to look back and see the man's leering face following him, the hooves of the horse bearing down on him.

"You'd better run." The words faded, and Gideon stopped running. His leg screamed in pain from the unexpected strain, and his breath rasped through his dry, scratched throat.

"Preacher?"

He looked up. It was Elijah. The boy stood, his cotton sack in one hand, and his eyes wide. Gideon glanced over his shoulder, but there was no one there. Isaiah Pope had ridden on to whatever task he'd been about. Gideon dropped to his knees and lowered his head to his hands.

He felt a hand touch gently on his cheek, then pull away. He glanced up.

"You okay, preacher?" Elijah asked.

Gideon saw that the boy's finger had come away from his face with blood on the tips of the fingers. He glanced back at his own hands and saw that his right hand was sticky and red. The cut stung, very suddenly, and he tried to rise. The rows of cotton stretched out endlessly and wavered. He saw Elijah standing close by, his face a mask of concern, but he couldn't bring the boy's face into focus. His stomach fluttered and he tried to fight back the darkness rising within. He failed.

When Gideon woke, the first thing he noticed was smoke. It spiraled above him into darkness stippled with brilliant points of light. Stars. He tried to rise, but a cool hand pressed to his forehead and eased him back.

"You need to rest."

He turned his head slowly, partly because of the pain in his cheek and the lump on the side of his head, and partly because he realized from his position that his head rested in Desdemona's lap. She watched him with dark, expressionless eyes, but her lips bore an expression of concern and a hint of repressed anger.

"What..."

"I told you they don't want you here, Gideon. The one you met, the boy they call Isaiah, is the worst. He was away during the war. He was too young, but he slipped away late one night because he wanted to kill other men. He was afraid the war would end, and he'd be stuck here, farming cotton and forgotten.

"Now the war has ended, and he's back. He still wants to kill, and the war did him no good. We stay clear of that one."

"There are others?" he asked.

"He has two brothers. Joshua is the eldest, nearly a man. He's married, and has moved in to town. He has a very young brother, Enoch. We don't see the boy often. They keep him near the plantation house. Isaiah and his father manage the plantation."

Gideon moved his limbs one at a time, straightening both of his legs, and then his arms. Nothing seemed to be broken, and though he was sore, and felt the dressings on his wounds chaff slightly as he twisted and flexed, there was no permanent damage.

"How bad is it?" he asked finally.

Desdemona glanced at him and raised one eyebrow. "You'll live," she said softly.

"I meant my face," he replied. He brought his hand up and touched the bandage. "There was blood. Elijah was there . . . is he?"

"Elijah is fine," she answered. She nodded toward the fire, and he turned again. Elijah was curled up in a blanket near the fire, sound asleep.

"He's been here all along. He and His mother helped me to get you out of the field, and some of the others made a litter of cotton bags. They dragged you here as gently as they could, but you are a big man. It took a long time, and he's tired."

"And my face?"

She smiled and leaned closer to him. Gideon's senses compressed into the space that encompassed the two of them so suddenly that the only sound he heard was the blood pulsing behind his ear. He breathed in her scent and met her gaze, and she reached out to brush the tips of her nails over his cheeks, to run them through his hair, and to draw him up slightly. He felt the warm, soft flesh of her thighs beneath him and they burned his flesh like fire.

He opened his mouth to speak, but never formed the words. Her lips pressed to his, her fingers gripped his hair, and she kissed him. It was a long, slow, luxurious moment. Desdemona pulled away, but only slightly. He felt her studying him and closed his eyes, just for a moment. His breath was harsh, the air suddenly heavy and reluctant to pass through his lungs, and he felt giddy.

Then she laid him back on her lap, and laughed. The sound was deep and throaty and primal. He remembered the clearing, and the fire. He caught the hint of the scent of the incense she'd burned in the perfume of her hair. He tasted the sliver of whatever it had been that she'd fed him by that fire on her lips and felt a brief sizzle in the back of his throat. His mind flashed with the brilliance of lightning on a single image. Interlocked, tumbled bones strewn across a mat of soil and grass.

Then it was only her eyes, deep, and soft, and close.

"It is customary in my faith to offer prayers of thanks for miracles," he said softly.

"And what would you be thankful for?" She asked.

Her fingers were still in his hair, twisting and turning it gently. The touch was soothing, but left trails of heat. He glanced over to where Elijah lay sleeping.

"There is time, preacher man," she said teasingly. "Are you always in such a hurry to take advantage of your blessings?"

He blushed, and she kissed him again. He pulled back, just for a moment.

"I need to speak to them," he said. "All of them. Everyone who picks cotton and lives in the camp. I need to let them know what has happened, and why. I want them to know that I am not leaving, and though any man who claimed not to be afraid would be a liar, I won't let the Pope family prevent me from opening my church. I want to tell them that I will be here for them, that I will do anything I can to help make their lives better. It's important that they know."

"What must they know?" she asked.

"That not all white men are like the Popes, and Sheriff Hawkins. That God is with them, when they work, and when they sleep, when they love and when they pray. Do you pray, Desi?"

It was a sudden intimacy, the shortening of her name, and it came to his lips unbidden. It felt right, but he felt her stiffen suddenly. She was very silent for a moment, and then melted beneath him.

"What is it?" he asked.

"Only my mother called me that," she said softly. "No one else."

"I didn't know," he said.

"It's good," she said, leaning down to wrap her arms around his shoulders. She rocked him like a child and stared off into the trees. "It is good to hear that name again, and it is good to hear it from you. I don't think that you and I mean the same thing when we say the word prayer, but yes. I pray. I dream. There is no way that I could do otherwise."

"Will they come?" he asked. "Will they hear me?"

"They'll come," she answered. "They already respect you. They'll listen, too."

"And you?" he asked.

"I'll be there," she said softly. "But I've already heard."

She sat up and placed a hand on his heart. It took only a few moments for his eyes to grow heavy once again.

He sat up slowly, and she helped him. She rose, laid a blanket out beside the fire, and he lay down on it. She curled in beside him, pulling a second blanket over them. Before he could think of anything further to say, he was asleep.

He dreamed of endless rows of cotton, the pounding of hooves, blazing eyes and the red hot flames of a fire. Then the dreams faded into a haze of warmth and comfort and silent darkness.

SIX

Gideon grew strong over the next couple of months. He returned to the fields, ignored the pain, and healed himself through the work. He walked to the fields with Desdemona at his side, and he returned with her every evening. Twice a week, Wednesday night and Sunday morning, he taught in the small, ramshackle church. He started slowly, beginning with stories from the Old Testament and lessons from the Psalms and Proverbs. They leaned forward in their seats and listened carefully when he spoke, and when he led hymns in his deep, baritone voice they joined in.

Desdemona sat in the rear of the church when he taught. She listened as the others did, but she watched him. They spent most days together, but by a Herculean effort, Gideon had not stayed with her after that single night, sleeping by the fire. He waited. He did not want to teach the people one thing and live a life that was another.

When the cotton was in, and the winter approaching, he came to her on a Saturday morning, very early, when most of the camp was only beginning to rise and start the day. She was seated at her fire, an old iron pot filled with water just coming to a boil. Gideon sat beside her and stared into the flames. She didn't look at him, but there was a smile curling the ends of her lips. He didn't know if was just because of his presence, or if she sensed why he'd come.

She added a small handful of rough-ground coffee beans to the water, and they watched together as the liquid swirled, swallowing the beans and emitting a wonderful aroma. She poured them each a cup, and for once, she avoided his eyes. He smiled, sipped his coffee, and watched the fire.

"I don't know your customs," he said at last. "I know the way things are in a small town very far from here, and I have a passing knowledge of how things were in Biblical times, though I wonder sometimes if I know anything at all."

"Seems like you learn fast," she said. She sipped her coffee and glanced at him furtively.

"A man can spend his whole life learning things, experiencing things, and believing that he's getting somewhere important," Gideon went on. "He sees things the way he's expected to, learns the ways of those around him and memorizes the rules so he can pass them on to new generations. A man hopes to have new generations to pass his truth on to, and there are rules for that, as well."

She said nothing, and he continued.

"What I'm trying to say," he told her, "Is that I've come to learn a new truth here—with you. I've come to understand that because a man learns things a certain way, or another man writes them down the way he's read them all his life and passes that on isn't enough to make a thing right. When the world changes—and our world is changing, there's no doubt of that, the rules have to change as well.

"I've been preaching since I was a small boy. They found out I had a gift, an ability to string words together and bring people closer. I spoke at revivals. My mother took me from town to town one summer, speaking in tents and sleeping in barns, spreading the word of God. That's what I knew then."

"Now?" she asked softly.

"Now the lines aren't so straight," he said softly. "Or maybe they're straight for the first time and stretching out further than they did before—actually reaching into the world. I was raised to believe a man grew up, found work, married, had children, and taught them to do the same. There were no Negro citizens in Random, Illinois. There were only Methodists and a very small group of Catholics, and even the Catholics were looked on with suspicion.

"You got no slaves back in Random?" she asked. There was genuine surprise in her voice.

"None," he said. "It's a very small place, and it was settled long ago by farmers and their families. They work their own land; they take care of their own crops. There are a great number of men and women in Random who have never seen a colored man or woman, and would be frightened for their lives if they did."

"Not you, though," she said.

"No, not me. I told you, my mother took me on the road with her. There were Negro families in a lot of the places we visited. Some places they came to the revivals. They stood off to the side, on their own, but they were there. A lot of places it was just like here, only with different work. There are a lot of folks back North who believe it is their duty to make things right to your people. Most of them believe this only so far as they can be involved without getting too close. Lip service is what I used to call it from the pulpit, though I was talking about service to the Lord at the time. They talk a good game, in other words. I was like that—it's how I ended up on the road.

"Somewhere along the way, things changed."

"You got a point to all this, preacher man?" Desdemona asked. Her hand trembled as she held her coffee, and Gideon reached out to lay his hand on her wrist and steady her.

"I do," he said softly.

"When I came here, I was already changed. I'd seen things on the road, and experienced others, that told me we lived in a little make-believe world in Random.   The God I thought I was serving either doesn't exist, or was waiting patiently for me to stand up and walk into the world. The bake sales and the Sunday dress-up will continue without me, but the world...the world needs men of God with the courage to act on their principles. This country, this new world we're building, needs men with the courage to stand up against Evil. I wish I was stronger. I wish I had a small army of righteous men and women standing behind me to face down men like Sheriff Hawkins, and Reverend Cumby.

"What I've discovered though is that I'm just a man. I'm a man like any other, and if I have work to do for God, I have to do it as a man. Setting myself aside as if I had some special dispensation, some right to the truth that others don't share—that was the sort of thing Reverend Cumby would understand, or the Methodist minister in town. Even the Catholic Priest back home in Random would nod his head and say I was right to take my place at the side of my God. A shepherd, looking out for his sheep. It's what they all do—it's what they understand. Without that belief, it's hard to face a room full of men and women week after week, telling them they have to act a certain way and believe a certain thing or face a pit of fire they couldn't possibly believe in—because if they did, they'd listen, and they'd act, and they'd do it more than once a week."

Gideon turned to face Desdemona. She looked up at him, her expression more fragile than he'd ever seen it, as if she were a bird, perched for flight, or a leaf ready to blow away in the wind.

"I've learned more in theses past three months," Gideon said, "than I did in the first twenty-five years of my life. One thing I've learned is that there are things that are real, and there are things that only seem real until you step into them and live through them.

"You mean the world to me, Desi," he said. "I lay down every night and I start to pray, but I end up thinking about you. I think about whether you are thinking about me. I think about how you dragged me out of that cotton—twice—how you took me in when the people who should have been my own would have beaten me to death. I think about what I saw out by the swamp, and how, no matter how right and real my faith feels, it has never shown me the types of things that you have shown me. I should feel as if those things are evil. I should want to convert you, to save your soul and drag you kicking and screaming into my church to have the dark spirits driven from your soul.

"All I want is to hold you to my heart and keep you there forever. What I'm saying, Desi...what I'm asking, is—will you marry me?"

She trembled so violently that her teeth chattered. Her eyes were wide and tears spilled out of the corners to swirl gently down her cheeks. The cup in her hand fell to the ground, but neither of them paid any attention to it.

"You can't," she said.

He took her hands, both of them, and gripped them tightly. She pulled back, a sudden jerk, but he held her, and with a small cry, maybe negation, maybe something else, she fell into his arms. He drew her close and wrapped his arms around her, pinning her to his chest.

"I can, and I will...if you will," he said. "I have never needed anything in my life. I thought I did. I thought I had been desperate, and hungry, and in pain, but here I've found that pain can be overcome, and hunger can make you stronger, but desperation only comes when you need something to breathe—when the blood in your veins tries to press out and find something just out of reach. Be my wife."

She laid her head on his shoulder. He felt her shaking it, and he reached up, ran his fingers into her hair, and stilled her. He kissed the top of her head gently and she pressed more tightly into his arms. They sat there for a very long time, saying nothing at all. The flames of the fire crackled, hissed, and died slowly to coals. The cups lay forgotten on the ground. The sun rose slowly, and the camp came to life.

No one interrupted them. Elijah came to the edge of the clearing, stood in the shadow of a large Elm tree, and watched for a few minutes. He smiled a sly, secret smile, and melted back into the trees.

After what seemed like hours, Gideon drew back and rose to his feet. He held out his hand. Desdemona's gaze was on the ground at his feet. Her hair fell like a dark shower that covered her shoulders, and her face, shielding her eyes. She sat very still, but he held his ground.

Just as he was about to turn, walk into the trees and never return, she shook her hair back and raised her eyes to his. Her eyes were still rimmed in tears, but her lips had curved into a delicate smile. He wasn't used to seeing her like this— vulnerable—and it melted his heart.

Then she took his hand. She clasped it in both of her own and rose, very slowly, so that she stood close against him. She rose up onto her toes and pressed her lips to his ear.

"Yes, Gideon, I will marry you. Whether your God strikes us down, or the Popes do it for him. Whether the spirits of the swamp burn us in our sleep or send the bones of the dead walking to drag us away, I am yours. There is no going back from a moment like this. This is not a question you've given me...there was never a choice."

"I know," Gideon answered.

Then, without another word, he turned. He held one of her hands firmly in his and he walked away from the fire. The others were winding out toward the fields, a few of them glancing over their shoulders. Gideon paid no attention to them. He walked through the woods toward his clearing, and the church.

Desdemona made no attempt to pull back, or to divert him. She walked beside him through the trees, drawing closer so that their hips brushed and her scent wafted up and around him.

"There is no one to perform the ceremony," Gideon said as they walked. He didn't look at her, but she sensed how aware he was and felt him tremble when their skin brushed. "I don't believe Reverend Cumby will come out here to oversee this union, and I've never heard of a man of God performing his own marriage. Tell me what your people do."

They stepped out into the clearing beside his church. "What do they do out here in the woods when they make a family? When they are in love? Do you perform a ceremony? Do they just come together, and everyone knows? Does Reverend Cumby actually marry them, or someone else—you?"

Desdemona shook her head. This time, she took the lead. She pulled him by their joined hands toward his small shack behind the church. She walked slowly, making sure that he had time to see her ahead of him, her hips swaying a little more than necessary, and her smile dark and hungry.

There were no more words. He opened the door for her, and she stepped inside. By the time he followed, and the canvas flap slid closed behind them, she was on his bed. Her dress fell away as if melting form her form and he stood watching. She arched her back, like he'd seen her do in the clearing, only this time her eyes were clear and her arms reached for him.

He slid down beside her and she worked quickly at his belt,

his pants and shift, and then his body. They kissed, and the world fell away, and in the Heavens he imagined he heard the soft voices of angels, or the dark voices of ghost, and knew that it did not matter.

In his ear, she whispered, "I do."

And it was sealed.

They weren't easy years. Word of the marriage trickled out to the gentry of Old Mill, and to the Pope family. Whenever they could, the Popes caused trouble for Gideon. If they caught him alone in the field, or the woods, they teased him or beat him, and they were constantly on the watch for Desdemona.

In some warped way, they believed she must be responsible for the union—that she must have used her swamp witch powers to steal the mind of a man of God and bind him to her will. No other explanation made sense to them, and Reverend Cumby, stung by the fact none of his freedmen congregation came to hear him when he pulled his wagon out to the fields, fed the rumor at every opportunity. He talked of demons, and of possession, and more than once he was on the verge of firing up a group of locals to take matters into their own hands...but each time someone interceded.

Even a blasphemy of the likes of interracial marriage could only hold their interest for long, however, and eventually it became a thing in the back of their minds, half-forgotten, but there just the same and ready to flare up at a moment's notice.

Gideon and Desdemona added on to his ramshackle church and built up the shack out in back until it almost resembled a city house. Gideon taught, and ex slaves from surrounding camps began to come around to hear him, and to learn. The camp grew, and though they didn't like having a social gathering of ex slaves on their property, the Popes found that they had no lack of labor when it came time for planting, or harvest, and that they had no trouble from the small community in the woods, so long as they let things alone, which they mostly did.

After the first year of their marriage, Desdemona gave birth to a son, and in the second year, a daughter followed. The boy was named Gideon, after his father, and the girl was

Gwendolyn. Both grew quickly, tall, strong, and light-skinned with their mother's dark beauty.

The two had children in and out of their home at all times. Elijah was like a son to them, and Sarah grew up to be a silent beauty. She still said nothing, and though Desdemona's casting of the bones predicted she would have great things to pass on, she showed no inclination to do so.

Things seemed to be easing up in town, as well. By the year 1887, Negro families could be found shopping from the street markets and buying some of their groceries from the Walz's store. Their presence was always met with disapproving stares, and sullen glares traced their movement through town until they were out and on their way, but there was no real trouble. Sheriff Hawkins had retired, and a younger man, Joe Thomas, had taken over. Thomas had come in with his family from the North, and had no love for farming. He took over the local law enforcement, a job no one but Hawkins had the stomach for, and while he kept the peace, he didn't share Hawkins' iron hand, or deep-rooted prejudice.

It might have gone on this way, growing calmer as the years passed and the old generations fell away. In many other towns, in many other places, this was the case. The prejudice was there, deeply rooted, and passed from mother to daughter and father to son with the government, church, and founding fathers putting on their separate shows of good will while turning their faces from the inequality all around them.

Things were much the same across the south, less so in the cities, and more like the old days on the farms and rural areas, with a trapping of change tacked on in front like the set of a bad play. Old Mill was no better, or worse than other places. There were bad apples in the mix, and just like anywhere else in the world, there were times when the wrong people crossed paths at the wrong time.

Gideon educated his children carefully. He wanted better things for them than working the Pope cotton fields, and he wanted them to be able to function in society when they moved north. He talked of it often, and though she clung to her children, Desdemona knew he was right. There was nothing for the next generation in their ramshackle village. She could never leave—they depended on her for healing, and for the rites and mysteries that her husband could not, or would not embrace, despite the truce the two had made over the years.

For once, it was the aged Reverend Cumby, so old that he had to be helped to the pulpit on Sundays, who foretold the tragedy most clearly, though it was nothing different than he'd predicted a thousand times before, year after year as his heart grew old and bitter and the fire and brimstone he spewed week after week finally charred what heart he'd had to start with.

"No good will come," he cried, "from the union of a man and woman of different race. That we allow such a thing on the very edge of our town is a tragedy. That we do nothing to set things right is a sin. No good will come of it, for it is an abomination."

No one paid any attention to the good reverend. It had been a long time since his fiery harangues had brought the heavy weight of guilt down on the heads of his congregation. The world was moving on, and he refused to step on for the ride, but this one time—this one last time, he saw clearly.

Young Gideon came to town once a week to shop for his mother. Usually his father or Elijah accompanied him—there was safety in numbers, and though there'd not been any real trouble in many years, it paid to remain cautious. One day in June of 1898, he went alone. It was a hot day, the sun beating down on the fields, and planting was in full swing. Gideon would have been in the fields, but his mother needed some things, and the best—the safest, they all believed—time for a single black man to walk alone into Old Mill was during a weekday when the men were working in the fields, and as few as possible would see him.

Gideon passes as often for not as a young white man. If you didn't look too close at his close-cropped hair, or the exotic tilt of his eyes, which were gifts from his mother, you could miss his race entirely. His skin was nearly as light as his father's, and his clothing was clean and mended. Everyone in Old Mill knew him, of course. They knew his father, or knew of him, and his mother. Gideon and his father were a part of local legend, the preacher beaten and left for dead in the cotton, rising to build a church in the swamp and marry a colored witch.

No one knew how to react to Gideon, so in most cases they chose not to react at all. He made it into town without a problem, and stepped into Walz' General Store with his hat in his hand and a smile on his face.

"Afternoon, Mr. Walz," he said.

The man who glanced up was Stanley Walz, Devon's son. Stan had been running the family business for nearly a decade. He frowned when he saw who had entered the store, but he remained civil.

"Afternoon. What can I get you?"

"I need a pound of corn, a bag of sugar, and some flour," he said. "Got the money right here."

The townsfolk regularly ran credit at Walz', but the freedmen were expected to pay cash.

Walz nodded.

"Right with you," he said. He leaned his broom against the wall and quickly packed the items Gideon had requested. He didn't want the boy in his store any longer than absolutely necessary. He didn't want others to see the two of them talking, or to get the wrong impression about how close they were. More than that, he didn't want his father to wander up from the diner on the corner and see him serving a colored man. It would mean another fight, and probably another telling of the old story about that long ago night in the sheriff's barn.

"I thank you," Gideon said.

"You're welcome to what you can pay for," Stan replied grudgingly.

Moments later, Gideon was walking down the sidewalk toward the edge of town. There was no one in sight, and that suited him fine. He wasn't really intimidated by the city folk, but he wasn't comfortable around them either. The way they stared at him, and the stories he knew they whispered as he passed itched at the back of his mind. Even when he couldn't hear them, it made him angry. He hated the way he was treated, and hated the way his father—a man of God—was shunned by these supposedly civilized men and women. It wasn't something he talked about, because no one in the town would have listened, and anyone in the camp he might have confided in, with the possible exception of Elijah, who felt the same, would have lectured him on biding his time, turning the other cheek, and studying so he could find a better life for himself. Somewhere else. Somewhere without his family, or the home he'd grown up in, or his father's church.

He kept his head down and walked quickly, and he made it to the Pope cotton fields without being noticed. Out across the field, he saw his friends and neighbors, his mother and even his father. Their backs were bent to the work, sowing the seeds that would become the next crop, all of which would be handed over for a pittance to men who didn't care about them at all. To men who would as soon kick them into a ditch or run them down with their horses as say hello.

Most days he paid close attention, particularly when he was out in the fields alone. He had brought the avoidance of the Popes to the level of an art form, but this particular day he was distracted. He had spent all of his concentration making it in and out of Old Mill without being seen. He let down his guard too soon and halfway across the last cotton field that separated him from home, he heard running footsteps. Even then, he didn't react. If he'd started running then he might have made it to the line of trees, and the path beyond. Some of the others would be there, there was always someone taking a short rest or getting a drink.

But he didn't run, and he didn't turn, until it was too late, and when he finally realized that the footsteps were dead on his trail, it was too late. He turned, and he stood staring at the red, blustery face of Bartholomew Pope. The boy was nearly a head taller than Gideon, and much broader. He had his own father's shoulders, and his tousled hair stuck out at odd angles, as though it had never been touched by a comb or a brush.

Of all the Popes, Bartholomew, "Bart," to his brother and their family, was the worst. Isaiah was nearly consumed with the farm now, married himself with a son, Enoch, and another on the way. Bart was different. He spent his nights out, rarely pitching in with work and when he did, only to bully field hands, or to offer useless advice to his brother. He drank, and he rarely bathed. His eyes were set too closely together, contorting his features into an eternal sneer. All of this Gideon could have lived with. He did, in fact, live with it, but there was more.

From a very early age, Bart Pope hated colored people. He had memorized all the standard insults by hanging out in town. He spent as much time as he could gathering stories from the old men in town, and the sons of those same old men drinking by the river. He'd said the words and laughed at the jokes for so long that they were a way of life to him. Gideon had his own theory.

Bart wasn't a bright boy. There was no danger that he'd ever run the farm; he was barely able to handle simple jobs, and he couldn't be trusted around the field hands because he couldn't keep his mouth shut, his hands off the women, or his fists off the men. He'd nearly beaten Elijah's nephew to death with a stick, and only Isaiah's sudden arrival had saved him from being murdered in his own field, and causing the deaths of a dozen hands in retribution.

He was trouble. That was the front and back end of it, and by the time Gideon realized it, Bart Pope had set his broad body in the cotton row that separated him from safety. Gideon looked around quickly, but there was no one close enough to see him, and even if there had been, there was nothing he could yell across that field that wouldn't start the trouble he was desperately figuring a way to avoid.

"What you doin' out here all by yourself, nigger?" Bart asked. He was sweating from his short run, his shirt plastered to his shoulders and soiled. His eyes had an odd, piggish glitter that made Gideon's stomach turn.

"Just been to town, boss," he said quietly. "Had to get some things for my ma."

"It's funny," Bart said, staring off over the field and trying to look thoughtful. "All these fields out here that need seedin' and a big, strappin' nigger like you takes the day off and heads into town. That about the size of it boy? You shirking your duties?"

Bart spat the last word.

"I work hard," Gideon said evenly. "Someone had to go to

town. There were plenty of workers to get the seed in, and I'll be back out there this afternoon. I got to get this home to ma, though."

"That right?" Pope asked. He hadn't looked back away from the fields. He seemed to be watching the workers, but Gideon knew better. He was looking out of the corner of his eye, hoping Gideon would light out for the trees. It was what he was hoping for, an excuse to beat him, or worse. Gideon didn't intend to offer it.

"Yes sir," Gideon mumbled.

"You say something boy?" Bart asked, turning back. He didn't move quickly. He had one hand on his hip, the thumb hooked over his belt. He appeared to be trying to imitate someone, or something, that Gideon didn't recognize. Maybe some older man or some image he'd see from the war.

"I said yes sir," Gideon replied more loudly. He tried to imagine how a soldier would snap his answer to a superior. It gave him something to focus on, making it a game—not a shame. His mother had taught him that, and it had worked for him more than once. Not this time.

Bart turned to him and smiled, and Gideon started walking. It was too late, he knew, but he tried to slip past Bart on the right, moving the small package of groceries to his own right hand to keep them as far out of reach as possible.

Bart stepped to his left and blocked Gideon's way.

"I ain't done talkin' to you boy," he snarled.

"Sorry, boss," Gideon said, trying to keep his voice calm. "I just need to get this home."

"I heard you the first time," Bart said. "You got to get that package home to your swamp witch, nigger mom so she can cook up some dinner for that papa of yours, that right? The nigger lovin' preacher? That what she used to put the spell on him, or don't she tell you the swamp Juju?"

"I got to get home," Gideon repeated. He tried to slip over a row, use the furrows as a shield, and break for the woods. Bart lunged, grabbed Gideon by the arm, and swung him hard. Gideon cried out and swung his arm wide for balance. Pope was strong, too strong. He sent Gideon reeling. The package of groceries fell into the dirt, and Gideon swung his arms up to protect himself.

"What you think, boy?" Bart grunted. "You think you can just run away from me? Ignore me? You think you don't have to listen to me? You think you can just waltz into town and act like any white man, just because your nigger witch mom tells you it's okay?"

Gideon saw red. It was very sudden, and he couldn't control it. He fought to keep his breath even. He told himself to roll into a ball, to ignore the insults, to take the beating and hope someone heard him crying out, or saw what was happening and came to his rescue. It might be bad, but Bart had never killed anyone, so far as Gideon knew. No one on the farm, anyway. He tried to let it pass, but it just wouldn't go.

"My mother isn't a witch," he said. His voice cleared, the field hand dialect falling away. His father had trained him to speak proper English, and he was proud of what he'd learned. He didn't let on when he was in the field, and he didn't let on when he was in town, but when he was home, he practiced. On Sundays, now and then, he read from the scripture in his father's church. Now, as his anger drowned his sense, all pretenses fell away as well.

Bart swung. His fist was big, and though he was slow, and Gideon saw it coming, it still caught him a glancing blow. White hot pain shot up behind his eyes, and he rolled to the left. Bart dropped then, letting his weight press down on the smaller, younger man. Trapped, Gideon lashed out.

All the anger he'd been bottling up since the day he was born poured out of him in that instant. He screamed, and he struck. His fist plowed into Bart's eye, driving him back and to the side. The bigger man bellowed in surprise and pain. Gideon leaped to his feet and followed. He drove the toe of his boot into Bart's side, drew it back, and slammed it forward again. He dropped onto the man's back and started swinging, not aiming at any particular target, just pounding away.

Bart tried to crawl through the dirt and escape. He swung wildly, but missed with most of his shots, and the few that didn't miss didn't have any power. Gideon plowed through them and fought through it. They were both screaming, and it was only moments before others were running across the field. They cried out for Gideon to stop, but he didn't hear them. They called out to Bart to run, or at least for the love of God fight back, but the big man had dropped to a broken heap in the dirt. He rolled into as small a ball as possible and grunted with each knew kick...each new blow to his head, or his ribs.

It took three grown men to pull Gideon off, and he was a quarter of a mile away before he came to his senses—before he started to understand what he'd done, and what the consequences would be. As his mind cleared, he moved more quickly. He didn't know where he would go, or what he would do, but he knew if he stayed close to the fields, this might be the last day of his life.

About five minutes after he entered the trees, Elijah stepped out of the shadows ahead of him.

"Go to the church," he said. "Your mother is there; your father is on his way."

Bowing his head to hide the sudden flood of tears, Gideon nodded and ran.

SEVEN

Word spread in the fields and washed across toward the plantation house like wildfire. By the time Gideon reached the church, his parents were already there, along with his younger sister. A network of others stretched out toward the fields, watching and waiting. A small delegation had been chosen, mostly older workers who'd been with the Popes since they were children. They were making their way slowly toward the plantation house. Someone had to tell Isaiah and get help for Bart, but they didn't hurry. Others were caring for the boy—he wasn't dead, but he was unconscious. No one wanted to be there when he woke up, but still they took care of him. Anything less would have been a death sentence for all of them.

The clock was ticking.

Reverend Swayne stood just inside the door of his church and stared out past the clearing into the trees, watching carefully. He knew it was too soon for any pursuit. It would be a while before Isaiah heard the news, longer before they retrieved Bart, or he staggered out of the field on his own. Then the drinking would start. Maybe they'd just come after the boy on their own, maybe they'd go to town to the doctor and come back with a posse. Whichever way it went down, it was going to be bad. Bad for the elder Gideon, bad for his son—and bad for their people.

Desdemona hovered in the shadows at the rear of the building. Her daughter, so much like her they could have been different-aged, mirror-images of one another, stood beside her. Elijah sat with the younger Gideon on one of the plank pews. No one spoke for what seemed an eternity, and then the Reverend began to speak.

"We have to get you out of here. There's no other way. You have to go now, into the swamp. You can't be here when they come, and you can't come back—not soon, maybe never. When they come, people are going to be hurt. Our lives are going to be turned upside down, but Isaiah has enough sense not to kill off his workforce. Sheriff Thomas won't be able to stop them, but I think he'll do what he can. If they find you, though," Gideon turned to his son, "they'll string you up. No one will stop them, and no one will blame them. I can't let that happen."

The younger man nodded. His anger was boiling up again, but he kept it just below the surface of his mind. He knew his father was right, but he couldn't think about it. If he remembered Bart Pope's leering, hate-filled face, or the things he'd said, he'd never be able to concentrate enough to get out of town. He'd never be able to walk away and live.

"But what about you?" he said at last. "What about mother? What about Desi?" He nodded at his sister.

The older man lowered his head, and then raised it again. His gaze was level, and his voice was steady when he answered.

"Your mother and your sister will go with you," he said. "At least for now, it's the only way. They will come soon. Maybe as early as this afternoon, but I don't think so. It depends on how bad the boy is hurt. If he's up and drinking by tonight, that's when they'll come."

"What will you do?" young Gideon asked. "Will you come with us?"

"I can't do that," his father replied. "I have a responsibility here. Even if they didn't count on me for spiritual guidance, these people never asked me to bring all of this down on them. A long, long time ago in a little town in Illinois, I made a decision, and this is a continuation of that. It's mine to do. You'll need your mother to guide you in the swamp…without her you won't need the Popes to end your life."

"I don't want to go, Papa," his daughter said, stepping forward. Desdemona reached out for her daughter's arm, but was shrugged off.

"I want to stay with you. It's not me they're after and …"

Isaiah looked up as well, and Reverend Swayne felt the knife of his guilt stab deeper into his heart. He knew the two, Isaiah and his daughter, were all but betrothed. It would be a matter of weeks, maybe even days, before the boy asked his blessing. Now it was out of the question. As much as he would love to have Isaiah for his son, he couldn't allow it at the cost of his daughter's life, or worse. And there were worse things possible. He knew only too well the depths that the men of Old Mill could stoop to.

"You must go," he said. "You must go with your mother, and your brother, and it must be now. Take what food and water you can, take whatever you need. I will hold services tonight. I'll bring everyone together, and we will stand as one. I don't know what, if any good it will do, but it's the only answer I have. We'll pray, and we'll wait, and what comes will come, but I have to know that the three of you will be safe."

His wife glared at him from the shadows. He knew she was angry—he felt it radiating from her like heat from a flame. He also knew she was frightened, not for herself, and probably not for him, but for their children—and for all the others they cared for. She didn't argue. She stepped forward, grabbed her daughter by the arm, and simply said, "Come."

She turned and slipped out the door so quickly she might have been a shadow passing, and reluctantly, with a tragic glance over her shoulder, her daughter followed. Gideon stood, but Elijah held him back.

"Not yet," the man said. He rose, as well.

"You go with them into that swamp," Elijah said, "and you don't stop. You get far enough from here to be safe, and you take care of them."

Gideon nodded. Elijah shook him. "I mean it."

"Elijah," Reverend Swayne said, stepping closer.

"No sir," Elijah said, stepping back. "You let me talk. You need to hear this, and there may never be another chance to tell you. I love your daughter. I would go now and take her away and make sure she is safe, but my mama is here. My friends are here. Sarah is here. I can't leave them any more than you can leave them but I want you to know—I love Desi; I've loved her so long now I can't remember a time when I didn't know I'd spend my life with her.

"Now this happens. I lived my entire life one field away from that family, those white devils with their lying preacher and their evil ways, and I survived. I lived, and you lived, and we stood here, Gideon, together. We'll stand together tonight, but I'm telling you now, so you'll know. When it's over—when I'm sure that things have settled into whatever comes next, and the danger has passed, I'll be going too. Wherever she goes, I'll follow. Wherever she lives, that is where my life will begin, and end.

"So you," he turned to young Gideon, who stood pale and trembling under the sudden verbal assault, "will get them out of here safe. I want you to tell her for me, because if I tell her, she won't go—or I will—and it will end badly. Tell her I love her, and that I'll come for her. Tell her I'll watch out for your pa, and that we'll be together, just like I told her. Together forever. Now get out of here and don't stop. Don't look back. Don't wonder what happened, or think about stopping."

The boy turned then, and dashed from the church. He didn't look back, not at his father, the building, the clearing, or at anything. His eyes ran with tears and his mind raged. He didn't want to escape. He didn't want to run into the swamp, he wanted to run into the fields and scream his defiance to the Popes, daring them to come and take him. He wanted to fight, and feel the pain, wanted to be pounded until he was senseless and the guilt building inside him faded to a dull, throbbing ache, or was wiped away completely.

He crashed through the trees. Others watched over him, following him, closing in behind and keeping track of his progress. He nearly ran headlong into his mother, who stood very still in the center of the trail, waiting. At the last possible moment, she spoke his name.

"Gideon."

He saw her, and he saw his sister, and though he tried to run by them, to crash into the trees and into oblivion and let the swamp swallow him whole, his strength failed him. She spoke his name, and it was as if the breath had been slammed from his lungs, or he'd run into a tree. He stumbled, and he fell to his knees at her feet. She stood looking down at him for a moment, then stepped forward and pulled him close against her.

Desdemona stared back over his shoulder toward the church. Her eyes misted, and though her features betrayed none of her pain, it screamed for release. She closed her eyes and she sent her breath into the trees, sent it to the church and to the man she loved, the man who'd stolen her heart. The man whose God she'd come to trust, only to be betrayed in the end. So quickly. Like dry leaves in a fire, crumbled to dust in the space of an instant as if it had never been.

"Come," she said. She turned, and after a moment Gideon struggled to his feet. He saw that his sister had a heavy bag over her shoulder and another at her feet. She held it out to him without a word, her eyes warring between fear, anger, and something much deeper. She looked so much like his mother in that instant that he had to shake his head and close his eyes to clear the image.

The three of them diverged from the trail together. The swamp was about a mile distant, but that was only the trailing edge. It stretched up into Virginia and sidelong, skirting fields and other towns, farms and plantations. There were inlets and pools, bogs and marshes, places no man had ever walked and lived to talk about, and it was all that awaited them.

The news would spread further than Old Mill. When they didn't find Gideon in the camp, the sheriff would be forced to send out word to the surrounding farms. The boy's likeness would be displayed in general stores, on city streets, in taverns. They'd know him by name and they'd be looking for him, fair game. A nigger they could beat and not get into any trouble for it. Someone to take out the war, and the changing world they all shared on. He was a marked man, and even the swamp might not take him far enough away to outrun it—but he had to try.

After an hour, he stopped.

"Wait," he said.

His mother turned in anger and was about to speak; then she saw his eyes. His sister turned as well, staring at him. All emotion had gone from her features. Only her eyes smoldered.

It was his sister he addressed.

"Elijah told me...he said..."

"I know," she replied, biting the anger from her lips. She didn't want to be angry with her brother but she teetered on a madness that could send her over the edge of a very thin fence, and it could throw her in either direction. "I know, Gideon. He loves me. I love him too."

"He'll come," Gideon said simply. "When it's over—when it's safe—he'll come."

She turned her head bitterly, and he was across the small clearing in a second, gripping her tightly by the shoulder.

"He'll come. He's a good man, and he loves you. If he doesn't come, I'll get you back to him. I promise."

"You'd better not let your tongue get you in any more trouble," she said. She shouldered her bag. "You've done enough."

'Desi!' her mother almost hissed the word, and the girl reeled as if slapped. She didn't turn to her mother, though. She kept walking. After a moment, Gideon and his mother followed.

By the time the afternoon shadows grew long, they'd reached the outskirts of The Great Dismal Swamp and, without hesitation, crossed that dark border and disappeared from the world.

As shadows fell over the tiny clearing, the church filled steadily. They streamed in from all directions, the old, the young, some who worshipped with Gideon every week, and some he'd never seen except in the fields, or at a meal. Others had come from surrounding farms, or deeper in the swamp, men and women who hadn't worked the fields in years, but felt the need to be a part of what was happening on this one night.

They knew Desdemona. She had birthed their children, healed their sickness and spoken over their dead. When they were frightened, or needed comfort, it was she who cast the bones and lit the candles, or brought sweet smelling incense and sang the old songs. They had come to respect Reverend Swayne. Maybe they even loved him, but it wasn't for him that they came. The younger Gideon was Desdemona's son. He didn't share her gifts, or her site, but he shared her blood, and they owed her—many of them their lives. They might not be able to keep the Pope's away from the church, or the clearing, but they could make it as difficult as possible to get away with murder.

They tasted it on the wind. Lookouts had watched the Pope House for hours. Lights blazed in all the windows, and a number of men had been seen coming and going. Loud voices had been heard more than once, and just before sunset, Bart Pope had staggered out to the edge of the cotton field. He wavered, either still hurt and dazed, or falling down drunk, and he stared straight across the field toward the church. He screamed at them, but they were too far away to hear. Isaiah came and dragged him back to the house, but not before it became clear that, if he had to come by himself, Bart Pope would be visiting the camp that night and he'd be out for blood.

The church was lit with hundreds of candles. Some were held by those seated in the pews. Some lined the windows, still more sat on the small altar Gideon had created, working the planks by hand and smoothing them with a plane made from broken straight razor. It was the one thing in the ramshackle building that had been crafted with great care. It held the holy items Gideon had carried with him all the miles from Random Illinois. It held his Bible. With the candle flames dancing around the room, the open pages of that worn volume grew to huge shadows on the walls. Gideon stood behind the altar, his head bowed in prayer, waiting until the church was full.

He hadn't spoken since his family fled into the swamp. Even Elijah, and then Sarah, who had shown up to join them, hadn't been able to bring him around. He'd thumbed through the old Bible, running his fingers slowly across verses here and there, reading inscriptions from the ladies of his old congregation, or appearing to read them. His mind was a million miles away, following three sets of footsteps to a place he might never be able to follow.

The world had shifted so suddenly it took his breath, and his concentration, and he stood there as the pews filled and the air in the room grew heavy and close. A low murmur swept through those gathered, but he didn't try and decipher the words. There were too many, spoken too softly, and none of them could help. Nothing could help.

He sent his mind back across the years, through the trees and down to the edge of the slick green water. He dredged up memories of the candles and incense, the smoke and the power he'd sensed there, just beyond that dancing smoke. It seemed like a dream to him. Though he remembered it vividly, the flash of Desdemona's hands, the chanting song and the bones tumbling through the air in slow-motion arcs to embed themselves in the dirt. He glanced up and scanned the faces before him.

He stood very straight, suddenly alert. There was a hole in his memory that he had to fill, a thing he had to know that he'd never asked. He couldn't believe, thinking back on it, that it had never occurred to him before, but he latched onto it now. He couldn't do anything more to help his son, or his daughter, and his wife was gone from him, but there was something he could distract himself with if he could only find the right person.

He saw her in the second row. She was tucked in beside Elijah, whose broad shoulders towered over her. Gideon Swayne stumbled into his congregation, walking down the aisle and stopping beside the two. All eyes in the room followed him. The voices stilled. Gideon dropped to one knee, reached out over Elijah's lap, and took Sarah's hand in his own. She was nervous, but she didn't pull back. She'd known Gideon most of her life, and she trusted him.

"Long ago," he said, finding his lips and tongue dry and his voice cracked. It had been too long since he'd had a drink, or licked his lips. He fought to be understood. "A very long time ago, when I first came here—before this church was built, I went with her—with Desdemona—to the swamp. We went a long way, down the water. She drew a circle, and sang, and she cast a handful of old bones. She told me it was for you—that your mother had asked her, and that she had to do what she could."

He stopped, frustrated. He wanted to ask her what the bones had revealed. He wanted to know what Desdemona had told the girl's mother, and to know if it had been true. He needed to know, very suddenly, that the strength he knew so well, the power that glowed behind his wife's eyes, was real, and strong.

Sarah watched him carefully, but he knew she would not speak. He didn't know why she was silent, or what had happened to make it so, but he knew God was testing him with this. It wasn't his faith in his religion that was on the line, but his faith in his wife—in the swamp—in the people he'd come to love and trust. He patted Sarah's hand and rose slowly, turning back toward the altar.

He had gone only a couple of slow steps when a soft voice cut through the deep silence. He wasn't sure he'd heard anything at all, and nearly passed it off as a whispered comment from the rear of the room.

He turned. Sarah stood, gazing at him with wide, soulful eyes. She had a hand on Elijah's shoulder for strength, and the young man stared at her, his mouth open wide.

"What..."

Before Gideon could continue, Sarah spoke again. This time he heard her. They all heard her.

"She said I had a gift. She said..." the girl hesitated, choosing the sounds and forming them carefully into words. "She said I'd know when it was time to talk."

"Now?" Gideon asked. "Why...why now, child?"

"They're coming." She said simply. Her eyes widened as if speaking the words made the prediction true for her as well.

Gideon didn't have to ask who she meant. He stood for a long time, just watching Sarah's pretty face. She returned his gaze, but she trembled, and he saw she was terrified. He wondered if she'd always been able to speak, and only waited for the time to be right—for something truly important to say. That it was this—that it was a prophecy of this magnitude, was another tragedy piled onto a day of sorrow. He nodded at her and turned. He shook his head as if waking from a long dream.

When he turned, he swept them with bright eyes. The lethargy of only a few moments past was forgotten. They were here to help him. They were here to stand at his side against overwhelming odds. Many of them must have been terrified, he knew, but they were here. Energy filled the air, and he drew on it. He stepped to his altar and stood there, lit brightly by the candle flames.

"All of you know why we're here," he said. His voice carried easily. He felt strength and energy pour into him in a way he had only felt once before. He worried, just for a moment, that Desdemona had come back—that she'd been unable to turn away from him, and the people she loved—that she'd come back to fight. He brushed the worry aside. She was gone, his son was gone, his daughter was gone, but he remained. "There are limits to how far a man can be pushed. I know the Good Book teaches us humility. I know it teaches us to turn the other cheek. It also teaches us there is strength in our faith. It also teaches us that we must fight back against oppression. I can't condone what my son did today, but I can understand it. I can't change what happened in that field, and I would lay down my own life to have it taken back.

"This is a dark night. It is going to get darker. They will come—Sarah tells us they are already coming."

He stared out the still open door of the church directly ahead of him, down the aisle. More faces gazed in at him from the clearing beyond, and he thought he detected eyes beyond those, as well. There was no way to know how many they were, but the word that came to him was a name.

"Legion," he said softly. "They are Legion. Yeah, though I walk through the valley of the shadow of death, I will fear no evil.

"Let us pray."

Desdemona wasn't sure when her daughter disappeared from the trail behind her. She watched her son. His steps were clumsy and plodding. He stumbled, and his strength was fading. She knew the state of his mind, and her blood boiled at the way his spirit had been taken, and bent, and broken. She had to take care of him. She didn't know the exact moment that her daughter disappeared...but she'd expected it.

She didn't look back. She could do only so much. Her daughter was strong willed and had a touch of the same sight and abilities that she herself had been gifted, or cursed with. There was no controlling the girl, but she might save her boy. She knew that she might never see her husband again, but she had her son, and he was a part of the man she loved that she could protect. The rest had been lost to her the moment he'd decided to live near the swamp—it had just taken longer than she expected.

The boy barely knew he was alive. She saw expressions flit across his face, saw him shift emotions so rapidly his features rippled. She had to find a way to bring the light back to his eyes, those eyes so like his father's.

Desi watched her mother, and her brother, fading into the shadows. She hung back, not hurrying into the shadows, or turning from the path—just stopping until they passed on and left her. When she could no longer see or hear them moving off ahead of her, she turned and ran swiftly and silently back toward her home, the man she loved, and toward her father's church.

EIGHT

When they finally came, they came fast. Several men on horseback led the way. They carried farm tools—scythes, rakes, shovels, and they swung them like clubs, crashing through the trees and running down anyone and anything that got in their way. Isaiah Pope was there, seated high on the grandson of the horse he'd been on the day he nearly ran Gideon down in the cotton field. His eyes were black pits.

Bart was on foot. No one followed him too closely, or let him stagger too far in their direction, because he screamed like a man possessed and swung an axe back and forth in a massive figure eight motion. Those in his path moved out of the way easily but he was relentless, and he knew where he was going. They all knew. He cut a swath through the brush, notching trees and remaining upright by some demonic act of will.

Something inside him had snapped. He was drunk, but it didn't account for the manic, crazed way he stumbled forward, or for the screams. Isaiah remained silent, but he spurred his mount ahead with purpose. He didn't know if he'd ever have his brother back—at least the brother he knew. He didn't know the screaming madman following in his wake, and he didn't even trust that if he got too close, Bart wouldn't cut him down as readily as anyone, or anything else.

He knew what he had to do. He saw the preacher's face, the way he'd crawled off and into the cotton that long ago day. He knew he should have followed through. He should have done something that day, or soon after. He should have forced the nigger-loving preacher out of his woods and let things stay the way they'd always been.

Things had changed. The new sheriff didn't have the nerve to run things the way they should be run, and even Isaiah's wife, Jenny, had started to act as though there might not be any difference between the colored cotton pickers and her own people. It wasn't the same world as it had been when he'd first met Reverend Gideon Swayne, and now he believed that if he'd acted sooner, things might have been different. It still would have changed, but maybe not so soon. Maybe not until Isaiah himself was older and out of the picture. Maybe he and Bart would be sitting and swigging beer on the porch instead of out here taking care of a problem that never should have happened.

Ahead the clearing with the church flickered and glowed. It was so bright it looked as though it might be on fire, but he knew it wasn't. He knew they were waiting there, all of them. He sensed their presence and felt them flitting from tree to tree just out of site.

He wasn't alone. His brothers were with him, Bart and Bart's eldest son, Enoch. The boy was only fourteen, but he was tall for his age, and very serious. Isaiah hadn't wanted the boy with them, but Bart had dragged him bodily from the house and pushed him into the field. There were others.

Men and boys from town had begun arriving as soon as word spread about the beating. The nigger boy thought he was slick, but a lot of folks had seen him on his walk to and from Old Mill. No one liked that they came to town, and even less that they felt they could come in alone, during the day, when the men were out working the fields and mostly women and young children were left behind. It was wrong, and it was cowardly, and it made Isaiah's blood boil.

Bob and Fred Winslow were with them, the Fearing boys from across town, and half a dozen of the Bucks. There were a couple of field hands down from the Smoky Mountains for the picking season, hill people without much more social status than the nigger workers—but they were white, and they were big. The closer he came to the brightly burning candles and the church, the more he was glad to have them along.

Voices cried out now. They'd been spotted, and word was spreading like a wildfire back into the trees. He heard them crashing ahead of him and he spurred his horse forward. On his left he caught sight of an old man, limping slightly and falling behind those running to the church. Just at that moment he heard Bart. The boy screamed and it sounded like a wild animal, or a demon. Isaiah joined his voice to that sound and goaded his mount to higher speed.

The old nigger swerved once, and then stumbled, and in that instant, Isaiah was on him. He swung the scythe he carried in a quick arc without thinking. It caught the man in the center of the back. He felt the blade bite, and the man went down with a horrible scream. Isaiah yanked the blade free and rode on, bellowing with rage. His horse shied at the scent of blood, and he nearly went down, but somehow he clung to the animal, clenching his knees and ducking low over the mane. He shot through the last few yards into the clearing and pulled up hard.

"Gideon Swayne," he cried.

Faces swam before his eyes. He saw men and women staring out from the doorway of the church. He saw the pews stretching up toward the altar in the front of the building. The doors were open wide, and he saw Gideon Swayne, as well. The man stood, ignoring everything around him. His head was bowed. His hands were clasped before him, and Isaiah knew that if he were close enough he'd hear the man praying. Praying!

Someone to his left screamed, and he heard a wet smack, but he didn't turn. Bart stepped into the clearing and squared off, as if he might charge the wall of the church and crash straight through to the other side. Isaiah watched his brother for a moment, mesmerized. Bart held the axe easily in one hand. He'd slipped somewhere beyond his pain, and beyond the whiskey he'd been guzzling only a short time before into some other place. The axe blade dripped blood, but it was black in the candlelight, and Bart was half cloaked in shadow.

Isaiah glanced down at the scythe he still gripped so tightly the knuckles on his left hand were white. The blade was black. He couldn't see if it dripped, but he knew that somewhere behind him a man lay in the dirt, wounded and maybe dead, a hole the size and shape of that blade in his back.

In the church, Reverend Swayne raised his head and stared

straight out the doorway at Isaiah. He opened his mouth, and he spoke a single word. It didn't carry, but the men and women gathered before Gideon echoed it, sending it rumbling out like a wave of sound, gaining power and volume as it came.

"Amen."

It was too much for Bart. He broke and ran at the doorway. The axe swung up in a glittering arc, and suddenly something inside Isaiah snapped. Something in his stomach lurched, nearly unseating him, but he drove his knees into the horse's flanks. It screamed in sudden pain, and reared, then plunged ahead. Isaiah flung the scythe away and clutched the reins, rushing toward his brother, even as the wetly glittering blade of the axe whipped forward into the wall of the church. It bit deep, splitting one of the old planks and splintering the flame behind.

Inside, a woman screamed, and Isaiah saw the congregation rushing away from the door, away from the wall, where Bart drew back and swung again. Isaiah was nearly on his brother when the blade whizzed forward and broke through the wall. Wood rained on those too slow to move away from the wall.

Isaiah dropped to the ground and grabbed Bart by the shoulder.

"Bart," he cried out, trying to get a grip with his other hand as well. "Bart, stop. It's enough. Come away."

Bart turned, or at least, the man he held by the shoulder turned. There was no intelligence in the gaze, only rage. The axe rose again, and Isaiah shied away, stepping back. "Bart..."

The axe flashed forward again and bit into the frame of the door. Reverend Swayne was walking very slowly down the aisle toward them. His face was calm—serene, even—and his steps were measured. All around him his people squirmed and fought to get clear of the door and the wall Bart had attacked. Others swept up behind Isaiah and he turned, uncertain who to call out to, or what to say. The Fearings had shovels and they stepped through the door, shoulder to shoulder. There were three of them, dark haired and stout. Their eyes glittered, and they paid no attention to the madman on their right, swinging wildly at the frame of the church. It shook with each blow, but showed no signs of falling.

There were too many people inside for them to stay out of range. They split and Gideon strode through them like Moses. The Fearings didn't back down, they spread out, one on either side of the door, and the biggest, Ed Fearing, standing his ground in the center aisle. Isaiah backed away as more and more of his friends and neighbors poured from the woods and into the clearing. Some joined Bart, attacking the walls so that the frame of the building shook. Others tried to push their way in behind the Fearings, and still others moved around to the sides, guarding the windows and watching for anyone who might try to slip away.

"Give us the boy," Isaiah cried suddenly. "Reverend, give us that boy, or I won't be able to hold them."

There was no way he could hold them, with or without the boy, but Isaiah believed he might call them off—that he might prevent the thing happening before him if he could just focus them on the boy. The reason they'd come. None of them remembered now. None of them cared. He knew them all, but in that moment he didn't recognize anyone. No one, that is, but Reverend Gideon Swayne, who still walked slowly toward the door as if he feared nothing from the shovels and the axes, as if the power of his God were really running through his veins and would sustain him.

"Yeah," Gideon called out, "though I walk through the valley of the shadow of death."

Bart let out a scream. He swung the axe with the full strength of his broad shoulders. He bent his back into the blow and whipped the blade forward. The entire building shivered as the sharp steel bit deep.

"I will fear no evil," Gideon cried, holding his hands out and up, like some old world prophet.

Isaiah stared Gideon, then past him. He opened his mouth, and then closed it, unable to force enough breath from his lungs to form words. Unable to breathe at all as he backed away. He raised his hand, and he pointed into the church, but no one understood. They saw him back away, and they saw Gideon step into the doorway, his eyes open very wide, brows furrowed like some angry, ancient God. The Fearings had stepped aside as he approached, but they moved in behind him. All eyes followed his steps. All eyes but Isaiah's.

He backed another step, gulped air, and finally managed to scream.

"Fire!"

The candle light flickered, just as it had, but brighter. Gideon turned back, startled, but as he did so Ed Fearing stepped forward and shoved him. Gideon spun out the door, arms flailing. He tried to catch himself on the frame of the door, and failed.

Isaiah moved forward to catch him. The Fearings followed the preacher out the door, and seeing Isaiah reach for Gideon, surged forward to help. They believed Isaiah was going to claim the man for himself, and they wanted to be part of it.

"God damn it," Isaiah screamed at them. He stepped aside and let Gideon stagger back and fall, preventing the others from reaching him. "Turn around! The church is on fire!"

As if cued by his words, screams broke out from inside the building. The candles that had lined the window sills and ledges had tipped and fallen. Bart's repeated blows shook the structure and more candles fell. Those inside tried to stop it. They picked the burning sticks of wax up, flinging them at the windows and doors. Someone broke out the glass on the right side of the building, but grinning faces greeted them. Shovels and rakes slammed into the window frames, beating those inside back into the interior. The hot wax from the candles splashed those outside and enraged them.

Isaiah saw a woman stagger into the aisle. Her hair was on fire and it framed her face in orange flame. She screamed and stumbled toward the door, catching herself once on a pew. Someone grabbed her from behind, and pushed her down, as if they might roll her over or put out the flame, but where she fell, wax had pooled and burned, and she dropped into the blaze.

Screams echoed from the rickety rafters and the fire raged suddenly out of control. Someone inside broke and ran, diving through the window. His shirt was on fire, and the men outside cried out and fell back. More followed, coming out like rats off a ship, but too many were trapped. Too many burned, and Isaiah could only stand and watch.

Gideon regained his feet. He stared into the door, hesitated for only a moment, and then ran and dove back through. He grabbed the woman and lifted her, his arms searing and his shirt bursting into flame. He lifted her and shoved her toward the door, then he turned, and he disappeared into smoke and fire. Isaiah stood watching, and in that moment, Bart gave a hideous final scream. He swung the axe with all the maddened, crazed strength of his broken mind and it severed the corner support of the building. The roof caved in, dropping inward in a glowing, blazing avalanche of death.

Isaiah turned then. He saw his horse, shying away and nosing its way out of the clearing, and he ran to it. Without thought, without looking back, he swung up onto the animal's back. Amid screams and the roar of flames, he dug his knees into the horse's side, leaned close over its neck, and closed his eyes as it tore off through the trees, praying it wouldn't brush him off on a solid trunk.

Behind him he heard another roar join that of the flames. His brother was laughing, screaming his challenge to the night and laughing in the face of fire and death. The flames and smoke rose to blot out the sky.

Desi moved as quickly and quietly as a shadow through the swamp. She had learned from her mother, and she had learned from the trees, and the bushes, the slimy water, and the smooth, bleached white bones she carried at her waist. Her father had taught her as well; his strength and inner peace was the anchor of her world, but from a very young age she'd known there was something more. Her mother confirmed it, and though they kept it as quiet as they could around her father, it wasn't long before some of the others began coming to her when they might have gone to her mother. She helped when she could, and she kept her visions to herself—except around Elijah.

When her father ordered her from the church, she'd felt as if something vital had been removed from her heart. When she walked away, she didn't look back, because she felt his eyes— not her father's but Elijah's, burning into her back. A thin, golden thread bound the two of them at all times—something she sensed, and sometimes could even see, when they were alone, and there was no light. As she moved away, it stretched, growing thinner and thinner. When she stopped and turned back, it was just at the point she felt it would snap. The thought of that terrified her—and she knew that if it snapped for her, the pain would be as great for Elijah. She might have sacrificed herself to that pain to help her brother, but she couldn't sacrifice the man she loved. She knew her father would understand, and she knew her mother had already done so.

She passed from the damp ground near the marsh that skirted the edges of the swamp and onto the trail back through the trees. There was a scent in the air that she didn't understand, at first. Then, as the smoke curled through the branches of the trees and teased over her skin, she knew. She stopped, stood very still, and tasted the air.

Blood, and smoke. Pain and death. Then her eyes flew open and she screamed. She ran through the trees, feeling branches whip and slash her cheeks and arms, but she ignored it. She banged off the trunk of a tree, staggered, and continued, oblivious. The image of his eyes, wide and filled with pain and terror filled her mind, and she was unable to shake it. She ran, and she screamed his name, and she forgot her lessons. She forgot her caution. In the distance she saw the glow of the burning church and the rising cloud of smoke. They grabbed her a quarter of a mile from the church.

Jared and Zachariah Buck had hung back when the others assaulted the church. There wasn't any good way to join in without another axe, and when the screams started and Bart Pope let loose with a laugh that reminded them both of one of the demons old Reverend Cumby preached about on Sundays, they hung back. That laugh was too loud, and it didn't sound right. In fact, it didn't sound like Bart was ever going to be anything approaching "right" again. Men and women and children were dying in that church, and the boys figured it was time to become scarce, before someone managed to reach town for help.

Enoch Pope was with them. He was wide-eyed and half crazy himself with fear. His father and his uncle were at the church, but there was no way the boy was going near there. His eyes were too wide, and his lips kept parting, then closing, as if he had something to say, or scream, and couldn't scrape it off his tongue.

They retreated, and in doing so, they stood directly in Desi's path as she ran, screaming through the night, toward the church. She was on them before she realized it, and Jared grabbed her in a quick bear hug, stopping her flight. He was a big man, strong and quick, and he lifted her off the ground easily, though she thrashed and continued to scream.

"Well," he said, "what we got here, Zach?"

"Let me go," she screamed. "Let me go. Oh my god, he's burning let me go!"

"Not so fast, missy," Zach said. He walked over and inspected her as she struggled. "She's right pretty, Jared," he said. "It'd be a shame if we went back home without doing anything about this trouble out here, don't you think? How 'bout you, Enoch?"

He turned to the boy. "You think she's pretty enough?"

Enoch stared at Jared. He didn't speak, and he was obviously ready to bolt.

"I asked you a question boy," Zach said, taking a step closer. "You better root yourself there like a tree and listen to me, because if you run, I'm going to have to consider you might be thinking about talking to the wrong people, and I can't let you do that."

"We should go," Enoch choked out. "They'll be in to town, and they'll bring Sheriff Thomas. Just let her go."

He tried to put force behind his words. He tried to sound as if he was anything but a scared fourteen-year-old boy dragged off into the middle of the night against his will. He saw the terror in the girl's eyes, and somehow he knew that, even held as she was, she wasn't frightened for herself. Someone she knew was in that fire, someone she wanted to find, or to help.

"Let her go," he repeated.

Zach turned to Jared and shook his head. He leaned in close, grabbed Desi's hair and turned her so he could study her face. "Not just yet," he said, releasing her and turning. "We're going to spend some time getting to know her. Ain't no reason to be in a hurry I can see."

"Please," she said. Her voice broke, and squirmed wildly, but Jared held her off the ground and no matter how hard she tried to kick him, or bite him, he kept just out of reach.

"See," Jared leered, leaning down so his grizzled chin rested on her shoulder. "She's beggin' for it. Can't disappoint a lady."

The two brothers laughed, and Enoch backed a step toward the trees.

"You stand still, boy," Zach called out. "You're part of this, and don't pretend like you ain't. You think because you ran away after your uncle set that church on fire it makes you innocent? You're stayin', and you're doin' her too, or I'll take an axe handle to the back of your head and leave you out here so we can blame the whole thing on one of the niggers, out for revenge.

While his brother talked, Jared tore at Desi's dress. There was one wild moment when he was concentrating on tearing open the buttons and she nearly broke free. She lunged, spun, and ducked her head. Jared's hand slipped, but an instant later, Zach had her by one arm, and the two pulled her dress in opposite directions. The fabric ripped and they tossed it away, pressing her to the ground.

"Someone will hear," Enoch said. He was near tears, but he didn't run. He knew the Bucks, and he knew they'd do what they said without thinking about it. His father would find him, broken and bleeding in the woods, and he'd kill every man woman and child still alive in the woods. It would never occur to him to question a white man's word over that of a black cotton picker. He might not even care if he knew the truth.

"Ain't no one going to hear a thing," Jared growled, turning. His face was twisted in an expression born of warring emotions. Enoch had never seen anything quite like it, and his legs, already weak, turned to rubber.

"Get over here, boy," Zach said. He held the girl still, and Jared turned to her, grinding his knee in between her thrashing legs. He struggled with the waistband of his pants, and lowered himself onto Desi.

Enoch watched in horrified fascination as the girl fought and spat and cursed. Nothing she did helped. He wanted to scream. He wanted to rush over and drag Jared off of her, but instead he stood and stared.

"I said get over here," Jared repeated. Enoch took a step forward, hesitated, and then took another. "Get her other arm, boy. Hold her. You'll go after me."

Enoch stopped. His moth went dry, and he shook like a leaf in a heavy breeze. Then he was moving again. He stepped in close, avoided the girl's eyes, and grabbed her arm. He held her stiffly, afraid of hurting her and at the same time afraid of what the Bucks might do if he let her get away. His mind turned in on itself then, into darkness and heat. Where he held Desi's wrist, his flesh burned. He was mesmerized, and the voices of the Bucks blurred to incomprehensible grunts and moans.

At some point, Zach grabbed the girl's arm from him and pushed him down toward the girl's limp form. What came next he remembered later in fits and snatches of nightmares, and moments of sudden, shamed heat. Desi's eyes were closed, but just before he finished and rolled away, they opened, and he read the emotion, the hatred, and the questions that would sear themselves into him like a hot brand in those few seconds.

And he ran, crashing through the trees, fumbling with his pants. He slammed face first into a tree and reeled away, catching himself on a low-slung branch and running on. He had no idea which way he was running until he hit the edge of the cotton field. The sun was high, and he saw the smoke from the fire rising like an angry spirit over the trees. He ran until he hit porch of the family home, and fell at the door, sobbing.

Back in the trees, hurt and bleeding, Desi rose from the dirt and tied the remnant of her clothing over her body. Without a glance back the way she'd come, or in the direction her attackers had fled, she stumbled on toward the church—and her father— and Elijah.

She was too late. Some of the men who'd followed Bart ran for help. Others tried to find water, or to drag the trapped workers from the roaring flames, but they were all too late. Screams ripped through the night air, echoed off the trees, and died in the heavy, damp air of the swamp. There were no survivors. They dragged Desi away from the burning ruins of the building, but she broke free and escaped into the swamp.

The ruin of the church they left to rot. It clung to its roots. Gideon Swayne had built it with care, and the men and women who helped him, the souls he taught and protected, were craftsmen. They tried to rebuild it, but it was never more than a shadow of the building it had been, and God had left for brighter climes.

The bones of the faithful littered the ground beneath. The blood of Gideon Swayne soaked into the swamp. No one who visited that place ever returned. Things were heard—others were seen—skulking in the shadows. They call it the Preacher's Marsh, and one day, they say...he'll take to the road again to spread the word.

Some things can't be explained without blood, and candles, mud and the wind. In the Preacher's Marsh, the ghosts sing the gospel and the future is held in a handful of dried, whitened bone.

THE NOT QUITE RITGHT REVEREND CLETUS J. DIGGS

&

THE CURRENTLY ACCEPTED HABITS OF NATURE

A Tale of Old Mill, North Carolina

ONE

Near the Great Dismal Swamp, everything grows. Bugs thrive. Plants barely hesitate between frost and full, pollen-bearing bloom. A warm winter week can produce things that should sleep until summer. It's in the earth. Birth, rebirth—death.

Whatever grows must decompose. That is truth. As the sun set in a splash of deep violet and dark purple above the tree line, Jasper Winslow was contemplating that truth.

Some things decompose faster than others. Some things return to the food chain a few rungs lower than where they began. Boot leather, Jasper noted, was a durn site more resilient than denim, and a whole hell of a lot tougher than hide. Hair and teeth stood the test of time better than eyeballs or tongues, and were a lot less tantalizing to the aforementioned food chain, though bone seemed to have made it into a lower rung, at the least.

"Christ," Jasper observed eloquently. When he spoke that thought it came out more like "Keee Reist," but the meaning was clear. He was wishing some power greater than he were available to sort things out.

Reaching into his breast pocket, Jasper drew forth a battered pack of Zig Zag rolling papers and his tobacco. It was time for some serious thinking, and Jasper didn't reckon he should do that on an empty lung. Empty head was one thing; lungs needed smoke to survive—so his ol' Pap'd said. Jasper's fingers trembled, but he managed to roll a passable smoke and lit it with a match from the Red Apple convenience store out on 17.

Jasper had only been hoping for a good day fishing. The catfish were fat and hungry, and so was Jasper. It had seemed the perfect way to spend the day, despite the fact he was supposed to be fixing the air conditioning unit down at the Weller place. Air would still be there when he was done, near as he figured, and they could condition it as well tomorrow as today, though he knew he'd get an earful when he finally showed up. Things always got done in their time.

Glancing down at the edge of the swamp, where two size twelve (if they were an inch) Redwing work boots poked out of the weeds and trailed back toward the water and what remained of a man, Jasper sighed. No fish today, he knew. No air conditionin' neither. Nothin' to do but to think, just for a while, then decide what to do. One thing he knew for sure, he couldn't let this guy rot so close to his favorite fishing hole. Folks would find it, for one thing, and for another, who knew what rotted flesh would do to the water? It was a swamp, sure, but did that mean you had to by-God pollute it?

The cigarette he'd rolled burned low, flame slipping up one side cantankerously, and Jasper hurriedly licked the side that was burning so the other could catch up. He didn't want to waste the tobacco—it wasn't cheap.

He leaned in closer, letting the ash drop from his smoke onto the soaked denim of the man's jeans. There wasn't much to see from where he stood. The water sucked at the waist of the man's pants, and everything above the chest was obscured by plants and mud. Jasper didn't really want to know what was going on with the parts beneath that murky surface, but it didn't seem right to leave the man in the swamp.

He reached down, ready to grip those boots and yank the body free of the mud, and he stopped. It wasn't that he was squeamish, but what he'd just noticed sat him back on his heels. Jasper wasn't the sharpest tool in the shed, so his ol' Pap had said, but he had a good eye for things. What caught that eye just then were branches. Where the man's head should have been, there was the oddest set of branches jutting from the water that Jasper had ever seen. They weren't really like branches at all, in fact, but he couldn't quite put his finger on *why* they weren't like branches. They had the requisite slime and moss, and they were muddy as hell.

"Probably roots," he muttered to himself, not believing it for a second. The itch in the back of his mind was stronger, and he'd lost all interest in grabbing those boots. Another thought had imbedded itself in his mind, and he backed away with a quick grunt. Jasper watched a lot of TV. Not that reality Tee Vee, or any of that science fictiony crap, but the real stuff. Cops, killers, guns and drama. He watched WWE Smackdown, when it was on, but Jasper had other thoughts on his mind just that moment. This was a by-God crime scene. Unless the man he was about to grab had tripped face first in the swamp, turned on his back, and drowned one hell of a clumsy death, someone had dropped him here. There might be prints. There might be evidence. Hell, he'd probably trampled over half of it already, and wouldn't it be a wonderful thing to add his fingerprints to the mix? Then, there were those roots, or branches, or whatever the hell they were to think about.

Jasper looked down at the silent, motionless form, half-covered in swamp mud and slime, and shook his head.

"Huh uh," he grunted. "Ain't draggin' ol' Jasper into this one. No way."

Turning, he headed back toward his truck, wanting to break into a run and controlling the urge in a sort of half-stumble, half speed-walk that would have looked to even the most casual observer like a man on the lam from the Devil. Jasper had that level of cool. Of course, there was no one within a mile to see him, so the performance went unnoticed. He reached his beat up Ford pickup, climbed in, and fired the engine, even as he reached for a cold Milwaukee's Best from the cooler on the passenger side floorboard. With practiced ease, he snapped the top and poured half the can down his throat.

Hell of a thing, he thought. *Man finds a dead guy in the swamp and has to sneak a beer just to keep from being caught with it on the highway.*

Briefly, Jasper thought about going to the police. Then, with uncharacteristic wisdom, he glanced at the half-empty beer can in his hand, and thought again. There was only one place to go with this. There was only one man who might understand, or, barring that, take the matter off Jasper's hands and let him get on with his fishing.

Jasper slugged the second half of his beer, tossed the can out the window, and slammed the truck into drive. It was only about five miles to Cletus Diggs' trailer, and there were back roads all the way. That was another plus. With a grin, Jasper reached out and grabbed a second beer.

Jasper turned down a winding, rutted lane that curled around a stand of trees just off 17. If you were on the highway, you'd never suspect the place existed. Cletus Diggs was a private man, most times, and he liked folks to respect that.

There was a mailbox standing beside that outer road. Beneath the battered tin box, a string of small signs unfolded, like the credit cards from a city man's wallet. The Reverend Cletus J. Diggs. Cletus J. Diggs—Attorney at Law. Diggs Investigations—nothing buried so deep we can't dig it out. There were more. Nearly a dozen, by Jasper's closest guess. Cletus wasn't a man to let any dollar lie outside the circle of his influence. Jasper ignored the signs and turned into the long drive that led back to Cletus' trailer. To Jasper, Cletus was just Cletus, no more, no less, and no amount of mail-order schooling or chest-puffing would change that. Jasper and Cletus had grown up together, fished the swamp and hunted the hills since both had been short enough to arm wrestle a snake.

Cletus' Bronco was parked out front, and the old air conditioning unit was pumping its heart out. This was another reason Jasper wasn't impressed with Cletus. For all his prancing about and big words, it was Jasper who'd had to fix the air conditioning, re-pipe the plumbing and wire up the satellite dish jutting out at an odd angle from the trailer's roof. Among the signs dangling from the mailbox of Mr. Cletus J. Diggs, there were none that required an ability to work with his hands.

Jasper pulled in beside the Bronco and killed his engine. He grabbed what remained of the twelve-pack and crawled out of the truck. There was a doorbell on the trailer, but Jasper ignored it. Half the time Cletus ignored it himself and this was too important to get into a tussle over. This was big-time, Jasper told himself—the real deal. The man that never had a thing happen in his life had run smack into a wall of *something* and it was going to be up to Cletus to sort it out. That is, assuming Cletus wanted that AC pump to keep blowin' cold air all summer and his toilet to flush.

The trailer was dimly lit, half the illumination coming from a shuttered window across from the door, and the rest from a lamp at the far end. That lamp sat on an old wooden desk, canted to one side and held up by three legs and a stack of old law books. Cletus kept the law books around "for show," and though Jasper and several clients had pointed out that the law books were from Kentucky, and over 100 years old, Cletus just smiled and nodded, being Cletus. "It's not like I'm going to read the damn things," he'd say. "They just help with the ambiance of the office."

Office. Jasper had nearly snorted beer through his nose. The corner of that trailer was about as much a law office as his pickup truck was a NASCAR champion. There were papers scattered over every available surface and sifting into cracks in search of new ones. There were cups and cans, pizza boxes and cigar packs lying about in such profusion you'd have thought the trailer was a recycling bin for old paper products.

In the middle of it all, on the far side of the desk, Cletus Jehosephat Diggs looked up from where he'd been hard at work on the *Weekly World News* crossword puzzle, startled.

"There's an amazing new product," Cletus said, regaining his composure. "No bigger than a baseball. They attach it to the outside of your house, and those folks with more manners than a swamp rat push the button in the center. It announces their arrival."

Jasper ignored Cletus and slapped a beer on top of the pile of papers on the near side of his friend's desk. "This here swamp rat-mannered, no-account, don't give a fuck in hell about your announcement-buttoned doohickey redneck is gonna put you in a world of hurt if you don't pop the top on that beer and listen up.

Cletus frowned, but the expression didn't hold. Grinning, he grabbed the offered beer and leaned back.

"I take it this isn't purely a social call," he said, grin widening. "It is not," Jasper agreed, taking a long slug from his beer. "I'm in a bit of a fix, Cletus. I thought you might offer some professional advice."

"Get another of those Edenton girls pregnant?" Cletus asked, arching one eyebrow and watching his friend with interest. "Hit someone's livestock with your truck? You haven't been tippin' cows without me, have you Jaz?"

Jasper grunted. "Stop it, Cletus," he said. "I'm serious this time. I ran into something today—somethin' I'm not sure what to do with."

Cletus sat up again. Jasper was never serious. Never. There had been a tornado sweeping through the county a few months back, houses with the roofs sucked clean off and garages spinning on their foundations, and Jasper's idea of a good way to spend that historic moment had been to drive into the storm and see if he could hit the center. Luckily for Jasper, and every building and living being within range of the pickup, the storm had lifted off and left him with nothing but a rain of golf-ball-sized hail for his trouble. The insurance had refused, at first, to pay, and it was only Cletus' timely intervention on his friend's behalf that had gotten the damage repaired, and the claims adjustor out of an early retirement, courtesy of an irate Jasper.

"Okay, Jaz," Cletus said soberly, sipping his beer to belie the fact. "Tell me what's on your mind."

It didn't take Jasper long to fill Cletus in on the facts, as he knew them. This was mostly due to the *fact* that Jasper didn't really know a damn thing, except that there was a dead man sticking boots first out of the swamp, and that someone (not Jasper) needed to fetch the police and drag that guy out. That, and that there was a clump of roots poking long, slender fingers out of the swamp that was going to visit his dreams for a long time to come. He didn't mention that part. Cletus would see for himself, or he wouldn't see a damn thing. Jasper could wait to see which it was. He could wait a long damn time.

"You didn't touch him?" Cletus asked, not really a question. Jasper had the familiar sense that the gears in Cletus' surprisingly agile mind had engaged fully. The crossword was pushed aside and forgotten, the spreading ring of condensation from Cletus' beer defacing a photograph of two enormously fat people in shorts they should never have owned, standing on the cracked surface of a tennis court.

"TOO-FAT TWINS WRECK TENNIS CAMP—OWNER SERVES THEM WITH COURT" was emblazoned in bold letters across the top of the now sodden page.

Cletus was paying no attention to Jasper, or the *Weekly World News*. If the fat twins weren't looking for a lawyer, Cletus wasn't interested, and to explain the legalities of damage suits to Jasper would take more years and beers than either of them had left. Cletus was thinking. There were a lot of angles you could take on a dead man in the swamp, particularly if you were a man of as many talents and professions as Cletus Diggs.

Finally, gulping the last of his beer and sending the can in a failed arc toward the can in the corner, already buried in a pile of prior bad shots, he pushed back his chair and stood.

"You did the right thing, Jasper. I'll handle it."

Jasper nodded, still frowning at the fat twins in the article. "What you going to do, Cletus?"

"Not sure yet," Cletus replied. "First I'm going to go have me a look. Then I'm going to call the police and meet them there, see what I can find out when they haul our late friend out of the mud."

Cletus reached over and took a faded Fedora off the top of a particle board world globe bar he kept beside his desk and stuck it on his head at a cocky angle. Reaching to the front breast pocket of his shirt, he pulled free a small stack of cards. He shuffled through until he'd found what he was looking for, then stuck the brightly lettered PRESS card in his hat.

"That guy looked more in need of a priest than a reporter," Jasper commented.

"I'm not a priest," Cletus stood up, indignant. "I follow no Pope. I am a Reverend in the Universal Life Church. We don't perform last rites."

Jasper snorted. "Universal Life my ass. You are a Reverend in the church of send in your ten dollars and a coupon."

"Amounts to the same, in the eyes of the Lord," Cletus

replied with a wink. "Folks don't really mind who saves them, as long as they can go on sinning until their cards are punched."

Jasper shook his head, grabbed what remained of his twelve-pack, and headed for the door. "You give me a call, you find out who that guy is. And mind you, don't let them trample over my fishing hole."

"God forbid that the unclean should tread upon the sacred shoreline of mud," Cletus intoned, clapping his hand to his heart. "You have my word as a lover of catfish."

Then Jasper was out the door, and Cletus was close behind, the notebook tucked under one arm. The sun was dropping toward 4:00. Time waited for no man, not even a dead one.

Before he was even out of his driveway, Cletus had his cell phone to his ear and the number one memory button pressed. 911 rang once, then hit a tone and went to a busy signal. Cletus cursed and punched the number again. This time, after a short hesitation, he heard a series of clicks, and he was connected. Two rings and the phone was answered by a slow, sweet woman's voice.

"Hey, Colleen," Cletus cut in, before she could finish her spiel. "It's Cletus. I've got a good one for you."

"Hey Cletus. You shoot another poacher?"

"Nope. Didn't shoot anyone," Cletus assured her. "Yet. I got wind of something you might want to have checked out. Seems there's a man in the swamp off 17 that forgot you need to breathe to socialize in these parts."

"You pulling my leg, Cletus?" Colleen's voice had shifted from friendly to irritated as if handled by a double-clutching dirt-track driver. Cletus grimaced.

"Not at all," he assured her. "Got it on good authority. It's out past the Chester place, about a mile along the bypass. You turn off behind the Coles' barn and curve in around the trees."

"The fishin' hole?" Colleen asked.

Cletus grinned. Jasper thought that place was a secret, but everyone who'd lived in the county in the past twenty years knew the place well enough."

"Exactly," he said.

"I'll get Bob out there," she said with a sigh. "You'd better be tellin' me the truth this time. Bob'll have my ass if there's nothing there."

"I think you might want to call the Troopers," Cletus replied. "I don't think he tripped in the swamp and drowned."

There was a moment's silence, then Colleen continued. "You know I can't do that, Cletus. Bob'd have my hide. If there's something out there, he'll have to find it first, or we'll have hell to pay."

Cletus chuckled. He'd known this, of course. "Just thought it was my civic duty to provide all the facts, and the benefit of my long years of experience" he said. "I'll head over there a little later—give ol' Bob a chance to dig in and set up his "crime scene."

More silence. "He really tries, you know Cletus? He does. You shouldn't take that attitude with him."

Cletus didn't answer, but his grin widened. Then, before he hung up, he added, "You have yourself a wonderful day, Colleen."

The line went dead, and Cletus pulled back onto the road and headed for the highway.

When Cletus pulled in next to Bob's cruiser, he saw the young officer standing by the shoreline where swamp met the green grass and shrubbery, glaring down into the water. The marshy ground seemed un-intimidated by Bob's stern gaze. Flies buzzed and whirled around his booted feet, occasionally lighting on his face or neck. Cletus watched Bob swat at them in irritation for a few minutes, then he killed the engine and stepped out of his truck.

Cletus didn't speak at first, moving up to stand beside the other man and a little further back from the water. Up closer, he could see that Bob's normally brightly spit-shined boots were caked with slime and mud. His sleeves were rolled up to the elbows, and sweat rolled down his forehead, streaked his cheeks and slid under the top of his collar, where a damp, dark stain was slowly spreading.

On the bank, just as Jasper had described, a man's legs

protruded from the water and dangled over the bank. There were scrapes where Bob had apparently been attempting to tug the body free, but it was still submerged from the waist up.

About two feet beyond that point, an odd root formation— or the branches of some long-fallen tree, stretched up out of the muck. That sight, for some reason, itched at Cletus' mind. He nearly stepped back, but at that moment, Bob spoke.

"Hell of a thing," Bob said. He turned, and Cletus saw that something was wrong before the officer's words confirmed it. Bob spoke as if dazed, his voice slipping in from some point very far away.

"Hell of a thing," he repeated. "Just stuck there, Cletus. Won't budge. Like a fishin' line in a bramble patch. Just stuck."

Cletus felt something prickle in the hairs on the back of his neck. He stared down at the water, lapping gently at the shore, then slid his gaze out to that strange root formation. Or was it branches? Something about it was wrong, but Cletus couldn't quite nail it down.

"Let's get him out of there, Bob," Cletus said at last. "The two of us ought to be able to yank him free."

Bob didn't move at first. Cletus could see that the man sensed the "something" that was wrong as clearly as he himself did, and Bob had been standing there longer. Staring. Wondering. He'd had some time, in fact, to worry those thoughts around in his head. Finally, the man nodded.

"Reckon we could at that," he said.

Cletus leaned down slowly, getting a tight, if reluctant grip on one of the booted ankles protruding from the water. Bob leaned in with an equal lack of enthusiasm and gripped the other. Both men drew in deep breaths, steadying themselves for what was to come, then Cletus said, "Now."

They heaved. At first, nothing happened. Cletus strained, and he felt his fingers slipping. He concentrated on *not* concentrating on the feel of dead, slimy flesh. Beside him, Bob was grunting with his own effort, and it seemed as if it might be for nothing. The dead guy wasn't budging.

Then, all at once, there was a loud sucking sound and Cletus felt the world tilt. The body came free, slid up the bank and sent the two men reeling backward, fighting for balance, and fighting even harder to not be under that wet, rotting mess when it came to rest on the bank. Cletus released his hold on the ankle and lurched to the side, barely managing to keep his balance.

Bob had better luck, to one way of thinking. He was standing off to the other side, an empty, sodden boot in his hand.

The mud must have slicked his skin, Cletus thought absently. It was about then he noticed that Bob wasn't standing still. Bob, in fact, was backing away from the shoreline, taking shaky, uneven steps that grew quicker and less graceful as each moment passed. His arm dropped to his side, and the wet boot brushed his thigh. Bob screamed. Not a yell, or a manly holler, but a scream, full-throated, up from the diaphragm (as Miss Dozier had taught them so many years before)—long, loud and enough to make Cletus' eyes bulge.

Bob tossed the shoe aside like it was a snake, and turned, shooting off toward his squad car like he was chased by a bullet.

"Bob?" Cletus asked, his voice far too soft to be heard. Bob wasn't listening, that was clear enough, in any case.

Then Cletus turned, and perfectly good beer, courtesy of his buddy Jasper, resurfaced as bile and threatened to shoot between his lips in a geyser.

"Jesus Jumping Jehosephat CHRIST" he managed, nearly releasing the bile after all his effort to stop it.

Bob didn't hear him. Bob wasn't there. He'd reached his squad car and was leaning against it heavily, pointedly ignoring the water, Cletus, and the thing that lay on the bank. The thing that had looked so much like a man. The thing that had been wearing flannel and work boots—dead, yes indeed, dead as a doornail—but a man, for all that. The thing that no way in hell was a man. Bob wasn't looking at it, thinking about it, or even believing it, at that moment, but Cletus was doing all those things, and his eyes watered with tears from the stench of it.

Everything was normal up to the shoulders. Big, yes, a strapping, big fellow with bulging, well-muscled arms and a blue tattoo of a cross on the left wrist. Two hands, ten fingers, as close as Cletus could tell, everything inventoried and in order, just as it should be. Except . . . well, except that no man Cletus had ever known had sported an eight point rack. Not even a nub of antler had he witnessed in all the years of his life, other than on four-footed creatures. What lay before him in the muck appeared to be a man, with the head of a white-tail buck, dripping slime, moss and muck into a puddle that dribbled back toward the swamp. Flies flitted around those impossible horns, and slimy weeds trailed down and away behind, back in the direction from which they'd tugged him—it—free.

There was no way to tell where man ended and deer began. The furry neck dipped beneath the sodden flannel collar. The eyes were glazed, milky and beginning to rot. Cletus' stomach churned, but he moved closer in morbid fascination. He had to know—had to see. He leaned in close, holding his breath against the stench, purposefully avoiding the rotting, rheumy eyes staring lifelessly toward the heavens, and gripped the collar of the shirt. He didn't bother with niceties. He gripped, and he yanked, feeling the buttons on the front of the shirt give way with a soft, wet sound. No loud tearing—it just came away revealing the thing's neck.

A ragged line, like a scar, but sloppy and rough, ran around the man's throat. The head attached just at the base of what would have been his neck, rolling down in back toward the muscles of his shoulders and dipping with a "v" of fur down the center of his chest. Everything above that was adult Bambi, abuzz with flies now that it had been dragged free of the water and stared lifelessly into the later afternoon sky.

Cletus turned slowly. Bob leaned against the side of his cruiser. The microphone of his radio dangled loosely from one hand, and his forehead was on his other arm. The man's hair was tangled and matted with sweat, and he wasn't moving. Cletus could hear the radio squawking, and for a moment he wondered if Bob had even called in.

Cletus didn't look back at the water, or the thing in the mud. He walked straight to Bob, watching his own boots carefully as he went, measuring each step by the number of heartbeats pounding in his head between strides. Bob didn't look up as he approached, and Cletus didn't expect it. He knew how Bob felt, and if he stopped for even a second, he'd be leaning on the squad car himself, listening to the radio talk to nobody and waiting for someone to come along and find them.

That wasn't an option. Cletus reached the squad car, and without hesitation, reached down and yanked the microphone from Bob's limp grip. The man didn't even flinch. From inside the squad car, he heard Colleen's distressed voice.

"Bob? Bob? Report please. What the HELL is going on out there Bob?"

Cletus keyed the mic and broke in.

"Colleen? This is Cletus."

Silence for a moment, then, "Cletus? What the hell are you doing on this frequency? Where's Bob?"

"He's right here, Colleen. We have a . . . situation."

More silence.

"Call the troopers, Colleen. Get their asses out here and now. I won't answer any questions, but you're welcome to talk to Bob some more. I don't think he's going to prove very communicative."

Cletus dropped the mic and turned toward his truck. He had a camera in the back, and he needed to get some work done before Colleen quit squawking and did as she'd been told. Bob never moved. Very low, Cletus heard the young officer muttering to himself. It sounded like prayer.

Chapter Two

The Cotton Gin was a low slung club set back from the road and tucked away on a side street just outside Old Mill. At lunchtime, they served up barbecued pork sandwiches and sweet potato fries. In the evening they served up whiskey and beer. Both crowds lined the parking lot with pickups, beat-up sedans, and motorcycles. Cletus pulled in and parked near the rear of the lot, scanning the other vehicles before climbing out for a stretch and a better look.

The regular crowd had arrived early. There were a few trucks Cletus didn't recognize mixed in, mostly with Virginia plates, and one old Mercedes coupe that almost certainly belonged to a salesman. Things in Old Mill didn't change much, and when they did, even the changes were predictable.

As Cletus crossed the gravel lot toward the entrance, he saw a familiar plume of gravel and dust approaching, and he grinned.

"Like a Yellowstone geyser," he said to no one in particular.

A moment later, he stepped aside as a baby blue 1966 Ford Thunderbird rolled into the lot. The paint gleamed, and the wide white walls caught the last of the late afternoon light nicely. The Ford pulled into a spot along the back, near where Cletus himself had parked, and a large, ruddy-faced man sporting a Stetson hat and a prodigious collection of well-digested bear beneath his belt stepped out.

"Evenin', Horton," Cletus called out. He stood and waited as the older man took a look around, then crossed to where Cletus stood.

"Evenin', Cletus. You're here kind of early tonight. Rough day?"

"Actually, Horton," Cletus replied with a grin, "I was hoping I'd run into you."

Actually, hope had nothing to do with it. Every Thursday without fail the local classic auto group met down south in Camden, and Horton was the treasurer. He hadn't missed one of those gatherings in the ten years they'd been going on, and Cletus knew it. He also knew that when the festivities broke up, Horton always came to the Gin.

When he wasn't tooling about the countryside in his T-bird, Horton Buck was the acting Coroner of Perquimans County. Cletus knew the body had gone to Horton first, he'd double checked with Colleen. Once she'd finished telling him how Bob had come in , spent the first half hour in the bathroom wasting what was left of his breakfast, and the rest of the day back out in the swamp with the Troopers, she told Cletus that Horton had been called to pronounce the body dead, and to haul it in to the morgue.

For once, Cletus felt sorry for Bob. He didn't know if he could have kept himself together after what he'd witnessed that morning with a bunch of stiff-necked State Troopers running him around the swamp and asking damned fool questions. Cletus didn't have to hear the questions to know what they were, and he didn't have to be a genius to know that those boys weren't going back to their own headquarters with anything approaching the truth, the whole truth, or anything in that neighborhood. They were going to find the simplest explanation and run with it. They were going to keep it as far from the press as they could, as well as the fine citizens of Old Mill, until they had some idea what they had on their hands.

Horton skirted the bar and headed for the booths in the back. The table furthest from the bar had a small sign on it that read "Reserved." Horton grabbed the sign, placed it in the back of the booth, and spun it around. It now read "Occupied," and he grinned up at Cletus, who slid in across from him with a chuckle and a shake of his head.

"Even the Coroner's Office has its perks," Horton said. "What's on your mind, Cletus?"

"I think you know the answer to that, Hort," Cletus said.

Horton looked at his clasped hands, his already flushed face reddening. A waitress approached them and sat a large pitcher of beer and two glasses between them, then disappeared back into the noise and smoke. They might as well have been sitting behind a wall.

"I can't talk about that Cletus," Horton said. "You know that. There's lines you don't cross."

"That isn't going to cut it, Hort." Cletus leaned closer for emphasis. "You weren't out there this morning. I was. What I saw...I can't explain it. Hell, I doubt if you can explain it, but I know you know more about it than I do. I need to know what's going on."

"You working this for someone?" Horton asked.

Cletus shook his head. "I told Jasper I'd look into it. I called Bob, and we both went out there. We pulled that...body...out of the swamp. I've never seen anything like it, and I hope I never do again, but damn it Horton, I want to know what the hell it was. I mean, at first it looked like someone had just sewed a head onto a dead body, but just before I left, I got a closer look. I'm no medic, but I've seen cuts, and stitches. Those were healing."

Horton took a long drag on his beer and sat back. He blinked, swallowed, and emptied the glass in the second gulp. He glanced around the bar as if there might be spies lurking in the shadows. Cletus almost laughed, but managed somehow to hold it in. No one in the county, and least of all in The Cotton Gin gave a hoot in Hell what Horton said or thought, and they sure weren't going to break up a good game of eight-ball to eavesdrop on him.

"What do the troopers say?" Cletus asked. "I assume you told them what you'd seen?"

"I tried," Horton said, glowering and taking another swig of beer. "Lord knows. They're already off on a five county hunt for a crazed taxidermist. They plan to question folks with hunting licenses and they're going to contact the FBI to run a search through NCIC. The body is headed to the State Bureau crime lab up in Raleigh. They're hoping for prints."

"You didn't see any?" Cletus asked.

"I asked if they had a double-D Goddam database for hoofprints," Horton snorted, finishing his second glass of beer. Cletus drained his first. Getting useful information out of Horton was an iffy proposition at the best of times. He hoped the Gin had enough beer.

"So," Cletus said, "we both know that skin was healing. We both know that skin could no way in hell have been healing. We both know men don't come to the Dismal Swamp for head transplants on a regular basis, and, even though the *Weekly World News* is my Bible, I swear on Bat Boy's honor I've never read of *any* head transplant that took. Barring the possibility that some rednecked hunter tried his computer scanner on the buck he just shot and 3-D Photoshopped it onto his cousin, you got any ideas?"

Horton looked at Cletus and blinked, then glanced down at his beer glass as if seeing it for the first time. He placed the glass carefully on the table and steepled his hands, looking off across the bar as if Cletus wasn't there at all.

"Most folks," Horton said softly, "think I'm something of an idiot, Cletus," he said softly.

Cletus was taken aback by the comment, but held his silence. He knew he should probably have denied the truth of the statement, but they both knew if he did it would be a lie. Horton saved him the trouble by continuing.

"Fact is, I didn't have to come back to Old Mill at all. Had offers from Raleigh, Richmond up in Virginia, even an outfit out in California. There was a time I was going places, and this wasn't one of 'em. Then I met Clara, and things changed. You knew her folks, didn't you Cletus? Harry and Jenny?"

Cletus nodded. "They took care of me a few times when my pop was out to sea. They were good folks."

Horton nodded. "They were, and Clara? She was my angel. She might have moved with me to Raleigh. She might even have gone to California, but she'd have been miserable the whole time. Her life was here, and my life, as it turns out, was with her. So I stayed. Anyway, there's a point to all of this. I know a thing or two about medicine, and biology, and a bit about wounds.

Cletus had a thousand words on the tip of his tongue, but he kept them to himself. This was a side of Horton he'd never seen, and he had an idea he was about to learn some other things as well.

"I worked with a surgeon once," Horton said, "who specialized in transplants. I learned a lot during that internship. I saw a lot of lives saved, a lot of others lost, and I paid attention. One of the biggest fears in a transplant is that the body will take a perfectly good organ and reject it. Sometimes it happened so fast the patient was dead before they could get them off the operating table. Other times things seemed fine, and then degraded. It was always faster near the end. We know a lot about the human body, but for the most part it's just a game of educated guesses. We save a lot of lives, but every time we operate, we learn something we didn't know before, or we find out that something we thought we knew is bullshit.

"That man you pulled out of the swamp—and he was a man, at least he started out that way—didn't die because the transplant was botched. He didn't die because it was impossible. He died because his body rejected it. Maybe it goes deeper than that. Man of science or not, I like to think there's more to a man than the flesh he carries around with him. Maybe his soul rejected it—who can say. The inflammation around the stitches was something I've seen before. The blood wasn't matched. He tried to live...or something tried to live in that body...but it just couldn't do it, Cletus."

Cletus' skin had gone clammy, and for the second time that day his stomach was on the verge of doing some rejecting of its own.

"What are you saying, Horton? Bottom line?" he asked.

"I'm saying it isn't the fact some psycho doctor out there sewed a damned deer head onto man that scares me, Cletus. It's the fact it almost worked."

Horton stood up very suddenly and turned away from the table. Cletus started to follow, then thought better of it. He didn't know what to say. Horton tottered across the bar, swung wide of the pool table, and headed for the door. When it closed behind him, Cletus was still watching. Then he sat back, poured another beer, and lost himself in his thoughts.

The Gin wasn't busy, but business was steady. Men came and went on their way home from work, or out from home. A local trucking company softball team breezed through, downed several pitchers of beer, and rolled back out. Cletus sat and watched them, and he thought. He watched them because they were all alive, and moving, and if he closed his eyes and quit watching, even for a moment, he heard the wet, sucking sound of swamp mud releasing its hold on those damned antlers, and he saw the jagged line of stitches across the man's chest.

He shouldn't have been sitting and drinking so far from home, and he shouldn't have been spending his time worrying over a dead man, even one sprouting antlers. No one was paying him on this one, and with the State Troopers in charge and the FBI on call, it wasn't likely that Old Mills' finest were going to call him in as a consultant. He had mail-order courses to finish. He had a couple dozen "magic" talismans to mail to fill orders from his advertisement in the latest *Weekly World News*. There were dozens of more important things he could have been doing, but somehow he couldn't pry his dead ass out of that booth and get to it.

Finally, when things started to get ugly near the pool table, he rose and dropped a ten on the table behind the empty pitcher. When the action moved to the south side of the table, he moved around the left, narrowly avoiding jostling a woman twice his size in blue jeans half her own. In the clear, he breathed a little easier. He glanced toward the door and saw a tall man in a New York Yankees baseball camp slip out the door.

At that moment he heard a loud crack behind him, and he turned, half-expecting he'd been too slow, and that he'd meet a pool cue teeth first. When things got a bit too drunk out, the Gin was famous for what Cletus liked to term "Redneck Olympics." He'd watched them at it more than once, and he knew better than to stick around when things started to run south of sane. The night he'd stayed to watch, five big men, two farmers, a trucker, and a mechanic from down at the Ford dealer put ten bucks apiece on the bar. Sadie, who'd been tending bar that night, had held the money. The game was simple. They each chugged a glass of beer. Whoever took the longest to down his drink was "it". Once this formality was behind them, they turned to the front door. Whoever walked through that door next, woman, man, sheriff, or Hell's Angel, the man who was "it" had a choice. He could step forward and take a swing, no warning, and no mercy, or he could match the fifty bucks on the bar. If he swung, and knocked whoever it was down, he got the fifty bucks. If he chickened out, or if it was someone's grandmother, and he just couldn't do it, he matched the pot, and they drank again. The night Cletus had watched, they'd matched twice before Amos Lester said "Aw Hell" and swung before the door was even all the way open. He hooked his ham fist around the corner and caught one of three marines who were coming in flush on the jaw. The marine went down, and Amos took his money quick. Then the marine got up.

The Gin was not a watering hole for the weak of heart.

The fight at the pool table had gone past the cursing stage. The big woman he'd missed the opportunity to do the bump with had her pool cue, tip down, gripped like a club, and she was advancing on a big man with so much hair it erupted from the collar of his shirt and spilled over his shoulders. He leaned on the wall, holding his head and screaming. Blood seeped through his fingers.

"Time to go," Cletus muttered. He turned and hurried out into the parking lot, just in time to hear a loud cry for help.

Cletus made a habit of being observant. It was necessary for about half the jobs he performed, and a good idea for the other half. It was the kind of ability that kept you from getting the butt-end of a pool cue up side your head, and that kind of advantage was important.

When he stepped out of the bar, he noticed two things immediately: a ratty old pickup truck hitting second gear, chewing gravel and shooting out of the parking lot and on toward Highway 17; a big man in a t-shirt that failed to reach his belt by four inches running straight at him, screaming and bellowing at the top of his lungs. His belly swung from side to side, and his voice was a harsh blast of air forced past a burning need to breathe; Jasper running his truck into the ditch as the first truck shot past, nearly taking off his rear-view.

"Damn," Cletus said.

He didn't know the fat guy, and he wasn't fast enough on his feet to give chase, so he took off at a run toward Jasper. The big guy saw him, tried to switch direction and met the sad reality of gravity. His back leg caught in the gravel, his front twisted, and he went down. Cletus saw this out of the corner of his eye, but he was too far away to prevent the fall, and about a hundred pounds shy of a serious attempt, so he kept moving.

"Hey!" the man got out one word, and then a sharp cry as he hit the ground, trying in vain to break his fall with his hands. Cletus almost stopped then. He heard the gasp of pain and knew something was likely broken, but just then he caught sight of Jasper, and he went on to the ditch.

Jasper was bent forward over his steering wheel. Cletus couldn't tell if he was moving, but it looked bad. The pickup was buried nose first in the mud at the base of the ditch. It was about four feet down, and Cletus took it at a slide, catching himself on the driver's side door, grabbing the handle and yanking it open. Jasper turned then, dazed, and Cletus saw a trickle of blood on his friend's forehead.

"Take 'er easy Jasper," Cletus said. "Just sit there a minute till I get a chance to look you over."

"Cletus?" Jasper asked.

"Yeah Jaz, it's me," Cletus said. "I was coming out of the bar when that asshole ran you off the road. You get a look at him?"

Jasper shook his head, and his face screwed itself into a pained expression as the stupidity of such a gesture made itself known.

"Didn't get a good look," Jasper said at last. "It's dark, and I was tryin' not to get my ass killed. Funny thing though, Cletus. I didn't see the guy who was driving—but there was a couple fellas in back. I nearly missed the turn when I saw them. I swear they was white—you know—like them *Mime* assholes you see on TV, or Gene Simmons from Kiss back before they washed their faces. Spooky as hell."

Before Cletus could question him further, the man in the

parking lot let out a scream. Cursing, Cletus stepped back from the truck.

"I got to go see if I can help Shamu back there, Jaz. You take it easy till the cops get here."

"No cops, Cletus. I got to get out of here."

"Why in..." Cletus stopped mid sentence. The floor of the pickup was littered with beer cans.

"Go sit in my truck," he growled. "Can you walk?"

"I think so," Jasper said. "Thanks Cletus."

"'Just get over there. I have to check the guy in the parking lot and get him some help. I also want to find out if he saw anything. Maybe you can find that guy and his to clown-painted friends and get some money to fix your truck."

Cletus spun away and headed back to where the fat guy was flopping in the gravel like a beached salmon. Cletus reached him just as he managed to pull himself back to a seated position.

"Hold on there, Bubbah," Cletus said, putting a hand on the guy's shoulder. "Just stay down there and try not to move 'till we see if all the parts are still where they belong."

The man saw Cletus, and his eyes grew wide. Despite the obvious pain it caused, not to mention damage to the parking lot, he choked out a single word, something that sounded like "llyn" and started back-stroking like a grounded Olympic swimmer.

Cletus stood, dumbfounded, and watched him go.

"What the hell did you say?" he asked.

When there was no coherent answer, Cletus gave chase with a curse.

Chapter Three

"Aliens!"

Cletus stopped in his tracks so fast he nearly lost his balance and joined Bubbah on the ground. He stared, and Bubbah stared. The front door of the bar popped open and one of the bartenders glanced out. He still held a towel in his hand, and he didn't look happy.

Cletus glanced at him, then back at the guy on the ground.

"Calm down, Bubbah," he said, and tell me what you saw.

"My name ain't Bubbah," the guy spit. His lip was still quivering, but as Cletus came fully into carbon-based alcohol fueled life-form focus, he looked a little less crazed. He stared up at Cletus, blinked, and went on.

"My name ain't Bubbah," he repeated, "and you ain't an alien."

"Two for two," Cletus replied. "You want to tell me what the blue Jesus you're talking about?"

"Name's Earl," the guys said. "Earl Suggs."

"Nice to meet you, Earl," Cletus replied. He caught movement out of the corner of his eye and knew that either the bartender, or someone else from the bar, was approaching quickly. "You want to tell me what you were screaming about? And while you're at it, why would you think I was an alien?"

"Abduction," Earl said, as if he hadn't heard Cletus at all. "It was a goddamned abduction, right here at the Gin."

Cletus thought fast. He had about thirty seconds before half the drunken population of The Cotton Gin closed in on the two of them, and after that he probably wouldn't get coherent word out of Earl here.

"Tell you what, Earl," he said. "My name is Cletus Diggs. Sometimes I write stories that get into the *Weekly Globe Examiner*. Your alien story might just get you on the front page, if you're interested."

Earl looked interested, but Cletus didn't waste time waiting for an answer.

"You come with me, Earl. My buddy Jasper just wrecked his truck, so the two of you could both use some lookin' after. We'll go back to Jasper's house—his daddy was a medic in the Coast Guard. I'll get you a beer, and you can tell me about the aliens, what do you say?"

Earl blinked, then he glanced over at the small group of drunks trickling out of the bar. He looked back at Cletus.

"You write for the *Weekly Globe*?"

"Cross my heart," Cletus replied. "I'd swear, but I'm a man of the cloth. It's a long story. You comin' Earl? If those guys catch up with us there's going to be a lot of questions. Now, I believe you, but what do you suppose folks are gonna say if you start yappin' about aliens?"

"But I saw 'em," Earl whined.

Cletus reached down and took the big man by the hand.

"I'm sure you did," he said. "But after what I saw going on inside by the pool table, that crowd isn't going to be your target audience. Best get movin', Earl."

Earl glanced a final time at the door, then nodded, gripped Cletus' hand, and hauled himself to his feet. He nearly crumpled, and Cletus caught him, slipping under Earl's shoulder and bracing for shock.

"It's my ankle," Earl said. "Twisted it when I fell."

Cletus didn't answer. He just turned and started across the parking lot toward his truck with Earl limping along at his side. The crowd from the bar stopped to watch them go. A couple of good old boys took a few more steps in pursuit, but apparently the call of beer was too strong. By the time Cletus helped Earl up to the side of the truck, and Jasper opened the door for them.

"Jasper," Cletus said, "Meet Earl. Earl Suggs. Mr. Suggs saw the folks who ran you off the road."

Jasper helped haul Earl up onto the seat beside him. Cletus

stepped round and clambered in behind the wheel.

"We're headed back to your place," Cletus said. "You got beer?"

"Pap brought home a case just this morning," Jasper replied. "There ought to be a few left."

Cletus stared at his friend.

Jasper stared back.

"What?" he asked. "We like beer, okay? No law against that."

"Nothing, Jasper. I was just thinking maybe if you'd had a few less beers, your truck might still be rolling under your ass, instead of nose deep in that ditch back there."

"I ain't drunk," Jasper said, blustering. "I only had..."

"They was aliens," Earl cut in. "In that truck? Aliens. Guy in front was all covered in some sort of black coat. He had a hat pulled down low. Those other two, though, they had their faces pressed against the window. I know they saw me. That guy wasn't from around here, but he didn't deserve to be abducted by no aliens."

Jasper fell silent and stared. Cletus kept his eyes directed at the road and fought back the urge to grin. Whatever Jasper did, and Cletus had an idea or two on what that might be, Cletus himself could not afford to seem anything but sincere. He had no idea why he was keeping after this case, but since he was, he needed every advantage he could wrangle.

When Jasper remained silent, Cletus jumped in quick.

"Earl here saw the truck that ran you off the road, Jasper. He also saw them grab a man out of the parking lot at The Gin. He was going to describe them to me, and I figured I'd take some notes and get something off to the *Weekly Globe*. I'm sure we'll need to get down what you saw too."

"They got meetings for this," Earl cut in. His breath was still a little ragged, and Cletus thought his ankle was hurting like a son of a bitch. "Every week, they got meetings down at the Dreaming Dragon Tattoo parlor. They bring in speakers—people who've been abducted. One day they brought a speaker from the CIA ... well...ex-CIA. He worked out there in Arizona at Area 51."

Jasper turned to Cletus.

"What the hell is he talkin' about Cletus? You want me to give him beer? Sounds like he's had a few too many already."

"I think he saw what he saw," Cletus answered slowly. If it hadn't been such a long shot, he'd have hoped Jasper would catch the tone in his voice and play along.

"The hell you say," Jasper said. "You think I was run off the road by aliens and some guy dressed up like Alex Baldwin in that movie "The Shadow" was behind the wheel. Tell me somethin' Cletus. Just when did aliens start abducting folks with pickup trucks instead of saucers?"

"Might've been a saucer," Earl cut in helpfully. "Could have been using a cloaking device. I seen one of them on *Star Trek*."

Cletus bit down hard on his lip and kept driving.

"Let's get us that beer," he said. "God knows, I need one."

They turned off highway 17 toward The Great Dismal Swamp. In the distance, back in the direction of The Cotton Gin, sirens cut through the night.

Back at Jasper's Pap's farm, they circled the coffee table in the sparsely furnished living room and broke out the beer. Both Jasper and Earl drank deep, but Cletus sat back and sipped his. When he figured things were as calm as they were likely to get, he cleared his throat and sat up.

"First things first," he said. "Earl, you were the first one of us to see that truck. You remember anything about it? Color, scratches, dents, bumpers stickers?"

"Did it glow green and whistle like on the Jetsons," Jasper offered. "Or maybe it just sort of phased in—like from the transporter deck?"

"Shut up, Jaz," Cletus snapped. "This may be a lot more serious than you think."

Earl didn't look upset. It appeared that it might not be the first time he'd been scoffed at, and possibly Jasper wasn't even the best who'd tried. His brow was furrowed, and he was thinking hard.

"You gonna write it down?" he asked at last. Cletus, who'd had the forethought to pull the small spiral notebook he kept in his hip pocket, and a stub of pencil, nodded solemnly.

"It was black," Earl said. "Black as night. I remember thinking it was strange, because it wasn't shiny black, like you'd expect. It was kind of dull."

"Like primer?" Cletus asked.

Earl frowned, then nodded. "Maybe, yeah."

"You didn't notice anything else strange about it?" Cletus asked.

"Nope," Earl said. "Not the truck—just looked like all the others in the lot. That guy came out of the bar and sort of staggered across the parking lot right when I was headed in. He walked past me, skinny fella with short hair, like a sailor—or maybe Coast Guard. He was parked right next to 'em."

"You see any flashing lights?" Jasper cut in.

Cletus glared at him, but Earl only took another long swig of beer.

"So," Cletus said, "We have a flat black pickup and a guy from out of town. Did you see what happened?"

"It was pretty quick," Earl said. "I didn't have any reason to care about that guy. The only reason I looked back was that I heard a crunch of metal. It was the door of the truck. They slammed it open and cracked it into that guy and his car. The two in back—the ones with the white faces?—they jumped outta the back quicker'n greased pigs. They had him up and was draggin' him into the back seat before I really knew what I was seeing. I started after them, but the driver had 'er in gear before I made two steps. They drove right at me. That's when I yelled and started running."

"Sounds like a good plan," Jasper commented. For the first time he didn't sound sarcastic.

"I turned once," Earl said. "I wanted to see if they was really gonna hit me, so I looked over my shoulder and that's when I saw 'em. The driver was all dressed in black. He had one of those black hats that looks sorta like a stetons, but not so big."

"Fedora," Cletus offered.

"Yep, that's it," Earl agreed. "I couldn't see him at all. Saw them others though. Faces white as snow. They had their faces pressed to the glass of the back window, all smushed up. Ain't never seen a man looked like that. Had to be aliens."

A loud "pop" sounded from the kitchen door, and they turned, startled.

Jasper's Pap stood there, staring at them over a beer, his eyes narrowed. "Black pickup and white faces, huh? Don't sound like aliens to me. Sounds like them two boys out Eternity way. Cain't remember their names, but I've seen 'em down town a couple of times. White as sheets and odd as a three dollar bill."

Pap burped then, and turned to Jasper. "You gonna sit there like a lump all night, or you turnin' on Smackdown?"

Cletus stood up, chugged his mostly full beer, and waved.

"I'd love to stay," he said. "Supposed to be a hell of a cage match in the main event, but I have some things I have to take care of. Earl, you need a ride back to your truck?"

"Smackdown's on?" Earl asked.

Jasper was already reaching for the remote. "Yep."

"Mind if I watch?" Earl asked.

Jasper looked at Papa, who shrugged. "I'm gonna have to go down sometime after midnight and tow my truck outta that ditch when the sheriff ain't around. You can ride with me."

Pap went for three fresh cans of beer, and Cletus headed for the door.

"You gonna get me in the *Globe*?" Earl called after him.

"When I finish the story," Cletus said, turning back with a wink, "you'll be the first to hear."

"Don't forget them aliens!" Earl bellowed.

Cletus paid no attention. On the way to his car, he pulled out his cell phone and dialed the sheriff's office. Colleen answered.

"Get Bob on the line," Cletus said.

"He isn't taking calls, Cletus. Not since he got back this morning, and the troopers took over. Hasn't been out of his office, not to eat, not for coffee. I'm worried."

Cletus stopped by his truck and stared back down toward the highway.

"I'll be right there, Colleen. If he comes out, don't let him leave. Me and ol' Bob have to go on an alien hunt. You can tell him that."

He disconnected the call before she could question him or protest, climbed in behind the wheel of his pickup, and pointed it toward Old Mill.

Chapter Four

When Cletus reached the Sheriff's Office, Colleen waved him past her desk toward the inner office door.

"You aren't going to page him?"

"He wouldn't answer. Hasn't been out of there since just after lunch. I'm worried about him, Cletus."

"He'll be okay, Colleen. You didn't see what we saw."

"You didn't lock yourself in an office and pout," she pointed out.

"Well, that's me," Cletus said. "I've seen a lot of strange things. Hell, I've seen Jasper eat barbecue. Takes a lot to faze me."

"Well, I hope you can get him out of there. We've got three calls and Lester's running his butt off trying to handle it all."

"I'll see what I can do," Cletus said.

He turned to the inner office door, knocked once, and pushed it open.

Bob sat behind his desk, turned to face the one window in the office. The blinds were pulled down tight, and the curtains were drawn. A single small desk lamp provided the only illumination. An empty coffee cup sat on the desk blotter.

"Hey, Bob," Cletus said.

Bob said nothing, and Cletus stepped closer.

"You okay?" he asked.

For a moment it seemed Bob would remain silent; then he spoke.

"What the hell kind of question is that, Cletus?" he asked. "You saw that thing. Hell, we both had it by the boots."

"That's true," Cletus said. "Whatever it was, though, it's

gone now. I don't expect we're going to find too many more like it."

"Shouldn't have been even one," Bob said. He didn't so much speak the words as spit them. "How can I go out there, Cletus? How can I know? What if I pull over a speeder out on 17, walk up to the driver's side window, and see antlers through the glass? What if it's something else? Something worse?"

Bob's hand shook. Cletus had seen the onset of panic before, and he knew he had to stop it quick, or it might get ugly.

"Then you give Bambi a ticket and get on with your life," he said. "What are you doing, Bob? We got a dead man on his way to Raleigh, and he was killed right here. Troopers are out scouring the county for crazed taxidermists, and here you sit. You think it was some guy got tired of mounting heads on his wall and decided to use his brother-in-law instead?"

"No," Bob said flatly. "I don't think it was a taxidermist. I don't think it was a hunter. I pray to God it wasn't anyone from Old Mill at all, but there you go, Cletus. He was in the damned fishing hole. Our fishing hole. Someone dropped him there, and whoever it was is a hell of a lot crazier than anyone I've run across in my short but illustrious career as Sheriff."

"Okay," Cletus answered slowly. "I think that's a fair assessment. Now what are you going to do about it?"

Bob turned. He glared up at Cletus through tired, sunken eyes, his teeth gritted.

"Do?" he said. "DO? Nothing, Cletus. What is there to do? We found him, State Investigative Service took him, and the troopers are currently running all our buddies in because they have a lifetime subscription to the Herter's Fish and Game catalog in their den and half-assed jackrabbit mounts on their Tiki bars. There isn't a damned thing I can do...why the hell you think I'm sitting in here?"

Cletus met Bob's gaze levelly.

"I think you're sitting in here on your ass because you're scared of what you might find if you don't. You know as well as I do there's someone out there more than a bubble off plumb, you going to let him get someone else? You going to trust those troopers to do your job? They don't know folks here, and they don't know the swamp. They might be the only men in the county that didn't know where the fishin' hole was before we told them. They aren't going to find this guy, so maybe we'd better."

"We?" Bob said.

"We," Cletus agreed. "We need to get going, Bob. We need to get you some food, and some rest. Tomorrow morning we need to take a spin out to Eternity."

"Now who's a bubble off?" Bob asked. "Eternity? Just why in hell would we go to Eternity."

"Aliens." Cletus said solemnly. "I'll fill you in on the way."

Bob stared up at him, blinked, then shook his head.

"Fine, but you're buying the food."

Cletus grinned, turned, and leaned out the door, giving Colleen thumbs up. Moments later he and Bob were headed through the outer office in search of food. Colleen frowned, staring at the pile of call slips on her desk.

"Tell Lester I'll make it up to him," Bob told her. "Al will be in in a couple of hours, and I'm in no shape to be making house calls. We'll sort it out tomorrow...right after Cletus and I get back from Eternity."

"Tell St. Peter I said hey," Colleen replied, popping her gum.

Chuckling, Cletus followed Bob out into the darkness, trying not to stare into the shadows.

When Bob pulled up in front of Cletus' trailer the next morning, he had had two tall cups of strong black coffee from Muddy Waters over in Elizabeth City, and his color was back. Whatever he'd thought, dreamed, or told himself when the lights went out must have worked.

Cletus climbed into the Land Rover beside him and took one of the coffees gratefully.

"Dancing Goat," Bob said. "It's Friday's special. Damn good coffee."

Cletus nodded.

"So," Bob said. He pulled a quick U-turn in the driveway and headed back toward the road. "You going to tell me why we need to go to Eternity? I haven't been there more than a couple of times in my life, and both times I got out as quick as I could. Now you tell me because we find a corpse with a deer's head, we should go to Eternity to chase aliens, and for some reason I can't help but take you seriously."

"Well," Cletus began, "maybe not aliens. Albinos though."

He quickly filled the sheriff in on what had happened the night before outside The Cotton Gin, and later at Jasper's place. Bob listened carefully, and when Cletus was done, he nodded.

"I think Jasper's Pap is right," he said. "The only albinos I've ever heard of around these parts are those two boys. It might not have anything to do with our deer man, but if they abducted someone from the Gin, we'd best get out there and see what's what."

"There's more," Cletus said.

Bob turned right, away from Highway 17 and on toward the swamp.

"I'm listening," he said.

"I went on the Internet last night," Cletus said. "I knew I'd seen something about those boys, but I couldn't remember what it was. They went away a few years back. Seems the two of them are some sort of geniuses. Studied medicine, genetics, and a few others things. The papers up in Raleigh tried to make a big deal of it, but neither boy would give them an interview. Later that year, the two disappeared. No one could figure out what happened. All the reporters could turn up was a single picture of the two of them sort of glaring at a camera. It was strange enough I considered finding them myself and doing something for the *Weekly Observer*, but I never did get around to it.

"To tell you the truth, Eternity pretty much creeps me the hell out."

"It's no vacation spot," Bob agreed.

They drove in silence for a few miles, and Cletus pulled a spiral notebook from his hip pocket. He'd made a few notes. His experience with Eternity was pretty limited, and even Jasper's Pap, when Cletus called up to question him, didn't have much. The town had been rotting into the swamp until a certain Reverend Eli Dozier rolled into town, and ever since then every story that rolled out of the rumor mill was strange. Eternity wasn't so much a town as a gathering place. There was no store, no gas station, no post office, and there sure as hell were no street lights. There were a couple of warehouses just off the highway for crops, cotton, and supplies, but in Eternity, NC, there was only one thing that mattered. Eternity had a church, and despite the fact that you could spend a week of Sundays walking up and down their one stretch of road without seeing a soul, the pews of that church were full every time the altar candles were lit. The walls gleamed with fresh white paint, and the tin roof was water tight and shone in the sun.

There were a lot of families in and around the outskirts of the Great Dismal Swamp. Some of them have lived there all their lives; others have migrated in as civilization ran them out of older homes and deeper shadows. Freeways, cities, towns and farms surround that land on all sides. Some were on the run from something, or someone—others just wanted to be swallowed up and forgotten.

Bob drove slowly and carefully, weaving the Land Rover around large potholes. Once Cletus had to get out and drag a fallen log out of the road. When he climbed back in, he turned to Bob with a frown.

"You remember any wind last night, Bob?" he asked. "I don't remember seeing any branches down near Old Mill."

"It was clear," Bob replied.

"Someone put that log there, then," Cletus said. "Someone didn't want anyone coming in here today. You think maybe they were afraid they were seen?"

"Could be," Bob replied. He glanced over his shoulder at the shotgun hanging behind the seat. "Someone back here doesn't want to be found, it's likely they're not going to be. I figure we'd better try and track down that preacher. He'll know what's going on if anyone does, and he might be able to lead us to those boys."

Cletus frowned.

"Might be you're right, Bob, and I'll be damned if I can think of a better plan, but I haven't heard anything good about this preacher, Dozier. Things have always been close and quiet out here, but since he came in and started preaching at the church the stories I've heard sound more like something off *The Twilight Zone*. If there's something going on here, he'll know it alright, but he might be the one behind it as well."

"Yep, figured that too," Bob agreed. "We'll have to be careful with him, for sure, but I don't see us getting anywhere out here unless we go to him first."

The road they were on grew steadily worse as it turned in under the trees, then ran along the bank of the swamp. Cattails shot up from the ditch, and a sheen of green, greasy slime coated the stagnant water. Cletus saw a couple of frogs hit that water. They dipped through the muck and the surface went flat. No ripples. A Water Moccasin slithered off the road and into the ditch.

Bob reached for his radio and pressed the key on his mic.

"Four-One to base," he said. He waited a moment, then tried again. There was a crackle of static, and then—faintly—Colleen's voice came across the speaker.

"Got you weak and barely readable, Four-One, over."

"We're getting ready to pull into Eternity," Bob said, speaking quickly, as if afraid of losing their one contact with the outside world. "This might be related to a kidnapping last night over at The Gin. Stay close to your radio—if we find anything, we'll be calling for backup."

There was another crackle that might have been an answer, but there was no way to be certain. Bob glared at the microphone in his hand, jammed it back onto its holder, and turned his attention to the road.

They rounded the final curve and suddenly the ground beneath their tires was even and free of ruts. The road leading into Eternity was clear and smooth. The trees opened up into a large clearing, and at the far end of that clearing stood the First Church of Light and Starry Wisdom. Neither man had known it was called that, but that was what the large, hand-lettered sign beside the walk leading to the front door proclaimed. It was even spelled correctly.

The parking lot was paved with smooth river stones, and it was empty. There was no sign of a black pickup truck, or any other vehicle. The front door of the church was closed.

"You think anyone's home?" Cletus asked. "Damn place looks like it dropped here out of the clouds."

"It's weird all right. What the hell kind of beliefs you reckon they have in The Church of Light and Starry Wisdom, Cletus? You're the preacher, right? I've heard of about ten flavors of Baptists, Methodists, those fellas that go to church on Saturday, Catholics, hell, we got more churches in Old Mill than we have houses—but I've never heard of anything like this."

"It's a new one on me too, Bob," Cletus said. "I'll look into it when we get back."

Bob pulled in and parked near the door. They sat for a moment, then Cletus took a deep breath, opened his door, and stepped out. His boots crunched on the gravel. Bob followed, and they headed straight up the walk to the front door of the odd structure. The walls were constructed of rough hewn wood. Hand cut. Cletus thought about that, and he hesitated at the top of the steps, reaching out to run his fingertips over the surface.

"This is all handmade," he said at last. "I figured they must have run some supplies in from Virginia, or out of the county, but I'll be damned if they didn't cut this and shape it by hand. You ever seen wood cut like that, Bob?"

Bob didn't answer. He pulled the heavy flashlight off his belt and rapped the base of it on the wooden door sharply. Cletus fell silent, and they waited. There was no answer, and Bob smacked the door again, then shrugged. He grabbed the door handle, pushed on the latch, and it swung inward easily. Bob followed it through, and Cletus followed.

The light inside had a greenish tinge. There were no stained glass windows like the ones at the Methodist Church in Old Mill, but something had been done to the glass. It didn't look quite clear, nor was it colored. It was as if it had been soaked in something green and become infected. Cletus kept his mouth shut, because he knew it hadn't been that many hours since Bob had been ready to panic. No sense vocalizing the fact the entire place felt diseased, or that the light felt like it was crawling over his skin. Didn't really pay to be thinking about it either.

Cletus turned and stared at the altar. He tried to imagine standing behind that podium, staring out at the rough-hewn pews, his hand on a Bible and his mind on messages from God. The images wouldn't come. The place drew goose bumps from his flesh like pie drew flies, and there was a smell he couldn't quite make out that added to his unease. None of it made him feel closer to God.

"There's a door behind the altar," Bob said.

Cletus followed Bob's gaze. He wasn't at all sure he wanted to know what was behind that door, but there didn't seem to be many choices.

"Let's do it then," he said.

The two of them rounded the altar, and Bob reached out to knock on the door. He stopped just short, frowned, and gripped the knob, turning it and giving it a shove.

"Police," He called, stepping through. Cletus noticed Bob's hand resting near the butt of his gun. Normally he'd have thought it was an overreaction, but at that moment it felt like grabbing a marshmallow to throw at a bear.

They entered a short hall single file. Bob never hesitated; he opened the door on their left. It was a storage closet. He gave it cursory glance, closed the door, and opened the door on the right. He stepped inside, and Cletus followed close behind him.

The room was an office, furnished simply with a desk, a couple of chairs, a small table, and a window overlooking the swamp. There were a couple of papers on the desk, weighted down with a worn bible. There was a bookshelf filled with odd, leather-bound books. They didn't look to Cletus like the standard commentaries on the gospels, or the sermons of any long-dead preacher.

"We'd better check out back," Bob said.

Cletus nodded. He stepped closer to the bookshelf and leaned down. As he did, the sound of a door closing nearly scared him out of his jeans. He fell forward, banging his head on the bookshelf and jostling one of the leather-bound volumes free. It fell at his feet, but he didn't lean to pick it up. He turned.

Bob had his hand on the butt of his gun, but somehow resisted the urge to draw the weapon. Cletus had pushed the door nearly closed after they entered so he could see behind it. It opened, and a man stepped through. He was tall with dark, wavy hair tumbling out from beneath a black fedora. Despite the heat, he wore a suit jacket, also dark. His face was shadowed by the brim of the hat, but Cletus thought he could see eyes glowing in the shadow.

The man stared at them, then tipped his hat back and smiled. It wasn't a happy smile, or a friendly smile. It was the kind of smile Cletus associated with the villain in every dark movie he'd ever watched.

"Reverend Dozier?" Bob asked.

The man nodded.

"Reverend Eli Dozier at your service. Is there something I can do for you gentlemen?"

Cletus was glad Bob was with him at that moment. The sheriff pulled himself together nicely, never missing a beat, and it gave Cletus a chance to lean down, pick up the book he'd knocked off the shelf, and slide it back into place. He got a good glance at the cover, and nearly cursed.

"It's been a while since I've been out here," Bob said. "I thought I might check and see if everything was quiet. We had a bit of trouble last night over to the Cotton Gin in Elizabeth City. Got a report the fellows involved might have headed out your way. Don't suppose you noticed anything out of the ordinary?"

Dozier's serpent's grin widened.

"Can't say that I have, Sheriff," he replied. "We don't see much of anyone or anything out this way, except on Sundays. There being only one road, though, it's hard to figure how we could have missed them."

"My thought exactly," Bob said. "You sure you didn't see a black pickup come out this way last night, or hear it? Report said there might have been a couple of boys in the back seat with white faces. No circus around, so I thought of those twins."

"Twins?" Dozier said. He twisted his face in an almost comical expression of confusion, but just before he did it, Cletus saw him start. It was only a tiny, fleeting crack in the man's weird armor, but Cletus thought Bob had caught it too.

"Anyone else out here said they didn't know about one of

the families in your congregation, Reverend, I might tend to believe them. Never seen such a close-in crowd as folks here in Eternity, but I'd appreciate it if you didn't insult my intelligence. There can't be more than a couple pairs of albino twins in the history of this great country."

"Oh, you mean David and Weston," Dozier said smoothly. "The Calhoun boys. Quite the story, those two. Might be the only boys out of Eternity this century with college educations, for all the good it did 'em."

"What do you mean?" Bob asked.

"Well, they're back here, aren't they?" Dozier asked bluntly. "That doesn't qualify in my book as much of a success story. Haven't seen hide nor tail of 'em since they got back. It's like they drove on out of here, went to school, then melted right back into the swamp."

"They don't attend services?" Cletus asked. It was the first time he'd spoken, and he hoped that coming out of left field might catch Dozier off guard, but the man just smiled.

"Their ma and pa come to church every Sunday," he said. "I haven't seen the boys. They weren't big on worship even before they left—I suppose they learned new things to spend their souls on up in Raleigh. What do you think, Cletus?"

Cletus stopped and stood very still. He had never met Dozier in person, and hearing his name come from the man's lips took him by surprise.

"Just one man of the cloth to another," Dozier added. "You think those boys found something new to worship?"

Cletus turned, surveyed the bookshelf behind him, then glanced out at the swamp through the green tinted windows.

"Wouldn't say it surprised me if they did at that," he replied.

Dozier looked like he might chuckle at this, then he bit it back and grimaced.

"If that's all you needed, Sheriff," he said, "I have some things to attend to."

While Bob made a show of writing some notes in the small notebook he carried in his breast pocket, Cletus continued to stare out the window. There was a single bed of flowers halfway to the tree line and the swamp beyond, and there was something strange about it. He took half a step closer to the window and concentrated, but just then Bob laid hand on his shoulder, startling him.

"We'd best be going, Cletus," he said. "We have a few more stops to make on the way back. I want to see if any other folks out here might have seen that truck."

Cletus nodded, frowning, then he turned back to Dozier.

"One other thing," he said. "The guy driving that truck last night? He was wearing a dark jacket and a fedora. You know anyone fits that description, Reverend?"

Dozier's eyes narrowed until they were nothing but dark slits, and he dipped his chin so the brim of his hat shielded his expression. He didn't answer, and Cletus turned, leading the way back to the church, and out into the parking lot.

"He knows something," Cletus said.

Bob nodded. "We'll talk about it after we get clear of here."

"Don't have to tell me twice," Cletus muttered.

They climbed into the truck and Bob gunned the engine, cutting twin ruts in the carefully tended drive. Cletus looked into the side mirror. Reverend Dozier was watching them go. He was standing directly in front of the odd little flower bed. From that distance, he looked like a scarecrow, or some sort of weird, swamp wraith.

Then they rounded the corner, and the church was out of sight.

Chapter Five

Cletus waited until they were clear of the swamp, leaving Bob to concentrate on negotiating the bumpy, unpaved road.

"You see that book I knocked off the shelf?" he finally asked. "The one I was trying to pick up when he came through the door?"

Bob turned and glanced at him, the focused on the road.

"Nope. Why?"

"I don't know what it was, exactly," Cletus said, "but I can tell you one thing. The front cover was tooled leather. It didn't have a title, but there was a pretty good likeness of a man with a seven point rack burned in deep."

Cletus saw Bob's knuckles whiten as he gripped the steering wheel too tightly. The sheriff's mouth tightened in to a grim line, but at first he didn't speak. He turned off onto the feeder road and pointed the Land Rover toward Highway 17.

"There's more," Cletus said. This time he didn't look at Bob, but stared out at the road. "There was something wrong with that flower bed out in back of the church."

"The flower bed?" Bob asked. "You had a problem with their flower bed, Cletus?"

"You didn't get a good look at it," Cletus said. "I did. You see any other flowers in Eternity, Bob?"

The silence was all the answer Cletus needed.

"There weren't any other flowers. One, single bed, in a circle, halfway from the church to that back line of trees. There was something sticking up out of the middle. I might have figured out what it was, but Dozier walked in."

"What are you thinking?" Bob asked.

"Don't know," Cletus admitted. "I mean, hell, Bob, it could be a very small graveyard, or some weird shrine. There might have been a well there and they grew flowers around it to keep folks from stepping into it and drowning. It was strange as hell, and when you peeled out of that parking lot, Dozier was standing right beside that flower bed, watching like he was waiting for us to be out of sight."

Bob was quiet for a while after that, and Cletus watched traffic passing. As they turned down the road toward Cletus' place, Bob broke the silence again.

"So, what you think I should do, Cletus?"

There was no 'we'—and Cletus wasn't sure how he felt about that. He didn't really want anything more to do with Dozier, or Eternity, and he damn sure didn't want to pull anymore of Bambi's evolved cousins out of the swamp, but he didn't think he'd be able to sleep until they put an end to it. Maybe not then.

"I'm not sure," he said. "I don't think anyone's going to give you a warrant because I thought a flower bed was weird. You tell the states boys about that book I saw, you might get them to swarm the place.

"We could go back," Bob said. He didn't turn to meet Cletus' gaze, and his fingers were white on the steering wheel again, but his expression was one of tight determination.

"And stake out the posies?" Cletus asked, then immediately felt like a jerk. He'd been hoping Bob would keep him in the game, and now that the door was open he showed his customary lack of tact.

"We go back," he added, "we need us a plan, Bob. We also need to know more about what we're getting into."

"You got any ideas how we'll do that?" Bob asked. "I don't reckon we'll find the good citizens of Eternity too forthcoming. Fact is, I'm not sure I can find any of them at all. The only time they come out of the woodwork is on Sunday, and I don't think they'd take kindly to my stepping up to the altar to ask them questions."

"And that's four days away," Cletus added. "If that guy they took from the Cotton Gin is alive, I'm betting he won't be by Sunday. At least, not like he was, if you know what I mean."

Apparently Bob did. His complexion paled, and he rolled his window down a bit. Cletus was afraid the man was going to spew out into the driveway, but Bob got himself under control.

"I've got to go in and take my shift," Bob said. "I'm going to have to run in some drunks, settle a few home disputes, and break up a fight or two down at the Gin. I don't know if I can do that, but I'm going to try."

Cletus nodded.

"I'm going back to Jasper's place," he said. "I think his pap might be able to get me in touch with someone who understands Eternity, and the swamp, a lot better than I do. I'm also going to hit the Internet and find out what I can about horned men and Reverend Eli Dozier. If we're lucky, I'll find enough to convince someone with more firepower than we have at our disposal to hit that place like a scud missile. If not, we'll have to go back there and get some evidence on our own."

"Hell with that," Bob said. "We'll get us a posse—unofficial, of course. We can get Jasper, maybe his pap, and how 'bout that other guy who thinks he saw a truck full of aliens?"

Cletus snorted laughter and shook his head. "I expect we could get the lot of them," he said. "Can't say I'd feel any safer for it, but you may be right. We'd better take as many as we can get, and we'd better make sure someone knows where we are, and why. I'm thinking it might be a long time before anyone thought to come out toward Eternity to look for us."

He climbed out, and Bob backed the Land Rover up and turned back toward 17. Cletus didn't envy the man the next few hours. Old Mill could be bad enough on a good day—this wasn't one of those. When the trail of dust reached the end of his drive, Cletus climbed into his trailer. He fired up the beat up, stained, old Mr. Coffee, and then the computer, watching the screen roll through its boot procedure to a backdrop of hissing, dripping, liquefied caffeine.

While he waited, he grabbed his phone and punched in Jasper's number. Cletus knew better than to tell his old friend there was work to do. Instead of an answer, he got the whirring hiss on the line that signaled Jasper's Pap's gen-yoo-ine vintage reel to reel answering machine. The thing was a dinosaur, but Pap refused to let it go.

"I bought that thing brand new," he always said. "Found it nice and shiny on the shelves down at Woolworth's. Took me and Emma a year to figure out how to get it to answer the phone, and another six months to figure out what to put on the message. We used to sit around and watch the ding dang thing, ignoring calls and waiting for it to kick in and tell folks we was in the shower, or gone to Outer Mongolia in search of inner."

Cletus had been hearing the story of that damned machine for nearly thirty years, and it still brought him a chuckle if he thought about it too long. And the damned thing still worked. There was no way to argue with that—quality belonged to things of the past—an archaic term bandied about far too often and with far too little merit in modern times.

The phone's speaker crackled, and pap's voice came onto the line, wavering slightly from the stretched, aged tape it had been recorded onto.

"You've reached Jasper and his pap. Leastways, you'd have reached them if they was here. When you hear this contraption beep, leave a number. If it still plays when I see the light flashing, I'll call you back."

Cletus left a message for Jasper to get some beer and get over to the trailer. He told him to bring pap along if he was up to it, and asked if ol' Earl the alien hunter had left a number, or any way they could reach him to 'follow up' on the story. He didn't say anything about the sheriff, or Eternity, Reverend Dozier, or aliens.

Satisfied, he hung up, stood up, and poured a cup of strong, black coffee. He carried it to his desk, brushed the nearest piles of paper away from his keyboard, and logged onto his computer. Unlike his trailer, and the surface of his desk, his computer screen was almost bleak in its absolute order. He had folder icons lined up on the desktop that held his current projects. He had a hard drive full of the last year's files, and others he planned to follow up on. He also had a complex and nearly paranoid system of backups. Information was the central hub of his life, and he guarded what he had fanatically.

He glanced at his e-mail, saw the box was full of unread messages, missives, requests, and adds for cheap, Internet Viagra. Apparently, Abba Contiga Brezhnev, Contessa of some country he'd never heard of, had a few million bucks she needed laundered, and had gone straight past hello and howdy-do and on to calling him her dear. Nothing earth shattering, and he closed the program with a grunt. Time to get serious.

"Google don't fail me now," he muttered, and between sips of hot, black coffee, he set to work.

Chapter Six

The moon was almost full, and it trickled through the trees like luminous spider silk. The water at the swamp's edge lapped over an old log and sucked at the mud hungrily. In the moonlight, the wet surface beyond the log looked black and slick like an ebony mirror. There were no ripples, and though, very faintly, the screeching song of tree frogs scratched at the air, the silence felt eerie and complete.

A flash of white passed between two trees, and then again. Shadows crossed the grass, as though a huge tree had bent down to touch the earth. The buck stepped into the clearing carefully. He raised his head and sniffed the air. The moonlight caught the clear pools of his eyes, and glimmered on the felt tips of his antlers. He was huge, strong, wary—and thirsty. After a long hesitation, he moved in closer to the water.

He stopped at the edge of the water and shivered, as if he'd felt something crawl through the fur on his back, or a breeze had cut through to chill his skin. Then, slowly, he bent, and he drank.

In the trees behind him, two pale eyes appeared. A few feet further along the tree line, a second set flickered into view as silently as the first. The buck stiffened, as if he'd heard, or sensed something, but when there was no sound, he returned his attention to the water, lapping it up greedily.

In the trees, a woman stood, watching the animal drink. Very slowly, she raised a bow, keeping it parallel to the tree trunks. The buck shivered again, but otherwise seemed not to hear. The woman didn't smile. Her face was blank, like the surface of the water. With the same, slow, silent deliberation she pulled a thin arrow from a quiver dangling over her shoulder and resting against her back. The shaft of the arrow was very narrow, like a willow branch. She notched it to the bow and stood, still as stone, waiting.

The buck finished drinking and lifted its head. As it turned and slowly scanned the clearing, she sighted in on its chest and drew back on the string. Her arm didn't tremble, and there was no creak of bent wood, or thrum of the bow string. She hesitated only a moment, and then, with a whispered word too soft to be heard, she released.

The arrow shot across the clearing. The buck, fast as he was, barely had time to lift his head, eyes starting to roll back in their sockets, before the arrowhead dug into its flesh. The animal reared then, pawing at the air and screaming. The woman stood very still, watching calmly. The arrow was too small for killing—too narrow, and without a lethal tip. The tranquilizer it had been dipped in was more powerful.

The buck leaped for the trees. It was strong, and that first leap carried it across the clearing. As its front hooves struck the soft earth, its legs crumpled beneath it, and it fell forward, rolling hard. He tried to struggle back to his feet, but was only able to raise itself a foot or so before falling heavily on its side.

The woman was out of the trees in seconds, cradling the animal's huge head in her lap. She avoided a final flip of the antlers, stroking the buck's nose and staring down into the wild, fear-soaked depths of its eyes. Others slipped from the forest then. First was a slender girl with long stringy hair and wide, serene eyes. She moved to kneel on the far side of the animal and began to bind its legs together, all the time humming a soft tune. The old woman paid no attention.

A circle of others formed around them. A few stepped forward, muttered under their breath, and touched the animal, then stepped back. They waited patiently and silently as the old woman spoke softly into the animal's ear, and the young girl bound it tightly, front legs together, rear legs together, then strong leather thongs between the two.

When she was finished, she stood and stepped back into the surrounding circle. She raised her arms and the two men on either side of her took her hands. The circle closed in this manner, and, so slowly that it was difficult to detect, at first, they began to move in a circle.

In the center, the old woman still held the deer's head in her lap. She sang softly to it, and her fingers walked down its neck toward the chest, where her thin arrow still protruded from its side. She gripped the shaft near the base, thin, bony fingers tightening around it, the fingers of her other hand stroking the beast's muzzle. She continued like this for a few minutes longer, and then—with a swift yank—she pulled the arrow free. There was a ripple in the buck's muscles, but the paralysis held. Only in its eyes did the fear register, and there it was rampant. They rolled to white, and the woman stroked its brow. She leaned in again, spoke into the animal's ear softly, and it grew still.

She stood, and the circle broke. Dark eyed men stepped forward, caps pulled down to shield their eyes. They strung a long, sturdy pole through the leather thongs, and the others closed in at the front and rear.

"Carefully," the old woman said. "Gently. He must not be harmed. He must not touch the earth again until it is time. Do you understand?"

The men nodded. None spoke. They lifted the buck off the ground and turned, very slowly, carrying it back into the woods. The woman stepped into the trees at their side, and was gone.

Behind them, dancing across the ground where their booted feet passed, the girl followed. Her eyes were closed, and her arms were raised. Her lips moved but no sound emerged, and she danced through the trees with uncanny grace, sliding around tree trunks, and following the others into the shadows.

All that remained in the clearing was the dark, placid water, still trying to devour the shore, and the bloody arrow shaft forgotten on the soft, loamy ground.

Chapter Seven

Cletus's trailer wasn't suited for entertaining. He had a couch—somewhere. Most of the time it was covered with newspapers, books, boxes and packing material. His chair, aimed straight at the television, was the only horizontal surface he kept relatively clear. When Jasper's truck pulled up out front, the tire replaced, and the fender sporting a nice deep dent, courtesy of the Cotton Gin's ditch, Cletus stood up from his desk, looked around, blinked, and cursed.

He stumbled around the desk, cracked his knee on the corner, cursed again, and started grabbing papers and boxes and books, piling them precariously on his coffee table, the floor, and any other space not piled too high to take another layer. By the time Jasper pushed the door open, the couch was cleared.

Jasper's Pap had a twelve pack of Busch in one hand, and Earl, who stumbled along behind, had a bucket of KFC clutched like a football. Jasper looked around, saw the cleared couch and the piles of books, paper, and detritus that had been cleared off of it, grinned, and dropped onto it.

"Quick, Pap," he said, "before that crap starts fighting back and smothers us."

"Funny," Cletus said, unable to prevent the grin that split his face. "Give me one of those beers, and pay attention. We don't have much time, and we've got a lot to cover."

"You find them aliens?" Earl asked. "I got me a statement ready—for the interview."

Cletus turned and looked at the man. He started to speak, then just shook his head.

"Later, Earl. We didn't catch anyone yet, but I get the feeling that we're running out of time."

Over beer and chicken, Cletus filled the others in on what he and Bob had seen and learned in Eternity. Pap and Earl listened intently, but Jasper kept glancing longingly over at the television. Finally Cletus fell silent, watching his friend and waiting. It was a full minute after the silence began before Jasper turned and glanced up guiltily.

"What is it, Jasper?" Cletus asked. "All this talk about swamps and albinos boring you?"

"No," Jasper said. He frowned and looked back at the television. "Well, yeah. Hell, Cletus, I don't want to go mucking around in Eternity. You remember what they used to tell us about that place when we were kids. There's a race on tonight, and we got plenty of beer. Can't we just let Bob take care of this and get drunk?"

"We aren't watching any races," Cletus said. "Damn it, Jasper, you started this, so pay attention. We need to find out more about that church, and what's going on out there, and we need to do it fast. There's a man about to die, unless I miss my guess, and the FBI is probably going to try and lock up one of our neighbors for stuffing muskrats in his spare time and having a couple too many sets of antlers on his wall. We're going to stop it, and your fat ass is going to help."

Jasper tried a hurt look, but it wouldn't hold, so he grinned, grabbed another beer, and belched. "Fine. What do we do, then?"

"I wish I knew," Cletus said.

"How 'bout Nettie?" Pap asked.

"That ol' witch?" Jasper said. "What does she have to do with it?"

"She lives in the swamp near Eternity, for one thing," Cletus said, leaning back. "You might have something, Pap. You think she might help?"

"Never knowed her to be helpful, exactly," Pap said thoughtfully, "but I've heard if you show up on her doorstep with enough Bourbon, you can learn just about anything you want. You can bet one thing, she doesn't attend services at the good Reverend Dozier's church, or any other."

"I never heard of anyone named Nettie," Earl said, "But I've heard folks talk about a witch that lived out in the swamp. When I was little, my daddy used to scare us into behaving by threatening to take us out and leave us for her. I ain't in any hurry to do it to myself, now that I'm growed up. We all goin' out there?"

"Don't think that would work," Pap said. "We all show up out there, she's never going to show at all. She has a cottage not too far off the highway, just near the edge of the swamp. I don't think she lives there, but if you make enough noise getting out there, take that whiskey I mentioned, and wait on the porch, she'll show."

Cletus thought about it for a moment, then cursed under his breath.

"It's got to be me. I'm the one who saw that book in the church, and I'm the one that helped tug that—thing—out of the swamp. I'll stop by the package store in Hertford and get fifth of something on the way."

"What about the rest of us?" Jasper asked, glancing at the TV again.

"You need to get ready for a fight," Cletus said. "I don't know what's going to happen out there in Eternity, but I know they aren't going to let me walk in and stop it without a fight. You might want to get some more beer."

Cletus passed out of Hertford, glancing up at a banner slung across the road proclaiming the annual "Fall Harvest Festival" in bold letters, and turned onto Highway 17 just as the sun settled on top of the tree line. A few miles south, he turned off the main road and headed on back toward the swamp. On the seat beside him he had a fifth of Old Crow wrapped up in a plain paper bag. He felt like pulling over to the side of the road and chugging half of it, but he kept his eyes on the bumpy road. It had been a while since the county bothered to level it, and he took his time, winding around the bigger pot holes and cursing the ones he missed.

The road disappeared around a bend ahead, and he slowed,

taking a deep breath. The old cottage that Pap had mentioned sat back into the trees just around that corner. Cletus had been avoiding it most of his life, starting in high school when his friends had all dared one another to pay the old place a visit late at night, and continuing through the present. He'd almost come looking for Nettie to see if he could find a story for the *Weekly Globe Examiner*, but at the last minute he'd decided he'd rather sell blood or work a shift at the Red Apple than knock on that door.

Now here he was.

He passed around the end of the tree line. The cottage, more of a shack, was tucked far enough back into the trees that it was visible only as a shadow among shadows. There were no lights lit, and just for a moment, Cletus considered stopping, backing up into the ditch, and heading back to town. His hands trembled, and he gripped the wheel tighter. He slowed, took a deep breath, and turned off the road onto an even bumpier track leading back under the trees.

He parked, sat, and stared at the old place for what seemed like a long time. Finally, not knowing what else to do, he opened the door of the truck, grabbed the bourbon, and stepped out of the truck. The sun had dropped the rest of the way behind the trees, and all that remained was a red, rosy glow that only seemed to emphasize the shadows. He closed the truck's door and walked slowly up a pitted sidewalk of slate rock and grit to the front porch.

There were cobwebs on the rails. Where grass grew, it was tall and ragged, but most parts of the front yard were dead, as if they couldn't support anything living too close to the frame of the old building. The floorboards of the porch were solid, but very old. They were cracked in places, warped at the ends. There were two wooden chairs placed side by side to the right of the door. Between them was a short table made from the wooden spool from phone or electric cable.

Without really knowing why, Cletus stepped up onto the porch, brushed off one of the chairs and sat down. He pulled the bottle out of its paper wrapping and placed it in the center of the table. He wished he had a flashlight, or even a candle. The moon would be up soon, but he wasn't sure he would find that silver radiance any more comforting than the shadows.

He stared off into the trees to his right, wondering what the hell he was doing. There was no one here. From the look of things, no one had been in this place in a decade, maybe longer. He closed his eyes, rubbed the bridge of his nose, started to turn and rise, and grew very still.

The light had changed. It wasn't much brighter, but it was yellow, and it flickered, sending shadows skittering in all directions. Cletus turned back to the table, and across from him, watching him in stoic silence, sat a very old woman. She was thin to the point of seeming frail. Her hair was as white as snow, but thick, falling back over her shoulders and disappearing down her back. She wore a shapeless dress of some dark material that blended with the darkness and obscured her from sight. All but her hair, and her eyes.

Cletus backed his chair up and cursed. He started to rise, but quick as a snake the old woman reached out and laid her long, slender fingers over his arm.

"I'd sit down, I was you," she said. Her voice was soft, but it carried. "Don't think I'd take myself outside that circle," she added, nodding at the plank floor.

Cletus glanced down. A rough circle had been burned into the wood. It wound around behind the table and the two chairs. He stood very still and stared at it. He hadn't been paying much attention when he walked onto the porch, and the light had been even worse, but he'd have sworn he couldn't miss something like that. He was proud of his natural instincts; he often retained details about a thing, or an event, or a face that he barely remembered noticing. None of this made the circle fade from the floor. He glanced back at the old woman, and returned to his chair.

"Been waitin' for you," she said. "Knew you'd come when it was time."

"I don't know what you're talking about," Cletus replied.

"You do, and there's no reason to deny it," she said. There was no anger or accusation in her tone. It was straightforward— almost matter-of-fact. "You going to open that bottle, or just sit there? I'm thirsty."

Glad to have something to do with his hands, Cletus reached for the bottle. His hand stopped short. There were two bottles and two glasses on the table now. The candle burned behind Nettie, showing her profile with very few details. He focused and found he couldn't tell which of the bottles was the Old Crow.

He grabbed one, twisted the top open, and poured until one of the glasses was full. He reached for the second glass, then stopped short. His fingers trembled, and he came close to dropping the bottle in his hand when he saw that the second glass was full. Nettie slid it across the table to him, then reached for the first.

"It will be harvest festival soon," she said. "You remember the harvest, don't you Cletus?"

Cletus wrapped his fingers around the glass. It was chilled, colder than it should have been, and he shivered. He glanced up and met her gaze.

"Of course I remember," he said.

"I remember too," she said. "I remember your father, Cletus. I remember your grandfather too. He used to ride in to the harvest festival in a wooden buggy pulled by two of the finest horses you've ever seen. Merle Cornelius Diggs. He was a fine figure of a man, did you know that? By the time you knew him, he was old, but I knew him in his prime."

Cletus stared across the table, trying to pierce the shadows. He knew it wasn't possible. His grandfather would have been a hundred and twenty years old if he'd sat at the table with them. The woman he was speaking with was old, there was no denying that, but she didn't seem frail, and it was very difficult to imagine she could be more than seventy.

"You couldn't have known him," he said at last. "I didn't even know him."

"I know things that would drive you crazy," she whispered. "You say you remember the festival, but I know better. You remember the watered down, hollowed-out husk of it. Like a locust skin, hanging on a fence like it was alive, and looking like it might get up and walk away—all gone. Empty."

Her voice never rose in volume, but Cletus heard her clearly.

He took a long drink from the glass in his hand. The first thing he noted was that it wasn't Old Crow. It had a taste of corn whiskey, but there was more. He had no way to judge it, but was certain that he tasted clover, and something more. He thought fleetingly about spitting it out, but it was already sliding down his throat, and the taste was intoxicating. He tried to meet the old woman's gaze and instead closed his eyes.

The breeze kicked up, and it triggered a memory. At least, it felt like a memory. He was walking across a field. The field was ripe with cotton, and he had to wind his way carefully through the plants. It seemed as if they rippled and gripped his boots. He stumbled steadily forward.

In the distance, he saw a fire. The flames licked and danced up a huge pile of wood. Figures circled that fire, but from where he walked in the field they were nothing but indistinct shadows. Beyond the fire a spread of houses lined the skyline, and he stopped, staring. Something was wrong. He scanned the horizon, and realized it was Old Mill, but not the Old Mill he knew. The houses were spread out, and too low to the ground. None of the downtown buildings stood where they should have been. He felt a cold sheen of sweat, chilled by the breeze.

When he started forward again, he caught his foot in the cotton and stumbled. He tried to right himself, hopped over a row of tall, tough green plants, caught his foot again, and sprawled. He hit the dirt hard, unable even to get his hands up in time to break his fall. He cut his cheek on a sharp cotton stalk, and his chin hit the dry, soft dirt with a soft *Thunk!*

He pushed himself up quickly, spitting dirt. He turned and glanced down at the foot that had caught in the row of cotton. He didn't see his Red Wings™, but instead saw that he wore some sort of shapeless leather footwear he'd never seen. His leg was smaller, but for some reason that didn't bother him as much as the boots.

He stood slowly, carefully extricating his foot and purposely keeping his eyes aimed at the ground. It was then that he noticed how quiet it was. It wasn't the quiet he'd expect in an Old Mill field, or even down at the old fishing hole by the swamp. Cletus lived in a world of sound. There was traffic in the distance, the subtle hum of neon lights, the voices and laughter of thousands of people. He heard none of it. When he stepped forward again, the air seemed thicker. He felt the sensation of walking in deep water, his questions echoing about inside his head unanswered.

The bonfire had grown taller and hotter. The ring of people dancing about its edge was an indistinct blur. They didn't turn as he approached. He walked closer, circling around the fire and giving the dancers a wide berth. He searched their faces in the shadows. As they spun past, he caught glimpses of their features. Here and there he thought he saw features he recognized, but the images were fleeting, and they moved too quickly. And they were wrong.

Like the town.

Like the idea of a huge bonfire standing on the edge of Old Mill, and the streets with too few houses, some not even standing where he remembered houses standing. And there was something else, something he recognized, but could not place. Beyond the fire, on a small mound of earth, a pole had been planted in the ground. It wasn't just a pole, though, it was a carved totem, a twisted, forked pattern of sharp tips and winding branches. The trunk rose nearly seven feet into the air, and its extremities stretched out on either side like widespread arms.

Cletus stopped and stared at it. It reached out to him over the tops of the dancers. Their motion was slowing. He glanced at them and saw they were holding hands. Their eyes were closed, and they swayed. Some of them leaned back, letting the motion of the circle and the centrifugal force prevent them from falling away from the fire. Then he noticed the woman standing alone in the center, her back to the fire. The others hadn't noticed his arrival, but she stared right at him. Through him, maybe.

The dancers slowed again. The woman raised her arms and held them out to Cletus. He met her gaze, sweat suddenly running down his forehead and winding over his cheeks. Cletus tried to step back, to turn and head for the town, or back into the field, but his legs were rooted in place as surely as if he'd grown there, and then he stepped forward. He walked straight toward the fire, and by the time he reached the dancers, they'd stopped. Cletus didn't pause as he met that ring, and the parted for him. He had an idea they'd known he was there all along—that they'd expected him, though he couldn't understand how that could be true.

He stepped through, and he saw that he knew the woman. And he didn't know the woman. Her eyes were deep green, and her corn silk blond hair glistened in the firelight. It was tied back in an intricate braid. She wore a very short, very sheer smock, tied off at the waist. She seemed to be about sixteen, or seventeen. It was hard to tell because of her eyes. They were old eyes, filled with far too much to have been gathered in a short lifetime.

She took his hands, and Cletus felt a spark of energy leap between them. He tried again to pull back, but it felt as if he were someone else. His body ignored his struggles and attempts to turn and run. As he drew closer to the woman, he pulled her against him and felt the most powerful erection of his life. He gasped out loud and gripped the girl so tightly he felt his fingers dig into her flesh. She didn't pull away. Instead, she ground her hips into him. He nearly blacked out.

The dancers were moving again. He saw them out of the corners of his eyes, but his gaze was captured by the girl, the heat emanating from her flesh, the brazen press of her flesh. The dancers circled once, twice, and then parted again. They rolled off and away from the bonfire, which he suddenly felt, blazing hot against his back, and they formed a path leading toward the strange pole he'd seen earlier. From where he stood, he saw that the branches had been carved to resemble the horns of a huge deer.

The girl turned so that they were side by side, their hips pressed tightly together. Her arm slid around the small of his back and he felt her nails bite into his flesh. They stepped forward, entering a corridor of bodies. Before the pole he now saw that a wooden table of some sort had been placed. It was covered in blankets and pillows. He shook his head to clear it, but only succeeded in fuzzing the few details that had been clear.

His arm slid around the girl's body. Someone stepped from the crowd at his right, laughing brightly. He felt hands on his shoulders; fingers ran through his hair, and then he felt an awkward weight settle over him. He tried to pull away, but every time he moved, the girl pressed herself into him in some new way, or his hand slipped and pressed a new bit of her flesh, and he lost focus. He tried to glance up, to see what they'd placed on his head, but all he caught were tangled shadows. They made no sense, but he knew they were important. He knew he should understand. He turned to the girl, just as they reached the table. She turned to meet him and melted into his arms.

"What..."

She pressed her mouth to his, lips open wide and his words were swallowed in her kiss. She fell back over the low bench, into the blankets with her silky hair spread back over the pillows and her lips parted. Cletus loomed over her. Her ankles hooked behind his thighs and pulled him forward. When he bumped the table's edge, the weight on his head overbalanced and he tumbled forward. He felt a shock and tried again to look up. This time he was able to focus. The antlers stretched up from his head and butted up against the base of the huge pole. The girl beneath him squirmed, pressing up against him.

He felt the horns gripped and tugged gently, pulled back to allow him to settle over the girl whose robes had somehow fallen away beneath her. He caught himself on his hands, but lacked the strength—or the will—to push up and away. He sank lower, and she raised her head, brushing his cheek with her lips. She reached up and grabbed his belt, loosening it with a quick tug and yanking the snap of his jeans open. His erection pulsed painfully, and he gasped as she freed it. He met her gaze for a long moment, then she arched up again. He felt her engulf him, felt her teeth grip the lobe of his ear, and heard her whispering—her voice low, husky, and hungry.

"Your daddy knew the harvest, Cletus. Your granddaddy knew more. There has always been a harvest lord. There has always been sacrifice. It makes him strong. It fires your blood."

The voice shifted with every word. It dried up. It became

the sound of dust blowing over dry wood. The images faded much more slowly. The girl beneath him arched and groaned and Cletus responded, crying out, shaking his head and feeling the ponderous weight of the antlers affixed to his head tug him one way, and the back the other.

He gasped and closed his eyes. He climaxed so swiftly, and so powerfully, his thoughts flickered, died, and then flashed into a burst of light so bright that it burned. His head struck something solid, and he cursed. He pushed up and back and nearly toppled over backward. As he rose, his back struck the wall behind him and for the second time in as many moments, saw stars.

There was no sound. There was no firelight. He stood, leaning on the wall of the old shack, trying to clear his mind, and his sight. He turned, but the seat across the table was empty. Both bottles were gone. Cletus fell back into the chair. He felt a dampness in his pants he didn't want to think about. He remembered her eyes—her wrinkled, ageless skin. He looked down at the table.

In the center something had been scratched, carved quickly and crudely into the wood. He saw a rough rendition of the pole, and the antlers. He saw a church, also—identifiable by the steeple. Behind, and beneath it, there was another box. A room? It was beneath a tree, and a crude patch of flowers. Cletus stared, and his mind slipped back to Eternity. He closed his eyes and thought about the view out the back of Reverend Dozier's office.

He rose, wishing he didn't have that damp slick spot in the crotch of his jeans to think about all the way back to his trailer. He wished he could erase the image of that pole, and the heat of that fire. He wished he'd never looked into her eyes. He knew what he had to do next.

He stood shakily and staggered to his truck. Moments later he had it turned and gunned the motor, shooting down the bumpy road toward Highway 17 and Eternity.

Chapter Eight

Cletus drove back to his trailer in a daze. He was halfway to the highway before he remembered to turn on his head-lights. Trees loomed on either side of the road; again and again he flinched, nearly running into the ditch each time he over-reacted. He felt drained, as if he'd run ten miles, and his throat was parched and dry.

He managed to make the turn off to his trailer without an accident, and breathed a little easier. There were lights on, and he knew Jasper and the others were still there. He'd have to slip past them and change his pants—that might take some explaining—but he was glad he wouldn't be alone. He didn't know what he could tell them—didn't know if he could tell them anything—but he didn't want to be alone.

He pulled in beside Jasper's truck and stepped out, leaning heavily on his front fender until he got his bearings.

"Damn," he said.

The front door of the trailer opened and a shaft of light cut through the shadows. Jasper peered out, shading his eyes.

"Cletus? That you?" he said.

"Yeah, it's me," Cletus replied.

He stepped forward, climbed the steps to the trailer, and turned away from the light, shielding himself. He stepped around Jasper and headed straight across the room for the hallway leading to his bedroom and the bathroom beyond.

"Where you goin', Cletus?" Jasper called after him. "Jesus, what happened?"

"In a minute, Jaz," Cletus called over his shoulder. "I have to take a crap like you wouldn't believe, and my eyeballs are swimming. I'll be out in a minute."

There was no answer, but Cletus could tell from the shadow wavering just outside his bedroom door that Jasper was still there.

"What are you waitin' for Jasper?" he called out. "You thinking about coming in and holding it for me, or are you going to get me that beer?"

There was a grunt from the hall, the sound of something large crashing into the wall, and Cletus was finally alone. He grabbed another pair of jeans and some underwear and stumbled into the bathroom. He locked the door, turned on the shower, and stripped as quickly as he could manage in the small, cluttered room. Suddenly he couldn't stand the damp touch of his jeans, or the cling of his underwear. He felt limp and damp; his legs barely supported him. The only thing that kept his eyes open was the fear of the dreams that might come if he closed them. The fear that he might feel her again, pressing close to him and see the long, groping shadow of those carved horns stretching out draw him in—and down.

Cletus shook his head and stepped into the shower. The water was hot. Normally he'd turn down the temperature, but this time he welcomed the heat. He grabbed the soap and scrubbed. His arms were heavy, but he forced them into action, and before he knew it, he was grinding it into his chest, dragging it over his skin faster and faster. The water was too hot, and the coarse soap scraped and chaffed his skin, but he couldn't stop himself. The water poured down over him, and he leaned forward until he lost his balance, cracking his head into the side of the shower.

His blood roared, deafening him and he heard a loud pounding. What seemed like a long time later, he realized the pounding wasn't his heart. It was Jasper, and it sounded like he was ready to knock the door off its hinges. Cletus stood up, turned off the shower, and stared at the soap in his hand. His skin was red, raw in places. He ached over every inch of his body, but he was awake.

"Damn," he said again. Then, "Just a minute, Jasper, I'll be right out."

The pounding didn't stop immediately, but it slowed. "I'll be out in a minute," he growled. He knew it didn't sound sincere, but he didn't have any more energy to spare for it. He toweled dry quickly and gingerly, avoiding the worst of the raw areas from his bout with extreme showering, and pulled on the clean clothes. He turned the knob and opened the door slowly in case Jasper was still standing there, but the big man was seated on his bed, sipping a beer and watching the bathroom door.

"You want to tell me just what the hell that was all about?" Jasper asked. "You came crashing through here like you were on fire, locked yourself in the can and took a shower so long and hot, steam came out under the door and into the living room. Hell, Earl thought it was smoke—he was ready to call the fire department."

Feeling drained, but alert, Cletus tried a weak grin. "Let me get that beer," he said, "and I'll try to tell you. You're not going to believe it anyway, so there's no hurry."

"You find that old witch?" Jasper asked as they headed back down the hall.

Cletus nodded. "I did. Did you know the Harvest Festival was like a dried out locus shell?"

"Huh?"

Cletus stepped into the main room of his trailer, opened the fridge, grabbed a cold beer, and hit his chair hard. He didn't say a word until he'd popped the top and drained half the can.

When he looked up, he saw they were all staring at him. Earl's eyes were wide. He sipped his beer and stared like Cletus was a late-night movie. Jasper frowned and slumped back on the couch. Only Jasper's Pap watched calmly. In fact, Cletus was pretty damned sure the old bastard was smirking.

"I know where they have him," Cletus said at last. "I took her the whiskey, like you said, Pap, but she drugged me. I saw some crazy shit—and I'd be lying if I said I was okay, but I got what I went there for. At least, I think I did."

"What?" Earl asked. "She give you a vision?"

"You might say that," Cletus replied, taking another long swallow of beer. "Thing that matters is, she drew me a picture of that church out in Eternity. Remember I told you there was a sort of weird little garden out back by that tree? Seems there might be something there after all—an old root cellar, or something worse. I'm betting that guy who was abducted is down there, and I'm betting he won't be okay for long. The Harvest Festival is only a few days from now."

"What the hell does the festival have to do with anything?" Jasper asked. He belched, stared at the empty can in his hand, and lurched to his feet to get another.

"Toss me one," Cletus said. Then he continued.

"It isn't about funnel cake and bratwurst. At least, it wasn't always about that. That woman—Nettie—said she knew my dad. She said she knew my granpa too. What I saw—what she made me see, somehow—was old. I don't know how, but I swear she showed me Old Mill like it was a hundred years ago. Most of the houses weren't there, and there was a bonfire—a big one. It was outside town."

"You see that pole?" Pap cut in. The old man sipped his beer and met Cletus' gaze, but his hand shook.

Cletus fell silent and stared, then nodded. "I did. Damn thing looked like a telephone pole with antlers. I've never seen anything like it."

"Yes you have," Pap said softly. "You've seen it a hundred times, maybe more. You too, Jasper."

Cletus stared. Jasper looked like he was about to say something about his father's mental faculties, but before he could get a sound out, Pap went on.

"You've been down to the lodge, Cletus. How many times? Your daddy brought you there when you were no taller than a beer cooler. You telling me you never looked around that place? You never hid in the corners, or explored?"

"Sure I did," Cletus said, irritated at being interrupted. "So what?"

"You never hid up by the fireplace? Never looked up to the left?"

Cletus closed his eyes and tried to picture what Pap was talking about. He'd never joined the lodge—though his father had wanted him to. He'd been too busy, and it seemed like nothing more than a bunch of old guys convinced the border of Old Mill was the edge of the world. It was depressing, and he figured he'd save his time there for when he was pulling his pants up to the middle of his chest and farting in public.

The fireplace Pap was talking about was one of the most remarkable things about the lodge. It was huge, the mantle carved of stone with animals in relief below the ledge. The bricks were very old, and Cletus remembered they were scorched and black. He tried to remember the corners of the room to either side, and suddenly his face paled. He nearly dropped the beer Jasper handed him.

Pap nodded as he saw understanding dawning in Cletus' eyes.

"Yep," the old man said. "That's it. That damned pole is set into the corner of the building. They put it there to keep them from carrying it out to that field. They tried to come in and take it back, and our folks had to threaten to burn it—building and all. There's still some back toward the swamp who come down and stand outside the Lodge come Harvest. They stand across the street, and they stare. They blame us for what's happened to the cotton—the Mill closing, the crop being shipped overseas, the way the fields are drained to the point where even chemicals and topsoil and fertilizer can't bring it back. Sometimes, when I see their eyes…I wonder if they aren't right."

"You remember," Cletus said softly. "You know what I saw—what they were doing. That table—and the woman. Was it Nettie?"

"It hasn't always been her, not exactly," Pap said. He was staring at a point on the wall somewhere above Cletus as if he saw through to some other place, or time. "There were always two—an old woman, and a young girl. The girl was the harvest queen."

Pap grew silent then, and they all waited while he gathered his thoughts. It was obvious that some doorway, or window, into his past had been pried open. Cletus handed the old man another beer, and sat back.

"Your pa was supposed to be a harvest lord, Cletus. That was the year they locked away that damnable pole. Your grandpa was Harvest Lord before him, and he was never the same after. I was just a boy, you know...my memory is good, but that was a very long time ago.

"I remember the old woman, and I'd swear they called her Nettie, but I remember the girl too. She was a looker—thin and dressed in a sheer, cotton dress. In those times women didn't dress that way—not ever—but come harvest, the blinders went on and nobody noticed. Nobody said a thing."

"What was the Harvest Lord?" Cletus asked. He was afraid he already knew the answer, but he had to ask.

"You said you saw that table—that bed," Pap said softly. "Your grandpa Merle, he walked down that line, and that girl went with him. He didn't have the luxury you did of waking up. Can't say I remember how it ended—not exactly—but I remember this. It wasn't a week later I saw that girl, and she was carryin' a child. Not showing a little, like you'd think might be possible, but ready to pop. The old woman—I never saw her again. The girl grew up and when we took that damned pole, she moved out of town. Out off 17. She had a daughter."

"Nettie," Cletus whispered.

Pap nodded. "I think so. Leastways I can't figure any other way it could be. That shack where you were sitting on the porch? That's where they moved. For a long time, no one heard anything from them. Sometimes the women would go there, if they were sickly, or if there was something they needed. Sometimes even the older men would slip off to that cabin when the sun was down, bottles of whiskey in hand and things on their minds best left to the imagination—or forgotten altogether. She never came back to the Harvest Festival when they started holding it again. I never went either. It seemed empty somehow." Pap took another swig of beer and shook his head. Then he actually chuckled.

"What's so damned funny?" Jasper asked. He looked confused, and a little too drunk to piece together all he'd just heard from his best friend and his father.

"Just thinking," Pap said. "What Cletus said—what Nettie said—about a locust skin. It's exactly right."

"Locusts swarm the fields and eat everything in sight," Cletus cut in. "They raze the crops, leave people hungry, and if you walk out into them at the wrong time, they'll kill you."

Pap nodded slowly. "I know. I think maybe I'll get on over to the lodge and make sure things are locked up and secure. I haven't seen anyone standing down there yet this year, but damned if I don't get the idea they might. Maybe I'll take me some lighter fluid and matches, while I'm thinking about it—just in case."

"That might not be a bad idea," Cletus said. "As a backup. We've got us some work to do. Jasper, we have to get some things together. Earl? I'm going to ask you to do me a big favor. I want you to hightail it over to the Sheriff's office and get Bob."

They all rose, and Earl stared dubiously at the beer can in his hand. Cletus followed the big man's gaze and frowned.

"Ditch that," he said. "Get on the phone, call Bob, and tell him to get his ass over here. Tell him Cletus says he has a date with Eternity, and he'd better not be late."

"What about the Troopers," Jasper cut in. "Shouldn't we call them off their taxidermist hunt?"

"How you going to explain it to them, Jasper? You going to tell them it can't be a taxidermist because your ol' buddy Cletus, the fella out by the swamp who's a preacher, a reporter, a common law lawyer and likes rasslin' had a drunken vision on the swamp witch's porch, and he figures they should give up what they're thinking and head out to Eternity to raid the garden behind the church instead?"

Jasper stared at him, then guzzled the last of his beer. "You ain't gotta be a smartass, Cletus. And while you're at it, maybe you ought to think about the fact that you just described exactly what we're about to do."

"Yeah, Jaz," Cletus grinned, "but we're just a bunch of rednecked jackasses, so who will be surprised?"

He turned toward the door, and Earl headed for the phone, and Pap was already on his way out the door. Jasper tossed his empty at the trash can, missed, belched, and followed Cletus out into the night.

Chapter Nine

By the time Cletus and Jasper returned to the trailer, Bob's Land Rover was parked outside. Jasper's truck was still missing, and Cletus hoped that Pap was going to be okay. In the back of Cletus' truck several bundles were tucked up near the cab and covered with a blue tarp. The two of them climbed out and headed into the trailer.

They found Bob and Earl in front of the TV. On the screen, colorful cars roared in endless circles. Both men looked up—Bob with a frown, and Earl looking like he was going on his first Boy Scout hike.

"This better be good, Cletus," Bob said. "I'm on tonight—they're screaming for me to be out on 17 covering an accident, and I told them I was following something more important. Please tell me I'm following something more important."

Cletus started to answer, but Bob turned and nodded at Earl.

"Earl here tells me we're either going out to hunt aliens, or chasing off to Eternity after a swamp witch. I think when this is all over and done we should have us a talk about recruiting."

"Earl is the only witness to the abduction," Cletus said. "We may owe it to his family, his future wife and children, and the entire state of North Carolina to make sure he understands, before this is over, that there were no aliens in pickup trucks at the Gin the other night."

Bob shook his head and held his tongue.

Cletus quickly filled him in on his evening, including only the pertinent facts. He saw no reason to linger on the bonfire, or the girl in his dream. He didn't think it was the appropriate time to toss time-traveling visions into the mix if he wanted Bob's help.

"You know they're out there, Bob," Cletus said at last. "There was a hell of a lot Dozier didn't tell us when we were at that church, and I told you what I saw out back."

"I remember," Bob said. "You saw a tree and an oddly placed flower bed. The man was standing beside it."

"There's a cellar," Cletus said. "That's what Nettie was telling us, and I've got a feeling that if we don't get out there and open it up, we're going to have another floating deer man on the edge of the swamp, or worse. Maybe this time he won't die."

Bob stared at Cletus, and his eyes went flat.

"That ain't possible, Cletus, and I won't listen to it. You want me to believe there's a couple of albino geniuses carving a sailor up out in the swamp, I'm up for that. Maybe there is, maybe there isn't. You want me to believe some old witch traded you valuable information for a bottle of whiskey—that's good investigating, though I doubt the county would authorize me the whiskey. You tell me some guy with a deer's head is going to romp through the swamp, and that's where it ends. I'll pack up, head back to the office, and watch the rest of the race. We straight?"

Cletus stared at him for a moment longer, and then nodded. "We are. And if we do see something that shouldn't be moving, we'll make sure it stops."

Bob didn't answer, but Cletus knew they were on the same channel.

"Where you keep the shells?" Jasper called out from across the trailer.

Everyone in the room spun and stared. Jasper had a ten gauge shotgun under his arm, the barrels pointed slightly up at an angle over their heads. Cletus and Bob backed in opposite directions, cursing.

"Put that damned thing down, Jasper," Cletus growled. He stumbled across the room, but Jasper pulled the gun back just before he could get his hands on it.

"No way, Cletus," he said. "If we're going out to that church, I'm not going unarmed. I know you're packing, and Bob there has a gun rack full outside, and one on his belt. What was your plan—me and Earl as bait while you shot from behind the trees?"

Cletus stepped back. Jasper was right, and he knew it. None of them knew how dangerous this night might get. He turned to Earl.

"You know how to work a .45?" he asked. "I've got an old Navy issue in the dresser beside my bead."

"I can shoot," Earl said. He puffed up his chest and grinned like a schoolboy.

Bob turned away, shook his head again, and made an issue of looking through the papers on Cletus' desk. Cletus stepped out of the room and down the hall in back, returning with the pistol and handing it to Earl butt first.

"It's loaded," he said. "Safety is on. Don't take it off until we are OUT of the truck."

"Don't shoot anyone unless we're about to die," Bob growled at all of them. "Seriously, Cletus, I can see a hundred ways this can go bad, and not a one that makes it right. I can't deputize any of you without calling in and making reports and getting backup that they won't authorize in the first place, but that doesn't change the fact that I'm responsible for this half-ring circus. I don't want any of you getting hurt. We're going in, getting some answers out of Reverend Dozier, or whoever we find out there, and taking a look around that flower bed. If we find nothing, we're out of there, and that's the end of it."

"What if them aliens come after us?" Earl asked.

Bob turned to the door in disgust and pushed through, heading into the night. The door swung shut behind him with a clatter.

Cletus took a deep breath, patted Earl on the back, and followed Bob.

"Lock the door behind us, Jasper," he called. "No telling when we'll be back, and I don't need anyone digging through my stuff."

Jasper snorted.

"They'd have to bring a big shovel to find anything worth takin'" he said.

Cletus ignored him, and Jasper locked the door. Once outside, Bob was all business. He took Earl in the Land Rover, and Jasper climbed in beside Cletus. Cletus backed up so the two vehicles were side by side, and they rolled down their windows.

"You follow us in," Bob said. "I've got better traction, and if they see us coming, I want them to see an official vehicle."

Cletus nodded. Bob turned to Earl, grabbed his shirt and dragged him close.

"You say another goddamn word about aliens, and I'll kick your ass out on the road to walk home from the swamp. We clear?"

Earl gulped, but had the sense to nod. He started to say something, then bit it off. Cletus smiled.

Bob backed up quickly, spun and started down Cletus' drive toward the road and the highway beyond. Cletus took a quick half-circle and followed. The moon was full and high in the sky, illuminating the fields around them like a pale sun.

Jasper leaned down, grabbed something off the floor, then sat back up. Cletus glanced over just in time to watch the pop top on a Budweiser snap and fizz. He started to say something, and then held out his hand. Jasper grinned, handed over the beer and reached for another.

"Ooh fuckin' Rah," Cletus said, lifting his can just high enough it didn't show over the windshield in salute.

They drove in silence, and Cletus was eerily reminded of his earlier trip with Bob. Once they'd turned off of the main roads everything changed. It was like driving into the past, and it was harder and harder to remember even the semi-civilization that was his trailer in the face of the rich scent of rotted vegetation, the rolling hills and trees, and the hypnotic rise and fall of headlights as the two vehicles rumbled down the poorly maintained road.

When they neared the last corner that turned into the main road into Eternity, it was immediately obvious that things had changed. The glow of lights hung like a shimmering halo over the trees. As dead and empty as the town had seemed, it was now alive. It should have seemed more cheerful—at least that's what Cletus told himself—but it was impossible to push aside the sensation of standing too close to a buzzing beehive. The last thing he wanted to do was poke that place with a sharp stick.

Bob slowed before he reached the corner, and Cletus pulled

in behind him. He got out and walked up toward the Land Rover. He only noticed he was still carrying the beer can just in time to toss it into the trees beside the road as he stepped up beside Bob's window. Bob stared pointedly at the point where the can had flashed out of sight, shook his head, and let it go.

"There's something going on up there, Cletus,"

"I know," Cletus said. "I can see the glow from the lights. You think they're just having a late night service?"

"I'm not sure I'd want to be there, even if that's the case," Bob answered. "I just can't help thinking that if there's something twisted going on in or around that church, all of them are in on it. How would he hide it from them? We don't have enough manpower to take on the whole congregation."

Cletus glanced across Bob to where Earl sat.

'I'm not sure we have enough manpower to take on the empty church. What you want to do, Bob?"

The answer was cut off by the roar of an engine, closely followed by several more. Cletus stared at Bob, then turned and ran for his truck. Bob pulled ahead, and just as Cletus swung in behind the wheel again, he saw the Land Rover turn right, instead of left. He vaguely recalled that there was a rough trail leading off the main road, and he hoped that Bob had found it and wasn't going four-wheeling and leaving Cletus to follow on two.

Moments later he was bouncing down a narrow, single lane pair of ruts no one could charitably call a road, and clinging to the wheel grimly to keep the truck from bouncing off into the trees. Then Bob's lights went out, and Cletus killed his engine. He turned just enough to see a line of headlights approaching from the rear. He held his breath until the first swung to the right and disappeared down the road where he'd just been parked.

"Holy shit, Cletus," Jasper said, finding his voice. "What the hell is goin' on?"

"Damned if I know," Cletus muttered. He heard the snap of another beer opening and closed his eyes, waiting for the wash of headlights across his eyelids to stop and tell him everyone who was leaving the church had gone.

"Where are they going, Cletus," Jasper asked.

Cletus was about to snap at his friend, when something clicked in his mind.

"Damn it," he said. He stepped out of his truck and ran ahead to where Bob had pulled up against the trees.

"They're headed to Old Mill," he said. "Bob, I think they're after that damned horned pole at the lodge. Can you raise dispatch on your radio?"

Bob looked unconvinced, but he took Cletus seriously enough to believe there was danger. He grabbed the microphone and keyed it.

"Four-one to base. Come in base."

There was a squawk, and a quick burst of static, then silence.

"Damn it," Bob said. He tried again, but there was no answer.

"Hey," Earl said.

"Not now, Earl," Cletus snapped. "We have a serious problem here. You think if we drove back down the road a ways we could get through?" he asked Bob, who was fiddling with dials on the radio.

"Hey!" Earl said, raising his voice.

This time Bob spun on him, but before he could say a word, Earl thrust something into his face, and he bit his lip. Earl was holding a small cell phone, the type you buy at the 7-11 and pay for ahead of time. The lights were lit on the small dial, and even from where he stood, Cletus could see there were two signal bars.

"Use this," Earl said.

Bob stared as Cletus leaned over, snatched the phone from Earl, and started to dial. The glowing dial of his radio glimmered up at him, and he frowned.

"Just how in hell," he said.

Cletus held up his hand.

"Jim?" he asked. There was a short silence, and then Cletus cut off whatever it was that Jim had to say. "I don't have time for that now, Jim. I know I owe you, and I'll pay, but you've got to listen. This is important—not like Smackdown is on and we're out of beer important, but the real deal. You kapish?"

Another short silence, and Cletus nodded.

"Good. Get as many guys as you can and get over to the Lodge in Old Mill. Jasper's Pap is there, and I think he's in trouble. There's a whole convoy of the friends of Jesus of Eternity on their way in there, and I think they intend to burn the place down. See if you boys can't stop them. You can tell everyone these are the bastards that have the troopers running around hassling anyone who ever stuffed a deer, if that helps.

"No, I haven't been drinking. You going to do this, or do you want to talk to Bob. Yes....Sheriff Bob. He's right here with me. No...I'm not telling him that." This time Cletus did grin. "Tell you what, if we make it back to town in one piece, I'll let you tell him yourself."

Cletus disconnected the line and tossed the phone back to Earl.

"No wonder we can't get the drug dealers off the streets," Bob muttered. "They have all the high-tech equipment."

"I ain't no..." Earl started to protest. Bob held up a hand to silence him.

"Forget it," he said. "Let's get this over with before they come back."

Cletus returned to his truck and started the engine. It took a bit longer to back out onto the main road, but eventually he managed it. He backed far enough down the road that Bob could get out and followed the Land Rover on around the corner into Eternity.

There were lights on in the church, but not as many as there had been before. The door was closed, and there was a single vehicle in the parking lot. It was a black pickup truck. Bob pulled in beside it, and Cletus pulled in beside Bob.

Earl was out of the Land Rover before it came to a full stop, and as Cletus stepped out onto the parking lot he heard the big man speaking excitedly, and Bob trying to calm him down.

"That's it!" Earl whispered so loudly he might as well have shouted. "That's the truck they took him in. That's the truck that had the alie...albinos."

Cletus stared at it for a moment, and Jasper stepped up behind him.

"I think he's right, Cletus. I only saw it for a minute, but it was up pretty damned close, you know?"

Cletus nodded and turned to Bob, who already had the flap over his gun unsnapped.

"Cletus, you and me are going around back to check out that flowerbed. Jasper, you take Earl here, and get the good reverend's attention. Tell him you got drunk and turned the wrong way. You've had enough beer that he'll believe you."

"What if he don't?" Earl asked. "I ain't had as much to drink as Jasper."

"Ask him about the aliens," Cletus suggested, grinning. "Tell him you saw a saucer drop down out in the swamp near here, and you drove out to see if you could find it."

"Whatever you do," Bob said, "Don't let him come out back. Not until you see us. We'll either know what the hell is going on, or we'll know nothing is going on that's any of our business."

Jasper didn't look convinced. Cletus slapped him on the back.

"It's been long enough since you went to church, Jaz," he said.

"I come to your trailer all the time," Jasper said pointedly. "You ARE ordained."

Bob snorted, turned, and started around the side of the church. Cletus glanced a last time at the black pickup truck, then followed. Jasper and Earl crunched up the gravel walk toward the church. The silence surrounding them was as deep as a tar pit and twice as sticky.

Chapter Ten

Bob rounded the corner of the church with his gun drawn, and Cletus moved up close behind him. He wished there had still been some people milling about, or that there was light or sound from somewhere other than the church. It was like they'd stepped through the screen into some weird *Twilight Zone* adventure. There were a couple of lights on poles that lit the parking lot, and they hummed so loudly Cletus thought he could hear the electricity running through the wires. The sensation of being watched was so strong he couldn't help jerking his head around and looking over his shoulder every few seconds. There was nothing to see.

Bob seemed jumpy as well, but he was trained to this sort of work, and he moved steadily forward. He had his gun trained forward into the shadows, and he remained focused, trusting Cletus to watch his back. They reached the back corner of the building without incident, and then Bob did look back. He motioned Cletus forward so he could whisper.

"I'm going to cross over to that tree a quick as I can. You follow, but not 'til I'm over there, and we're sure no one sets off an alarm. If they see me, don't show yourself until you have to. We may need to get the jump on them, and I don't want to trust that to Jasper and Earl."

Before Cletus could answer, Bob stepped away from the building and started across the rear lawn of the church. He stayed in a crouch, but moved quickly and quietly. Cletus tensed, but there was no outcry. There was no flash of light to indicate doors or windows opening. There was no change in the deep quiet, or the hum of the lights overhead.

Bob reached the tree, disappeared for a second into its shadow, and then waved for Cletus to join him. With a last glance over his shoulder, that's exactly what he did. He tried to emulate Bob's crouching run, but his legs complained, and with a shrug he stood up straight and ran. Moments later Bob pulled him down into the shadows, and the two of them hunkered down in silence.

From where they squatted, they could see the rear window and door of the church. There was a light on in Reverend Dozier's office, but for the moment no silhouettes moved beyond it. Cletus hoped that meant Jasper and Earl had the good Reverend's attention in the church proper. All alternatives were bad.

"Keep an eye on the door," Bob hissed.

Cletus nodded, and Bob turned, using his free hand to root around in the leaves and flowers. There was plenty of light in the yard, but there under the tree they were in shadow, and most of the ground looked the same. Cletus wanted to be looking too. Squatting in the dark was last on his current list of favorite things, but he knew Bob was right. They couldn't afford not to keep a careful watch on the church. If Dozier came up behind them and caught them rooting around, there was no telling what he might do—or who he might have available to call for backup.

Bob let out a quick grunt of surprise, and Cletus heard him scrabbling for footing.

"Damn," Bob said.

Cletus turned. Bob was seated in the dirt, staring at the metal handle in his hand, and the wooden door that had risen from the leaves and brush when he pulled. He held onto it and scrambled back to his feet. There was a dim glow of light beyond the door, somewhere beneath them. They waited—but there was no sound. Whoever or whatever was down there had apparently not heard them.

Cletus glanced back at the church. The window still glowed like a big, empty eye, glaring out at them. No sigh of Dozier, or anyone else.

"You ready for this?" Bob asked.

"Nope," Cletus replied.

Bob grinned, pulled the door the rest of the way open and lowered it to the ground. He worked his way slowly around it and took a step down. Cletus took a deep breath, and followed. By the time he reached the steps, Bob was out of sight except for a dark silhouette moving down into a very dimly lit interior. Cletus wondered briefly if he should stop and pull the door closed behind them, but decided against it. They might need to get back out of there quickly, and the last thing he needed was to run head-first into a wooden door.

The second he started down the stairs, the stench hit him, and he nearly retched. It was thick, and viscous. Antiseptic, chemical vapors mixed with something more familiar. He couldn't trace the memory that itched at his brain, but he knew that scent, and it repelled him. Bob was already out of sight, and he knew he had to keep going, but every instinct he had told him it was a bad idea.

"Story of my life," he muttered. He took the remaining steps more quickly, pulling his .45 as he went. He hadn't heard Bob cry out, but that didn't mean there wasn't trouble. No sense walking into it without protection, for what it was worth. His eyes watered from the acrid fumes, and he wondered if the air below was even breathable, but it had been his idea to come here and investigate, and he couldn't back out now that Bob was in the middle of it, whatever "it" was.

As he reached the bottom step, he saw that a doorway opened on the right. The light beyond that corner was brighter. Whoever had designed the stairs and the cellar had clearly taken into account blocking the light from below from visibility above. Such forethought was a bad sign. Cletus rounded the corner, and stopped dead in his tracks. Directly ahead of him, Bob was stopped as well, his gun arm slack at his side.

Cletus barely noticed. He stared past Bob at a stainless steel table against the far wall of the cellar.

It was like a bad "B" movie nightmare. The surface of the table, which was about four foot square, was nearly covered by a large, round, glass tank. The tank was made of clear glass, or Plexiglas, and it was filled nearly to the brim with some sort of greenish fluid. Tubes and wires snaked over the top and into the liquid, which bubbled and frothed. Cletus hardly noticed.

In the center of the tank, staring at him with wild eyes rolled nearly to whites in its head, the head of a white-tail buck stared sightlessly back at him. There was no way the thing could be alive, but he saw its ears twitch. The nostrils flared, and Cletus was sure he saw movement under its skin, as if something were crawling up and down its throat.

"Jesus H. Freaking Christ," Bob whispered.

Cletus wanted to respond, but he couldn't find a single phrase in all his colorful cursing lexicon to cover it. Something splashed in the tank, and he felt as if his heart had exploded and all the blood, ice cold, had tried to seep out through his skin. It just wasn't possible—not that it existed, or that he could possibly wrap his mind around it. He saw the thing's shadow on the wall behind it, dark antlers stretching up toward the ceiling and out of sight.

"Amazing, isn't he?"

The voice was very close. It had no volume, and yet it snapped through the silent horror in the room like a whip. Cletus spun, but it was too late. As he turned, he heard the hiss of something being sprayed. He tasted something sickly sweet and his eyelids were instantly heavy. He tried to turn and lift his gun hand, but it was too heavy. He spun, and he couldn't stop the momentum. It carried him in a staggering circle.

Someone stood beside him, and he reached out, but the small, very pale man stepped back almost casually. Cletus rolled past him and fell. Behind him he heard Bob grunt, and knew it was too late for his friend, as well. The man who'd sprayed him with—what? He was one of the twins. There were two. The room spun and Cletus tried, and failed, to focus his eyes. Before he went out completely, he heard a heavy thud, and he knew Bob was down too.

When he came to, the first thing Cletus noticed was the smell. He couldn't place it, and he shook his head slowly, which was a mistake. He had a pounding headache that threatened to drop him back into darkness, or make him puke. He tried to move and found he was seated in a straight backed chair. His hands were bound behind him—it felt like duct tape. He closed his eyes, counted to ten, and opened them again. This time the room came to life, and he nearly tipped the chair over backward in shock and disgust, pushing back with both legs. Someone stood behind him, and they easily prevented him from moving.

Bob was tied in a chair beside him, already awake. The sheriff's eyes were glued to the table across the room and the strange tank. A small man stood beside him, young, and pale, white-blond hair unkempt and small, pink eyes blinking slowly. He, too, watched the tank, and Cletus followed their gaze. After a moment, he realized the guy was talking.

"He truly is magnificent, isn't he? Nothing like this has ever been attempted before."

"We attempted it, of course," a second voice chimed in from behind Cletus and to the left. "We attempted it just last week, with some success."

"But never before, brother, never before," the first man said, nodding and smiling, as if they were discussing a chess move over cocktails.

In the tank, the severed deer's head was showing more animation than it had when Cletus first saw it. He didn't know if all the lights and commotion had disturbed it, or if whatever they were doing to it in that tank had just progressed further, but the thing glared at them. The muscles of its neck rippled, and it lowered its antlers slightly, as if readying to charge. This motion was arrested by what appeared to be a network of bungee cords attaching it to the wall.

"Now now," the voice behind Cletus said softly. "Calm down. We mustn't damage ourself before the procedure is complete. Oh now, too much to do—too many people waiting on you."

"The Reverend is waiting," the first man added. "He is anxious to meet you, and the witch."

"She's not a witch," the second voice cut in. "Not exactly. There is an aspect of old world religious about her, but she is clearly attuned with the earth—the swamp to be exact."

"Yes, yes, but…"

That was all Cletus could take. He cleared his throat and put on the angriest scowl he could muster through the pounding in his head. His lips felt like they'd been glued together, and his words were garbled.

"I don't know who the hell you two are," he said, "or what that thing over there is supposed to be—though I have a pretty good idea on that. You boys made a mistake here, though. You've assaulted and abducted a man of the law."

"We didn't make a mistake," the first man said.

"Oh, no, that would be unlikely," the second cut in.

"Statistically," the first said, "we are correct about ninety-nine point two percent of the time. There are aspects of our training we are still fleshing out, but to be outright incorrect is..."

Bob was paying little or no attention to any of it. His gaze was glued to the tank, and his mouth hung open in a way Cletus didn't care for. It reminded him too much of the way Bob had stood over the body back at the swamp. Cletus didn't know how they were going to get out of this one, but he knew he had to get Bob back, and quickly.

"Yeah, just for the hell of it, why don't you boys tell us what you've made for the science fair?"

The voice behind Cletus belonged to another short, pale young man, so identical to the first that when he stepped around into view, it was like they were images facing one another in a mirror. Coupled with the way they finished each other's sentences, and the fact he could now see they moved like they were ganged together with gears and levers, the whole scene dropped fast towards *The Twilight Zone* without a parachute.

"He's our lifework," the first said.

"Actually, he really *is* our life, isn't he?" the second replied.

"You boys have names?" Cletus growled? "And while you're at it, you think you could finish one sentence at a time— or maybe tag each other when you change back and forth?"

Both brothers turned and stared at him. They didn't look angry. He could almost hear gears whirring as they processed what he'd said and tried to apply it to the situation through their own logic. Finally, the first brother said.

"I'm Weston," he said.

"I'm David," his brother chimed in. They walked toward Cletus, crossing as they passed around Bob's chair, and Cletus felt a moment of vertigo. He couldn't tell which was which. As they came to a stop directly in front of him, leaned in and peered at him as if he were in a giant Petri dish of his own, he decided it didn't matter. Until he figured out a better plan, he needed to keep them talking.

"Your buddy over the have a name too?" he asked.

They stopped, momentarily confused. Then Weston smiled—at least he thought it was Weston.

"It's an interesting question," he answered. "He has no name, but then, he isn't whole yet."

"The other has a name, I believe," David said helpfully. "Perhaps there will be enough left of him to remember?"

"Familial memory in the genetic code?" Weston asked.

"Residual synapses from the electro-chemical system they call a soul?" David pondered.

"Maybe one of you could tell me why that head isn't dead," Cletus said, trying to keep their attention.

Weston's head swiveled back and he smiled at Cletus.

"Of course we can tell you. We are responsible."

"A foolishly worded question," David agreed. "However, it is possible it's based on a genuine curiosity about our work."

Cletus nodded, not trusting his mouth in the area of self-preservation.

"It's simple, really," Weston said.

"Elementary," David added.

"The microbes we created, tiny nano-doctors, really, are reconfiguring his—its—molecular structure. It's like a computer."

"You can reprogram a computer to use a new operating system," David said.

"You can interface with the old hardware, as well," Weston continued.

"You're turning it into something else?" Bob blurted.

Cletus glanced over and saw that Bob's face, while pale and beaded with sweat, was animated again. For what it was worth, Bob was back in the game.

"More precisely," David answered. "We already have changed it into something else. It could exist as it is for a very long time, feeding off the fluids we provide and unable to release itself from the tank."

"Not as elegant as the whole," Weston added.

"Incomplete," David agreed. "We would never leave a work in such a state, but it is already remarkable."

"Unique," Weston suggested.

"Twisted," Bob muttered.

Both twins grinned at this, and Cletus wondered just what they really thought about the—thing—that they'd created. He wondered if they had a concept of God, other than an endless, two-voiced, single-minded conversation about cosmic entities. In the back of his mind, Cletus heard a muffled sound behind him.

Not sure if that sound was help, or just the Reverend coming to check up on his handiwork, he had to think quickly.

"How does it attach?" he blurted. "To the man? How do you make that—thing—bond with the body? Aren't transplants tricky, even with two humans?"

"Much better!" Weston beamed. If he'd heard the sound, he did not let on, and his face had taken on more emotion than Cletus had seen since they'd stepped from the shadows.

"Excellent," David agreed. "That is the point, isn't it?"

"What point?" Bob asked. He didn't seem to have heard the sound either, and Cletus started to wonder if it had all been in his mind, but he kept on.

"The subject must be fresh," Weston said.

"Not like the head," David agreed. "There must be as little disruption as possible in the central nervous system, so the microbes can assimilate the entirety of the logic involved."

"Very complex," Weston explained. "The human mind and body are much more difficult to control than, say, a portable computer. You can't reboot."

"No good backup system," David pointed out. "You get one shot."

Before Cletus could respond, there was a slamming sound from above. Muffled curses filled the air, and a huge clatter rose from the stairs. The two brothers turned, not moving from where they'd been standing. Weston blinked. David raised an eyebrow and frowned.

Jasper crashed into the wall at the base of the stairs, hit the wall hard, and rolled into the room, sprawled across the floor. He reached feebly for the rifle he'd held, but it was just out of his reach, and Weston was already moving toward it. He would have gotten the weapon from Jasper easily, if, at that moment, Earl hadn't roared around the corner, the shotgun at chest level, screaming like a banshee.

"Git 'er Done!"

David stepped back. Earl saw the deer's head, snout lifted to the air and eyes rolling. He stopped, just for a second. His jaw dropped, and then—without hesitation, he raised the gun and pulled the trigger.

The report of the shotgun in that tiny chamber was deafening. Cletus felt the buckshot whip past his ear and ruffle his hair, and he saw the deer's head explode in a spray of green fluid, fur, and flesh. Earl followed the shot into the room, bringing the butt of the gun against David's head in a solid crack of sound that toppled the man. He leveled the gun at Weston, who simply backed against the wall and stared.

Jasper rose slowly, rubbing his shoulder.

"Get us out of here," Cletus growled. "Jesus, Earl, you got that microbe crap all over everything."

"Technically," Weston commented, as if watching the entire thing from a balcony seat, "there is no crap. Excrement would not occur until the bodies were joined..."

Earl turned and cracked Weston hard in the head, shutting him up.

As Jasper untied Cletus, Earl stepped up and did the same for Bob.

"You find the guy?" Earl asked.

"No," Cletus said, "but there's a back room. He's probably in there."

"Cletus, you check it out," Bob said, standing and rubbing his wrists. "Take Earl with you. Jasper and I will secure these boys. Where's the reverend?"

"Tied up in his office," Jasper said. "Earl shot him in the foot."

Bob blinked. He started to say something, and the color returned very suddenly to his face, but then he held up a hand. "I don't even want to know," he said. "Let's get them out of here and into the Land Rover. We'll see what we can do about the good Reverend's foot on the way."

Cletus didn't wait to watch the brothers exit from their lab. He had bits and pieces of greenish deer meat and droplets of green chemical all over him, and he was nearly certain he felt his skin crawling. He needed to get this over with and get out of that pit—into some light and near to some water. Hell, he thought he might dive head first into the swamp if he needed to kill the double-D Goddamned MICROBES before they infected his system.

He pushed open the curtain leading deeper into the cellar, and Earl followed. There was a dim light in the next room, and almost immediately he made out a prone figure, bound, gagged, and lying on a hard cot in the corner. From where he stood, he saw the glint of the man's eyes, and knew they weren't too late. He rushed to the cot, knelt down, and quickly began unbinding the man's hands. Next he pulled off the tape they'd used to gag him, garnering a sharp gasp of pain as the sticky binding tore at the man's mustache and skin.

"Thank God." Cletus helped the man to his feet, and Earl turned, watching the doorway behind him as if he still thought the deer in the next room might re-assemble and come in after them.

"Let's get you out of here, friend," Cletus said, helping the man to his feet. He was stiff from lying in one position for too long, and Cletus figured the guy must have to piss like a racehorse, but they needed to get into the fresh air. They hurried through the outer lab and up the stairs. Above them, the moon was full and bright, and they could see the lights on in the Reverend's office.

"Let's get in there," Cletus said. "I've got to get this crap off of me, and we have to figure out what to do. The rest of the Good Reverend's folks aren't going to take this too well, and I don't want to be here when they return."

They entered the back of the church, and Cletus spared Reverend Dozier only a quick glance. He saw the man was bound to his own office chair, and that his face was pale and awash in pain. His shoe has been removed, and Cletus saw that Bob had applied bandages as best he could. The Reverend's prisoner, whose name they still hadn't even asked, dropped heavily into a chair across the desk from Dozier, who began looking, if anything, even more uncomfortable.

Jasper looked up as Cletus made a beeline for the bathroom. "You think Pap is okay, Cletus?" Jasper asked. "They've been gone a long time."

"We'll go after them, Jasper," Cletus said. "This isn't finished by far."

"You got that right," Bob piped in. He stepped out of the main room of the church and back into the hall outside the office. "I still can't get anyone on the radio, but I think we'd better high-tail it back to Old Mill and see what's going on. I can't get the image of that old carved tree out of my head, now that you put it there, Cletus. I don't know how, but I know that's what they're after, and something tells me that shooting that goddamned deer-in-a-dish down there was only the tip of the iceberg."

"Let's do it, then," Cletus said. "I've about had it with aliens and great horned gods, and if I don't get a shower soon I'm likely to end up as crazy as these three."

"You okay?" Bob asked, turning to the groggy, pale man they'd rescued.

"I don't really know," he said. "I'm Don, by the way. Don Watson. I think I owe you guys my life."

"You're welcome," Cletus said, "but we don't have time for this right now. You think you can walk?"

Don nodded. "I think so."

"Good," Bob cut in. "We'll call ahead for an ambulance and send the lot of you in to be looked at. Then we've got us one more stop to make before this is all over. Let's get going."

Earl and Jasper got Weston and David to their feet, groggy, wrists bound, but able to walk. Bob and Cletus supported

Reverend Dozier on their shoulders and helped him limp out through the church to the trucks beyond. Don followed a bit more slowly. He was weak, but he was recovering quickly.

"Those men shot me!" Dozier whined. "They broke into my church and shot me in the foot."

"You can tell it to the judge," Bob muttered. "My bet is he'll ask them why they didn't aim for your head."

They tucked their three prisoners into the back of the Land Rover and let Don crawl in between Jasper and Earl, then left the parking lot in a shower of gravel, turning down the swamp road toward Old Mill and driving as fast as the bumpy road and darkness would allow.

Chapter Eleven

The drive back to Old Mill was fast, and quiet. Cletus kept glancing over his shoulder to make sure the three in the back were still restrained, and quiet, but there was no trouble. Even Reverend Dozier had given up on trying to harangue them into setting him free. Bob had told the man if he didn't shut up he'd get shot in his other foot, and that had done the trick.

As they neared Highway 17, Bob keyed up his radio and called ahead.

"Four-one to base, four-one to base. You there Colleen?"

The radio crackled, then Colleen's voice filled the Land Rover's cab.

"Read you fivers, four-one, copy?"

Bob took a deep breath, then replied.

"Listen closely, Colleen, I don't have much time. Get me an ambulance. Send it to the Lodge in Old Mill, and do it quick. I have the guy who was taken from the parking lot at The Cotton Gin—his name is Don Watson, and he is okay. I also have the men responsible—three prisoners. All of them will need to be looked at. I also need someone to keep the three in custody and make sure they stay put."

"Where have you been, Bob?" Colleen answered.

"Later Colleen. Later I'll fill you in on everything. Get Randy into a squad car and get him over to Old Mill. And get me that ambulance."

There was further sputtering on the other end of the line, but Bob put the microphone back in its cradle and drove on.

"Where are we going?" Dozier asked. "You aren't taking me to the hospital?"

"You'll get to the hospital," Bob growled, "if your own people don't kill us all first. We're going to Old Mill to put an end to this once and for all. Just shut up, sit back, and try not to bang your foot on the back of the seat. I imagine that would hurt."

As if in his words were prophetic, the Land Rover hit a last rut as they bounced up onto 17 and the good Reverend howled in pain. There hadn't been a word out of the twins since they'd been tucked into the back of the jeep. They didn't seem particularly upset; Cletus wondered if, for all their genius, they had a clue in the world of the trouble they were in.

It was dark, but the moon was still high in the sky. There were few lights on 17, mostly from homes, a couple of gas stations, and small real estate developments that had sprung up over the years, despite the ground being lower than water level during a big rain. Cotton fields stretched out on both sides of the road, white tips glittering in the moonlight. They had less than ten miles to go, but it seemed to take forever, and every thump of tire on asphalt felt like a huge clock ticking away toward some disaster he couldn't quite face.

Behind them, Jasper had Earl trying to reach Pap on the phone, but there was no answer. They tried the lodge, and they tried Jasper's home line, but all they got was a busy signal at the first number and the answering machine at the second. The road wound around past an old church, and the turn to Old Mill was finally in sight. Bob took it too fast, bringing the Land Rover up on two wheels, then back down with a jarring thump that brought another howl from Dozier. Jasper slowed and followed. Once they were around that corner, he knew even Bob was going to have to downshift, if he didn't want to go off the bridge and into the Perquimans River.

There was no traffic coming in, or out, of the town, and even in a sleepy place like Old Mill, this was strange. The twist through town was also known as Business 17, and there were several smaller roads that branched off in the center of town, stretching to towns up toward Virginia and West toward Greenville. Someone was always rolling along that dark narrow stretch, and the empty, barren road and moonlight tipped ripples on the river sent a shiver up Cletus' spine. Nothing about this night felt right, and even with Dozier and the twins tucked safely in the back of the Land Rover, he didn't feel safe. There had been a lot of trucks leaving Eternity, and he expected he was about to learn where they'd gone.

"What's that?" Bob grunted, pointing across Cletus' chest toward the center of town.

There was a bright, orange glow that could mean only one thing. Fire. There were no sirens, though, and that was also odd. Old Mill had a volunteer fire department that sported a brand new hook and ladder truck. Usually those boys were flying down the road if someone barbecued too enthusiastically, but whatever was going on tonight had apparently not caught their attention.

Bob picked up the microphone again, started to say something, then dropped it back in the cradle and floored the Land Rover with a curse. Cletus hung on and prayed they survived to be of some help in whatever was coming.

Old Mill had two main streets running perpendicular to 17. Bob turned at the first, ignoring the red light. He met no traffic going either way, and gunned it down Temple Street toward the lodge. Ahead, flames licked at the sky, and a dark black cloud of smoke rose to blot the sky. There were bodies moving in and out of those clouds as well, lots of them. Cletus leaned out the window, trying to get a better look, but smoke wafted across the road and obscured his view.

"Slow down, Bob," he called out. "Jesus, whoever's in the road up there, you're going to knock them to hell and back."

Bob slowed, but he didn't look happy about it. In fact, he looked like nothing would give him more pleasure than to plow ahead into whatever lay ahead, drive straight through it, and out the other side. Maybe if he did, he'd just keep going and never come back to this craziness that had been his town only a few short hours before.

Bob cursed and pulled into the parking lot near the courthouse. Jasper pulled in behind, and moments later, the first sirens rose behind them. Cletus turned and saw Deputy Randy Barstow hurtling down the road in a cruiser. Randy was a bit over-enthusiastic in the performance of his duties, and normally Bob would have wanted anyone but his least favorite hothead on the job, but this was different. As Randy pulled up, Bob through him the keys to the Land Rover.

"Take them," he said. "Ambulance should be here soon. You follow along with them, make sure they are all taken care of, and make sure they are locked up tighter than a virgin's knees when you're done. You understand me, Randy?"

The younger man stared down the street, dumbfounded, watching men and women moving in and out of the smoke.

"The fire…" he said.

"Damn the fire," Bob growled, shaking him. "Get these boys to the hospital Randy. I'll take care of the fire. "And watch them. They're kidnappers, and probably murderers to boot. You don't want to give them an inch, you hear?"

Don walked up then, and Bob glanced at him distractedly, as if just remembering he was there.

"Randy," he called out. The deputy turned back.

"See that this man gets taken care of too, and call the Troopers. He's the guy that was abducted from the Cotton Gin. He's probably hungry, and I don't want *anything* happening to him."

"Yes sir," Randy replied. Apparently the deputy had gathered the seriousness of what was happening and was stepping up to the plate.

"Good damn deal," Cletus muttered. He stared at the hazy smoke where the lodge should have been, and something flickered. He couldn't quite make out what it was, but the urge to know was overwhelming. He started forward, not paying any further attention to Bob, or the others around him.

Meanwhile, Randy and Don climbed into the Land Rover and Randy stepped out to wave down the ambulance as it turned into the parking lot, attracted by Bob's flashing lights. Bob watched for a moment longer, then turned toward the fire and the smoke.

Cletus was already headed toward the lodge at a trot. He'd meant to wait for Bob, but something in the glow from the flames and the shifting, snaking clouds of smoke drew him forward.

He heard Bob call out to him, but he didn't turn. He stepped off the sidewalk and crossed temple. He pulled his shirt up over his mouth and nose, using the material as an inefficient filter, and squatted low.

The smoke was thicker than he'd expected, and he closed his eyes at the sting. It was a mistake. The moment the dim light was cut off, his boot caught on something and he tripped. Cletus cursed and waved his arms, reached out to break his fall, and landed hard. Something cut his hand, and his knees buried in soft soil. He opened his eyes and stared at the overturned earth, and the cotton plant gouging his palm.

The street was gone. He knelt in the dirt, and though the smoke had cleared some, the first blazed as bright as ever, dead ahead. It rose to the sky, and he saw the men and women of Old Mill, stretching into the distance, lined up on both sides of that fire like fence posts, guiding him forward.

Cletus turned, wild-eyed, and looked back the way he'd come. There was nothing there. The field stretched off into the distance where a line of trees was silhouetted against the skyline. He staggered to his feet and rubbed his eyes, hoping his sight would clear, but nothing changed. Hundreds of eyes watched him, lined up and waiting, and he took a step forward, then another. As he closed on the bizarre, impossible fire, he heard their voices, chanting low and steady.

He reached the first of those lined up waiting, and he scanned their faces. He knew some of them. They were men and women he'd known all his life, barbers and farmers, the kid who bagged his beer and groceries over at the grocery— and others. He didn't speak—something in their eyes told him they would not listen—that possibly they wouldn't even hear. Their lips moved in unison, and the chant grew deeper and more powerful as he passed through their ranks, approaching the fire.

Beyond the flames a huge form flickered in the shadows. Branches twined and rippled like snakes, stretching up toward the heavens. As he drew nearer, the shape rose over him, immense and dark. He knew the shape, but it was too large, the proportions were wrong. The totem had been tall when he'd seen it last, but now it seemed to touch the sky.

She stood waiting for him, and though his mind screamed at him to recoil from her, conjuring images of Nettie's wrinkled face and clawed hands, he could not pull away. Instead, he stepped forward and, smiling, she opened her arms to him again.

Then another stepped from the crowd, and he nearly blacked out. It was Nettie—old as she'd appeared on the porch of the old shack, old as she'd been since he'd known her as a child, old as his father claimed she must always have been. The girl he held squirmed in his embrace, pressing herself to him and others gathered near. Arms slid around him and nimble, urgent fingers plucked at the buttons of his shirt. His belt slid off and though he cried out softly in negation, the girl drew him forward and he stepped free of the clothing. Other hands stripped her simple gown, and she was beautiful.

A musky, heady scent filled the air and his body responded. She gripped him and he felt like stone in her supple fingers. She pulled him forward and fell back and he tumbled into her. He gazed into her eyes and they were wild, her lips parted and her back arched. He drove forward, burying himself in wet, moist flesh. She swallowed him, shivering up and down, pressing her shoulder blades and the balls of her feet into the wood of the table. The heat of the fire seared his back and sweat coated every inch of his body. He growled, unable to breathe without drawing more of the foul air into his lungs. It smelled of the forest, the swamp, the stables and so many other things at once he couldn't sort them out in his mind, and all the time he tried, he drove deeper and deeper into the writhing flesh beneath him.

When he climaxed, he couldn't see. His chest was on fire, and his breath seemed too thick to pass. He toppled to the side and cried out. Above him, he saw the totem, antlers dark and ropy against the sky. Carved wooden eyes glared down at him and glowed with an inner illumination.

Nettie stood over him. He saw that, old and frail as she was, she held the girl's body in her arms. She smiled at him and—in that moment—her face took on a beauty he could not

comprehend. Then, she stepped over him, and was gone.
His next lungful of air was blistering smoke. He heard a voice calling his name, and he rolled, trying to get back to his feet. He felt wood beneath his fingers, and it was hot. His thoughts reeled, and he tried to press up off the floor. He made it to his knees. His eyes burned, but he lifted his gaze.

Above him the ancient wood of the totem burned crazily. The deer's head was wreathed in flames that danced up the antlers toward the ceiling above. He blinked, and then his mind cleared. The lodge. He was in the lodge, and...

Strong hands gripped him under his armpits and yanked him backward. Cletus fought feebly. He tried to scramble to his feet, but more hands joined the first set, and whoever it was dragged him backward, bumping him along the floor. He felt splinters stab into his flesh, and he cried out, but the sound died in a cough that stole his breath. He tried one more time to scream, but the effort was more than his tortured flesh could take, and he slipped over the edge into darkness. The last thing he saw was the deer totem engulfed in flame and the antlers, crumbling into a cloud of black ash as they fell.

When Cletus came to, he was lying on his back staring up at the sky. Bob was leaning over him, and others stood near, Pap included, staring down at him like they thought he was already dead. He shook his head slowly, regretted it, then managed to part his parched lips.

"Bob?" he said. The word was too soft, and he coughed roughly at the effort.

Bob leaned closer. "Lie still, Cletus," he said. "There's time to talk later, and believe me, you're going to tell me just what in hell happened in there. The last thing I saw was you walking off into the smoke."

Cletus turned his head and saw the black smoke still rising. Fire trucks were on the street now, and plumes of water arched into the air to fall sizzling on the flames. Cletus let his head fall back, and he closed his eyes. When they didn't open again, Bob checked for a pulse, found it strong, and stood up.

The ambulance siren rose for the second time in an hour,

and he stepped to the curb to wave it down. In the back of the crowd gathered and watching from a distance, an old woman with wispy gray hair stood very still. Her expression was serene, and her lip curled in an enigmatic smile.

Chapter Twelve

Cletus typed the last few words of his article, read back over what he'd written, and clicked "save" to preserve the work. The article was a long one, filled with references to things that hadn't actually happened, but that made good copy. There were photos imbedded in the text—the twins, Jasper and Pap, the burned lodge, and the cellar laboratory. It should have been big news, and Cletus knew that better than anyone, but the bigger papers had turned away from it in horror. Even if it was true, how could they present such a fanciful pile of crap to the reading public?

In the end, the news agencies had reported an abduction, and had managed to ID the first 'victim' as well. They chalked it all up to craziness in Eternity, including hazy details about a cult and mutilation, but neglecting to mention that the first dead man had apparently begun to heal with Bambi's head slapped onto his neck, or that another such head had lived a short life in a Petri dish beneath the First Church of Light and Starry Wisdom.

Reverend Dozier was on his way to jail for a long time, along with the twins, who Cletus was certain would end up locked away in some government lab, working on things Cletus didn't want to know about and finishing one another's sentences. It was how things worked—no one was going to toss away genius over a little genetic experimentation. Hadn't that same government slipped Nazi scientists into the US after WWII?

At the top of the article the byline read : Cletus J. Diggs & Earl Suggs

The article wasn't likely to launch Earl into a literary career, but it had made the big man happy, and for blowing the crap out of Bambi the Zombie , he deserved it. Besides, the story was featured in the *Weekly Globe Examiner*, bumping even the doctored photograph of a giant grasshopper held up by its back legs and displayed by a grinning West Virginia farmer. It was big time, and it helped pay the bills. Cletus was all about paying the bills.

Jasper had his arm in a sling from where he tumbled down the stairs, and Pap was still getting his wind back. His story was almost as strange as Cletus' own. He and about a dozen others, thanks to the call from Earl's phone, had holed up in the lodge and they were there when the trucks from Eternity showed up and started parking in a circle around the place. None of them seemed to know for sure when the fire started, but Pap was certain it began outside. He clearly remembered a ring of fire around the entire building and smoke so thick they thought they'd never get out.

In the end, it was like a corridor opened up in the flames, leading out the door. That was how Cletus had made it in, and how those inside had gotten out. Miraculously, no one had been seriously injured. Cletus still had trouble drawing a deep breath without coughing. The smoke had burned his lungs, and he still had a couple of raw patches on his arms and legs from the heat. All in all, he figured he'd gotten off pretty easy.

Bob had been given a citation by the Governor of NC for bravery, and for solving the abduction case. He'd been damned close-mouthed about the details of the investigation and the rescue in Eternity. He took credit for Earl's shot through the Good Reverend Dozier's foot, claiming the prisoner had tried to escape. Bob said he'd warned the man to stop, but had been forced to take a non-deadly shot when Dozier dove toward his window. No one questioned this, particularly since Bob had eyewitnesses, and the only detractor was Dozier himself.

All around three counties, hunters were resting easier, though there had been a decided drop in sales of hunting and taxidermy supplies. The Harvest festival had come and gone, a muted, calm affair that hardly raised a social blip. Cletus did not attend, nor did Jasper. They stayed in and watched a race on Cletus' TV, washing remnants of soot and ash from their systems with cold, cheap beer.

Despite all of this, something haunted Cletus, and he knew that writing the last words in the article wasn't going to change that. There were things left unfinished, and there was no time like the present for taking care of business. He turned off his computer, stood, and headed for the door, and his truck beyond. On his way past the table, he grabbed a brown paper bag, gripping it where it was twisted around the neck of a bottle of Jim Beam.

The shack was just as he remembered it. The table was bare—no glasses, and no trace of the bottle he'd brought the time before. Cletus climbed out of his truck and stepped up onto the creaky porch, placing the bottle in the center of the table and looking around carefully at the old home, and the woods beyond. It was late afternoon; he hadn't been willing to come at night, but somehow he didn't believe anyone would be 'home' if he came at noon. It was the closest compromise he could make.

This time the sense of urgency was displaced by one of inevitability. He didn't need to be anywhere in particular. He'd brought his own glass, as well, so he didn't have to wait to begin drinking. There was plenty of courage in the Beam bottle to get him through the evening, he thought, and if nothing else came of it, he'd be drunk, and that would be enough.

As it turned out, he didn't have long to wait. He poured a double shot into the first of the two tumblers he'd brought, placed it on the table, and filled the second halfway. He took a quick gulp, and gazed out at the woods, watching the sun set slowly toward their leafy peaks.

Her voice nearly made him spill his drink.

"I knew you'd come," Nettie said softly.

Cletus didn't turn at first. He continued to watch the sunset, and he took another, longer pull on his drink. He didn't really know why he'd come. He didn't have any clearly formed questions, and he figured it would be best just to let her lead him wherever it was she was planning to take him and get it over with.

Finally, her silence drew him in.

"Why did you help me?" he asked. "Dozier could have brought back your horned monstrosity out in Eternity..."

"What he was creating was an abomination," she said softly. "You know that. You can't build a God in your basement, and every time you try, you end up with less—and more—than you bargained for. "

"You helped him too," Cletus pointed out.

"To a point," she said. "It's a matter of belief, Cletus—what do you believe? I remember a time when men and women knew the importance of the old ways. The Great Horned one walked the swamp through the power of their minds and their dreams. He fed on their faith, and in turn he gave them children, and crops—far more and stronger than anything that exists today. You smelled him—I know you did. You saw him in that fire, too—but it wasn't a stick, buried in the corner of the building you saw—he is much greater than that—much more powerful, even now that the belief has faded. He's almost lost to us, you know. It won't be long before the world moves on, and leaves him a dusty shadow in the swamp."

"We slowed that down," Cletus said.

He turned, and he saw that she nodded. Her glass was empty, and he filled it again.

"There's folks now, for a while, that will believe," she went on. "No one that knows what it is they are believing in, exactly, but even those strange, pale boys in Eternity helped. No one who saw what they created will ever forget it. No one who watched that fire, or worshipped with Reverend Dozier, will be able to erase it from their memories, and they'll pass it on, weakened and distorted, but they'll tell the tales, and he'll walk a few years longer. It's all I can do—I'm a very old woman, and I'm tired."

Cletus stared at his drink. He wanted to ask at least one more question, but he didn't know how to word it. A creaking floorboard broke the spell of the moment, and he glanced up.

Behind Nettie, a young woman stood. She as young, no more than twenty. Her hair was so platinum blonde it nearly matched the nimbus of gray surrounding Nettie's ancient, wizened face. She watched Cletus with wide, unblinking eyes. She neither smiled, nor frowned. Her hands rested protectively on Nettie's shoulders. Then she stepped up beside the table, and Cletus saw the bulge of her belly. She was with child—far along from the look of it. He grew pale and gulped what was left of his whiskey.

Nettie started laughing. "Yes, Cletus, you are a part of this now. He worked through you, and the line that I have been a part of will pass on through the generations. You'll feel him if you stand too long in the fields, or if you spend too much time fishing in the swamp. He'll watch over you—he's part of you now, as you are part of...the future."

Nettie reached out and laid her hand gently on the girl's swollen belly.

Cletus shuddered. His fears that he'd lain with Nettie had been replaced by a deep-rooted, chilling sensation of connection to a darkness he couldn't see. He suddenly felt as if the shadows the rising moon had spread across the road and his truck were not all the product of light and limb, but cast instead by antlers, branching up and away into the night sky. The air thickened, just for a moment, and he smelled the musky, rutting odor of animals and the scent of fresh mown grass and fields at harvest.

He stood quickly and stumbled toward the steps with a cry. He caught himself on the rickety railing, glanced back, and saw that the table was bare. No one sat across it; both bottles and glasses were gone.

He hurried to his truck and slid in behind the wheel, checking to be certain all the doors were locked and the windows tightly closed. Then he sat, steadied his breath and his heartbeat, and started the engine.

Backing slowly, he aimed the truck at the road, and the highway beyond. As he pulled away, he couldn't shake the sensation of eyes watching him from the shadows and a powerful, hovering presence just outside the groping limits of his mind.

About the Author

David Niall Wilson has been writing and publishing horror, dark fantasy, and science fiction since the mid-eighties. An ordained minister, once President of the Horror Writers Association and multiple recipient of the Bram Stoker Award, his novels include Maelstrom, *The Mote in Andrea's Eye, Deep Blue, the Grails Covenant Trilogy, Star Trek Voyager: Chrysalis, Except You Go Through Shadow, This is My Blood, Ancient Eyes, On the Third Day, The Orffyreus Wheel,* The DeChance Chronicles, including *Heart of a Dragon, Vintage Soul, My Soul to Keep, Kali's Tale* and the stand-alone spinoff *Nevermore—A Novel of Love, Loss & Edgar Allan Poe.* His novels in the O.C.L.T. series include *The Parting, Crockatiel,* and the novella *The Temple of Camazotz* .He is also the author of the memoir / cookbook *American Pies: Baking with Dave the Pie Guy.* David can be found at: www.davidniallwilson.com and can be reached by e-mail at david@davidniallwilson.com .

Curious about other Crossroad Press books?
Stop by our site:
http://store.crossroadpress.com
We offer quality writing
in digital, audio, and print formats.

Enter the code FIRSTBOOK
to get 20% off your first order from our store!
Stop by today!

www.ingramcontent.com/pod-product-compliance
Lightning Source LLC
Chambersburg PA
CBHW060404180626
46817CB00007B/2513